HELL'S HALF ACRE:
COLD-BLOODED

HELL'S HALF ACRE: COLD-BLOODED

William W. Johnstone
with *J. A. Johnstone*

PINNACLE BOOKS
Kensington Publishing Corp.
www.kensingtonbooks.com

PINNACLE BOOKS are published by

Kensington Publishing Corp.
119 West 40th Street
New York, NY 10018

PUBLISHER'S NOTE
Following the death of William W. Johnstone, the Johnstone family is working with a carefully selected writer to organize and complete Mr. Johnstone's outlines and many unfinished manuscripts to create additional novels in all of his series like The Last Gunfighter, Mountain Man, and Eagles, among others. This novel was inspired by Mr. Johnstone's superb storytelling.

All Kensington titles, imprints, and distributed lines are available at special quantity discounts for bulk purchases for sales promotions, premiums, fund-raising, educational, or institutional use. Special book excerpts or customized printings can also be created to fit specific needs. For details, write or phone the office of the Kensington sales manager: Kensington Publishing Corp., 119 West 40th Street, New York, NY 10018, attn: Sales Department; phone 1-800-221-2647.

PINNACLE BOOKS, the Pinnacle logo, and the WWJ steer head logo are Reg. U.S. Pat. & TM Off.

ISBN-13: 978-0-7860-3595-3
ISBN-10: 0-7860-3595-1

First printing: June 2015

10 9 8 7 6 5 4 3 2 1

Printed in the United States of America

CHAPTER ONE

"My dear Senator Jennings, you can't stand fifty-three criminals against a wall and shoot them down with Gatling guns," Major General Thomas Lambert said. "The public would never allow it."

"It's all about money, General," Senator William Jennings said. "We can't afford the dollars to keep the scum alive any longer."

"I am aware of that," Lambert said. "And I've been in touch with the warden of Huntsville and I'm very sympathetic to his problem."

Lambert was a beautiful infantry officer, resplendent in blue and gold. A trimmed, spade-shaped beard spread across his chest and his great mane of iron gray hair fell in perfumed ringlets to his shoulders.

"There's always the Indian Territory," Jennings said. In stark contrast to the army officer, Jennings was a thin, spare man with the aesthetic face of an English Lake Poet.

"Out of the question, my dear sir," Lambert said. "We have quite enough problems with outlaws and renegades in the Territory as it is. We will not allow you to send us more miscreants." He smiled. "Add fuel to the fire, so to speak."

Rain drummed on the roof of the senator's private railcar, which had been pulled into a siding two miles north of Houston. Outside, the capes of the army guards glistened in the light cast from the carriage windows, and their fixed bayonets gleamed.

Inside, the car smelled of cigar smoke and brandy and of Senator Jennings's sweaty frustration.

"The cost is outrageous, General," he said. "It's out of all proportion to the number of men involved. Murderers, rapists and outlaws of every stripe. I can't lease them out as labor. No one will hire them because they represent such a danger to the community. Those men out there in the cages require extra guards around the clock, another vast expense that Huntsville, indeed the great state of Texas, cannot afford."

"Then I have two suggestions to make," General Lambert said. He turned to his aide. "Major Holt, please read them to the senator."

Holt was young, eager, the son of a senator and very much a political soldier. He had seen no action nor did he desire any. Washington was his battlefield, a mahogany desk his steed.

"General Lambert suggests thusly," Holt said. He read from the paper in his hands. "The prisoners be returned to Huntsville and there be hanged one by one under the greatest secrecy."

"There is no secrecy in Huntsville," Jennings said. "I have been told to make the prison less costly, but hanging fifty-three in one go would certainly cause a riot. Gentlemen, conditions in Huntsville are vicious, brutal and cramped. The governor tells me he currently has two thousand men in one hundred and thirty cells, each cell designed to house just one man. Convicts are lashed, starved, chained in solitary for months at a time and revolt is in the air. Fifty-three hangings could tip them over the edge and the impact on neighboring communities would be horrendous."

Lambert took that with a nod, Holt with a smile.

"My other plan," the general said, staring at the glowing tip of his cigar, "is that you drive the convicts into the desert somewhere and shoot into the cages. Then you leave them there. The wounded will soon die of thirst."

"Wise solution though it may be, I have a problem with that, General," Jennings said. "Like the hangings, the word will get out. When men drink they go on the brag and a secret like that will not be kept. With an election growing ever closer you can imagine what a field day my opponent would have. Why, I'd be crucified in his newspapers as a mass murderer."

Lambert opened his mouth to speak but Jennings held up a silencing hand. "Perhaps at this juncture I should note that none of these criminals are condemned men. No, they are all serving sentences of thirty years to life."

"A damned disgrace if you ask me," General Lambert said. "They did the crime and should pay the penalty."

"Blame the judges," Jennings said. "Just lock them away where they can do no more harm and let the citizens of Texas pay for them. That's the modern attitude in the law courts these days, I'm told."

"Damned impertinence," Lambert said. "Coddling criminals like that."

"Can I speak?"

This from a thickset man wearing an old Union greatcoat, a bowler hat, and a muffler around his bull neck. Under the coat he wore a checked jacket and pants and he carried a Colt in a shoulder holster. He was a scar-faced man in his midfifties and looked like a vicious criminal himself.

"Yes, you may," Jennings said. "General Lambert, this gentleman's name is Herbert Coffin. He's been hired to supervise the transportation of the prisoners to . . . well, wherever we can take them."

Both officers in the car glanced at Coffin as though he smelled like something dead, a result of the soldiers' disdain for civilians and an acute awareness of their gulf in class. Earlier, Coffin had not been offered brandy and cigars.

Jennings saw the expressions on the officers' faces and thought his employee's bona fides would help him rise in their esteem. He made matters worse.

"During the war Mr. Coffin served the Union as a camp guard at Point Lookout," he said. "He knows how to deal with prisoners."

It was the wrong thing to say to Lambert, a fighting soldier who had served in the war as a major of infantry and had battled both Comanche and Apache since.

"I heard that in two years fourteen thousand prisoners died at Point Lookout, the result of disease, starvation and beatings," he said.

Coffin shrugged. "They were rebs. What did they expect?"

Lambert's face flushed with anger but Jennings deflected the general's wrath. "What was it you wished to say, Mr. Coffin?" he said.

"I've got a solution to your problem, Senator. You want to dump fifty-three convicts, so dump 'em in a place where they'll never be noticed."

"And where might that be?" Jennings said.

"Two hundred and fifty miles northwest of here there's a dunghill of a town called Fort Worth. And its worst area is the Third Ward, a stinking slum they call Hell's Half Acre."

"I'm aware of the town," Jennings said. "But I've never visited there."

"Your only interest should be the Acre," Coffin said. "I've spent time there and it's full of saloons, bawdy houses, dance halls and opium dens. It's a haven for gunmen, highway robbers, card sharks, whores and con artists." Coffin reached inside his coat and produced a newspaper clipping. "Here, Senator, read that to the military gentlemen. It's about the Acre."

Jennings glanced at the clip then read aloud, "'It's a slow night which does not pan out a cutting or shooting scrape among its male denizens or a fatal morphine experiment by one of its frisky females.'"

Jennings handed the paper back to Coffin, his face bright. "We dump the convicts there?" he said.

"Those boys out there will fit right in, Senator. In the Acre they'll be among their own kind and nobody will even notice them. I reckon in a couple of months or so, they'll all be dead."

Jennings clapped his hands. "Brilliant! What do you think, General Lambert? I believe we have found the answer, thanks to Mr. Coffin, solved in the space of a moment."

"It is an excellent solution to your problem, Senator," Lambert said. "Dump trash among trash and no one will take heed." He grudgingly looked at Coffin and said, "How long to get your wagons there?"

"Two weeks, I reckon," Coffin said. "Good weather or bad. I'll drive 'em, by God."

Jennings said, "Good! I think that calls for another drink. Mr. Coffin, a brandy with you?"

"No," Coffin said. "I reckon I'll step outside and check on my prisoners."

CHAPTER TWO

Herb Coffin left the railcar and walked into the lashing rain. An army guard nodded and Coffin nodded back. "Going to check on my prisoners," he said.

"Hell to be a prisoner on a night like this," said the soldier, a middle-aged man with a cold clay pipe in his mouth.

"Hell to be a prisoner on any night," Coffin said. Lightning scrawled across the sky and thunder rumbled.

There were three caged prison wagons, the fifty-three convicts split among them. Murderers and robbers were confined twenty to a wagon, the remaining wagon more sparsely occupied with six rapists, the remainder blacks and Mexicans.

No attempt had been made to shelter the wagons from the rain. They were parked out in the open and their occupants were soaked, a few of them coughing.

Coffin lit a cigar and stopped at the first wagon. "How many of you boys are still alive?" he said.

"All of us," a man's voice said from the darkness. "We won't cash in our chips until we get our hands around your throat, Coffin."

"Maybe you'll get your chance," Coffin said. "I'm taking you boys for a long drive in the country. You'll like that, won't you?"

Coffin took a billy club from his pocket and slammed it into the bars. The prisoners were packed so closely that he hit heads and shoulders and men cried out in pain.

"Answer me when I ask a question," Coffin said. "You'll like that, won't you?"

A few of the prisoners muttered yes, but then a wide-shouldered man with a ragged prison beard pushed his way to the bars of the cage and said, "I'm going to kill you, Coffin. I swear, I'll gut you like the swine you are."

Coffin grinned, the rain in his face. "Well, if it ain't Major Ford Talon, the hero of the South. After the sixty lashes I gave you at Huntsville I thought for sure you'd be dead by now."

"You cut my back up, Coffin. But I wouldn't let you kill me. You hear me, I willed myself to stay alive until the day I could get a bullet into your miserable carcass."

Coffin said, grinning, "You're a walking dead man, Talon. We're all going to a place, but you ain't never gonna get there. Study on that for a spell until your guts turn into jelly."

"I'm not a boasting man, but I don't scare easy. I'll get to where we're going, Coffin, and by God, then I'll get you," Talon said.

Coffin pulled his Colt and pointed it at Talon's head. "Pow!" he said.

He walked away laughing, the heedless rain falling around him.

CHAPTER THREE

"I don't want no trouble from you, Casey," Luke Short said.

Sheriff Jess Casey nodded. "Very commendable of you, Luke."

Short studied the wanted dodgers on the office wall and said, "You can take that one down. Poke Ritter got all shot to pieces by lawmen a month ago up in the Indian Territory." He shook his head. "Pity. Poke was a good man."

"Says there he was a murderer and a bank robber," Jess said.

"Ah well, to each his own, I guess," Short said. "He was still a good man."

"Luke, you didn't come in here to keep me up to date on my wanted posters," Jess said. "What can I do for you?"

"So that everything is aboveboard and out in the open, I want your legal permission to shoot a man."

"What man?" Jess said.

"You know Banjo Tom Van Meter? He played in my orchestra at the White Elephant for a spell. He's the one who cut up Bill Tate that time."

"No, I can't say I've had the pleasure."

"Well, no matter. The thing is he took Lulu Lanahan away from me, plans to pimp her himself. As a gentleman I can't let that stand. It's a matter of honor."

"And you want me to say it's all right to put a bullet in him?" Jess said.

"Sure I do. Banjo Tom always goes around heeled, so it will be a fair fight," Short said. "Hell, if it helps, I'll let him draw first."

"No matter, Luke. I can't give you the law's permission to kill a man. Let Banjo Tom be and find yourself another Lulu."

Short's face registered his displeasure. "If Tom Van Meter asked your permission to kill me would you give it to him?"

"Probably, Luke, probably."

"All right, then from this day onward we're enemies, Casey," Short said.

Jess smiled. "I thought we were that already."

"Oh yeah? Well now we're even worse enemies than we were before."

Luke Short slammed out of the office and Jess listened to the departing thud of his shoes on the boardwalk. He nodded to himself. It might be a good idea to have words with Banjo Tom and warn him that Luke made a mighty dangerous enemy.

* * *

A strange restlessness in him, Jess stepped to the window and looked out on crowded Main Street. People promenaded on the boardwalks and the wheels of commerce, the heavy freight wagons, trundled past, trace chains rattling as the great Percherons leaned into their collars. It was still early morning but dust clouded the air and beige streaks of horse dung lay everywhere.

Things had been quiet in Hell's Half Acre for a week now. The only incidents of note were a cutting at the Silver Garter saloon, Kurt Koenig's place, and a minor shooting scrape on Rusk that left no one injured except a passerby who got his left thumb shot off. The shooter, a businessman named Miller, paid the victim compensation and later a fifty-dollar fine for the discharge of a firearm in a public place. A pregnant woman gave birth in a dance hall after taking part in a polka and there was a suicide by hanging at a slum tenement on 12th Street. And of course, Luke Short wanted to kill a man legally.

For the first time since he'd arrived in Fort Worth Jess Casey felt bored. Yet he was uneasy, on edge, a jumpiness in him. As any lawman will confirm, when things get too quiet something real bad is about to happen. It always works that way. As surely as night follows day.

* * *

The prison wagons were twelve hours from Fort Worth when Herb Coffin called a halt to feed and water the prisoners. Around the wagons stretched a vast expanse of hilly grasslands broken up by mesquite, stands of wild oak at the higher elevations and sumac and bois d'arc along the creek bottoms.

Including the drivers, Coffin had six guards up on the cage wagons and two more mounted. The guards deployed, carrying belt guns and rifles, before the cons were allowed to crawl out of the wagons and stretch their aching bodies. Breakfast was hard biscuit left over from the war and cold salt pork speckled with green mold.

As he always did, Ford Talon sat away from the other prisoners, his face turned to the burning sun. He opened his eyes when a shadow blocked the rays and saw, haloed by dazzling sunlight, the mounted form of Herb Coffin.

"This is where you get off, Major Talon," he said. "It's the end of the line." Sweat ran down Coffin's face and his smile was vicious. "You killed Thomson and Burt real easy, didn't you? That's because they were stupid enough to let you close. I won't make that mistake."

"They died like the pigs they were, Coffin. And so will you," Talon said.

"Now that's hardly likely, is it?" Coffin said. "I'm the man with the rifle." He grinned. "You know, Thomson and Burt kicked him all right, but he didn't die until I stomped his head to a pulp. So all was in vain, Major. You never avenged your brother at all."

Talon knew what Coffin wanted. The man was trying to goad him into an attack so he could justify the killing to the other guards. But Talon refused to play Coffin's game. He sat where he was, the taste of rotten salt pork in his mouth and a heart full of hell.

Coffin said, "Soon. If you got any prayers, say them, Johnny Reb."

He swung his horse away and left Talon to his thoughts.

His brother Johnny had died at Lookout Point, kicked to death by Coffin and two other guards. He and Johnny had been posted to different cavalry regiments and he didn't learn how Johnny had died until he talked with veterans who'd been locked up with him in that dreadful place.

After that Talon took to the vengeance trail. He'd killed one of the guards, Burt, in a saloon in El Paso and had tracked another, Thomson, to Kansas, where he worked as a deputy sheriff. Talon had been wounded in that shooting scrape but had killed his man. Later he'd been arrested in Galveston and tried for murder and had been sentenced to thirty years in Huntsville. He'd not heard anything of the third guard, Herb Coffin, until the man was put in charge of the prison wagons. His experience with beaten, starved men had stood him in good stead.

Now he'd caught up with Coffin but it looked

as though the man was right. His vengeance trail ended right there. Talon was on the wrong side of forty and not afraid to die—he'd seen too much of that on a dozen battlefields—but the thought of Coffin going free made him sick to the stomach.

The prisoners were shoved and kicked back into the wagons, except for Talon and a man who'd died sometime in the night.

"You men go on," Coffin told the guards. "I'll catch up after I've concluded my business here."

This brought cheers, jeers, and much grinning from the guards, but Coffin's face was serious. Executing a man took some mental preparation.

The wagons rolled across the long grass, then swung east, headed for the Trinity. Ford Talon glanced at the blue denim sky where the sun burned like a red-hot coin. Insects made their small music in the grass and high up a hawk glided like an angel, but its searching eyes were full of deviltry.

Herb Coffin drew rein a few yards from where Talon sat. "Stand up and die like a man," he said. His Colt was steady in his gun hand.

Imagine a rough-bearded man dressed in rags, gaunt with hunger, black shadows under his eyes from the effects of the lash, iron shackles, and constant abuse from men who had no respect for him and considered him barely human. Imagine a man at the end of his tether who looked as though he no longer cared if he lived or died, and you have a pretty fair mental picture of Ford Talon that summer morning on the Texas plains.

But a man like that has nothing to lose . . . a thing Herb Coffin should have taken into account.

"Talon," Coffin said, "I hate your guts, just as I hated your brother before you. See, the damned reb didn't know when he was beat and I was glad when I killed him and I'll be doubly glad when I kill you. But your dying will be slower than his because I'm gonna give it to you right in the belly. One shot in the guts and you'll scream like a pig for hours, maybe days."

Coffin thumbed back the hammer of his Colt, the triple click loud in the morning quiet. He grinned. "Are you ready?"

Talon noticed a subtle change in Coffin's voice. The man was about to shoot. He made his move, already aware that it was a forlorn hope. From his sitting position he stood up and rushed, not Coffin, but his horse. He charged directly at the zebra dun's head, screaming like a banshee. Startled, the horse jerked up his head and his front hooves left the ground. Coffin held on, his legs clamped around the barrel of his mount. He leaned out of the saddle and got off a shot. Talon took the hit and, driven on by pain, shrieked even louder. Scared now, the dun swung wildly to his left and Coffin, not an expert rider, grabbed for the horn. It was all the chance Talon needed. His arms extended, he threw himself at Coffin and tried to wrestle him from the saddle. But his strength was not what it once had been and Coffin brushed him off and slammed downward with the Colt. Talon saw the danger and moved his head at the last moment, but the gun barrel scraped cruelly down the right side of his head, tore his ear and thumped painfully onto his shoulder. Coffin tried to steady himself for another shot. But the dun would have none of it. Thoroughly frightened now, he reared and his rider fell backward out of the saddle.

Coffin landed hard on his back, winding him, and Talon was on him like a starving wolf. Now was a time for tooth and claw. Both men wrestled for the gun in Coffin's hand, but realizing he didn't have the strength to best the man, Talon bit down on Coffin's wrist and at the same time he jammed his thumbnail, long untrimmed, into the man's left eye. Coffin screamed and tried to bring his revolver to bear, but Talon bit deeper into the man's wrist, drawing blood. Afraid for his eye, Coffin grabbed Talon's right forearm. But Talon, fighting for his life and nothing left inside him that was human, dug deeper until blood trickled onto Coffin's cheekbone.

Coffin shrieked and arched his back, bucking violently like a rodeo mustang. He threw Talon off, breaking his hold, but the Colt jerked out of his hand and thudded onto the grass. Talon made a dive for the revolver and beat Coffin to it by a fraction of a second. He rolled away from Coffin, putting distance between them, but the injured man staggered after him, blinded in one eye like an enraged Cyclops.

Three years in Huntsville had not eroded Talon's gun skill. Shooting from his back he put his first bullet into Coffin's right knee, knowing it would drop him. Bone shattered and Coffin screamed. He didn't fall, but stood where he was, unable to continue.

"This is for Johnny," Talon said.

He pumped bullets in Coffin until the hammer clicked on an empty chamber. The man still didn't drop, but he swayed on his feet, stunned at the manner of his death. Then he crashed to the ground like a felled oak, groaned once and died.

CHAPTER FOUR

Ford Talon lay on his back and stared at the sky. He'd killed all three who had murdered his brother and it had left a hole in him that he did not know how he was going to fill. For years he'd been dedicated to his quest for vengeance, but now that was over there was nothing to take its place. He had neither wife nor child and no friends to be glad at his coming and sad at his leaving. Talon was a man alone and now what he feared was life itself.

He got to his feet. The fight with Coffin had drained him and he felt tired beyond belief. The dead man offered no solace but stared at him with dull, accusing eyes. Despite his rags and bare feet, Talon could not bring himself to wear Coffin's clothes. His hatred ran deep and the duds the man wore were unclean things.

He did ransack Coffin's pockets and found a wallet that contained more than two hundred dollars. He took the money and the man's shoulder holster. He loaded the Colt with cartridges he found in the pocket of Coffin's greatcoat and shoved the big revolver into the holster.

The zebra dun grazed close and Talon had no problem grabbing his trailing reins. Smelling blood on him, the horse raised his head and white arcs showed in his eyes, but Talon had a way with animals of all kinds and his gentle hands on the dun's muzzle reassured him and he calmed right down.

Talon swung into the saddle and considered his options. To say they were limited was an understatement. Finally he summed things up by deciding that he needed a bath, shave, new duds and then a slap-up meal. He didn't look into the crystal ball any further than that.

The wallet with the two hundred dollars made a reassuring bulge in the waistband of his string-tied pants as he swung the dun and followed the wheel tracks of the prison wagons.

After Jess Casey had solved the mystery of the homicidal Dr. Sun, the grateful mayor of Fort Worth, Henry "Harry" Stout, had awarded Sheriff Casey a new gold badge that was now pinned to the front of his faded blue shirt. Later he'd also been presented an oak rocker that Stout claimed had been purchased "at great expense" by the city. As Jess had learned later, the chair was about to be thrown out along with other City Hall garbage before Stout rescued it.

Jess now sat in the rocker on the boardwalk outside his office and watched Fort Worth go by, as he'd done many times before. The Acre's sporting crowd was still abed and only the respectable element populated Main Street. This made the ragged, unkempt Ford Talon stand out all the more, especially since he rode a good horse.

Jess was surprised when the man stopped and nodded. "Good-day to you, Sheriff," he said. "I'm looking for a bathhouse."

Jess gave the man a quick once-over. He looked to be in his seventies but could be half that age. He was dirty, bearded, ragged and it seemed like he'd been at hard labor for years and had missed his last dozen meals. Yet he rode a five-hundred-dollar horse and the expensive Colt in his shoulder holster made an emphatic statement. His feet in the stirrups were bare, the toenails long and rimmed with black.

"Passing through, are you?" Jess said, his eyes wary.

"Don't know," the stranger said. "I'll decide that after I get cleaned up and get some grub into myself."

Suspicious, Jess said, "Where you from, stranger?"

Talon didn't hesitate. "Huntsville State Penitentiary. Before that wherever my hunt for three killers took me. And before that I was an officer in the army of the Confederacy. Did I go back far enough?"

"You came across, no doubt about that," Jess said. "Are you on the scout?"

"Those three men I told you about, I killed the last of them a day's ride west of here. He was a Huntsville employee, so yes, I guess I'm on the scout. By the way, anybody ever tell you that you're a ringer for General George Armstrong Custer?"

"Yeah, too many times. No paper on you?"

"Not yet."

"What name do you go by?"

"Talon. Ford Talon. A war ago they called me Major Talon."

Jess thought that over then said, "I'll show you where the bathhouse is at. I've got nothing better to do this morning." He rose from the rocker and said, "But first I want your pistol and the Winchester rifle from under your knee."

"I must look like a mighty desperate character, Sheriff," Talon said, reluctantly shucking his guns.

"You do," Jess said. "Believe me, you do."

CHAPTER FIVE

Dirty Sammy's Bathhouse and Sporting House was situated behind a cattle hide storage yard on Calhoun Street. It was a large white tent with a wooden sign above the entrance that pronounced:

HOT BATH – 10 cents
CLEAN WATER – 10 cents extry
SOAP – 10 cents
TOWEL – 20 cents
CLEAN TOWEL – 10 cents extry
BAD WHISKEY – 20 cents
GOOD WHISKEY – $1

This establishment is staffed by young ladies of gentle breeding.

~SAMUEL J. HOWE, *prop.*

Ford Talon looped his horse to the hitching rail and said, "Looks like this will suit me just fine."

"Any kind of water will suit you just fine," Jess said.

The moneyed sporting gents would not stir until after dark so the daytime staff of the bath-house was composed of three ladies chosen for brawn rather than beauty.

"This here gent wants the best of everything," Jess said. "And shave him while you're at it."

A muscular woman, her dark hair pulled back in a severe bun, stripped off Talon's filthy rags and then sat him in a bathtub. Her two colleagues poured in water from steaming jugs, which made him jump. "Hell, that's hot!" he yelled.

"Cold won't do you any good," the dark-haired lady said. "Wait until the scrubbing with lye soap starts."

"Your best whiskey and cigars for the gent, ladies," Jess said. "And leave the bottle." Then to Talon, "Let me have your wallet."

"What for?" Talon was suspicious and it showed.

"You want to get nice and clean then dress up in those stinking rags again?" Jess said.

"I never thought of that," Talon said.

"I'll go talk with Nate Levy," Jess said. "He was a boxing manager but now he's opened up a used clothing store. Nate will fix you up."

Talon swallowed a shot of whiskey that made his eyes pop. "My God, and this is the good stuff!" Then his voice on fire, "It's rotgut."

"This ain't Buckingham Palace, Your Majesty,"

the dark-haired woman said. "It's a bathhouse. Rotgut is what we sell in this joint until the posh gents of refined taste like you come in later."

Jess picked up Talon's wallet and said, "Where did a raggedy-ass like you get all this money?"

"I saved it," Talon said.

"Somebody saved it," Jess said. "I'll bring it back with your new duds."

"You don't even know my size," Talon said.

"Medium height, skinny build, that's all Nate Levy needs."

"Sheriff, why are you doing all this for me?" Talon said, his voice bumpy as a woman pummeled soap through his hair.

"Because I saw a man scraping the bottom of his last barrel who badly needed a break." Jess smiled "You reminded me of me."

"Well, I'm beholden to you," Talon said.

"I'm not saying that I won't arrest you later on suspicion of highway robbery and possible murder," Jess said. "But first things first. I won't have a smelly tramp in my cells."

"I didn't murder anybody," Talon said.

"Then you've nothing to worry about, have you?" Jess said.

"Well, what do you think, Jess?" Nate Levy said. "An incredible transformation, I say." Then, to Ford Talon, "The sack suit is all the rage nowadays and the vest, bow tie and bowler hat set it off to perfection."

Talon looked at himself in a mirror held by one of the ladies. He'd been clean-shaven except for his mustache and that had been combed and trimmed. "I look better than I thought I would," he said.

"You look good," Jess said. "Like an officer and a gentleman. Who knew that under all that hair a handsome face was waiting to reappear?"

"I was an officer and a gentleman once," Talon said. "But that was a long time ago." He smiled. "And now I'm about to faint with hunger."

"Good, because lunch is on you," Jess said. "Nate and me didn't go to all this trouble for nothing."

Ford Talon fell on his food like a starving wolf and for a while Jess Casey and Nate Levy sat back and just watched him eat.

After Talon shoveled down a huge steak and half a dozen eggs with plenty of bread and butter, then two wedges of apple pie, Nate said, "I'd rather buy his clothes than feed him. Even my boy Zeus didn't eat that much."

"I've been hungry for a long time," Talon said, dabbing his napkin to his mustache. "Three years to be exact."

"Why were you sent to Huntsville?" Jess said.

"And more to the point, how did you get out and when?"

But Talon didn't have time to give an answer because a towheaded boy rushed into the restaurant and breathlessly yelled, "Sheriff, Mad Dog Rankin is at it again!"

CHAPTER SIX

"How many times is this?" Sheriff Jess Casey asked big Boone Hart, the owner of the Pony Cart Saloon, a modest establishment at the corner of Rusk and 15th.

"Third time in my place," Hart said. He was a grossly overweight man with a magnificent pair of muttonchop whiskers that framed his round, scarlet face. "I can't speak for anyone else." Then, "He's got Nancy Nairn in there and three others."

Nancy Nairn, the Nacogdoches Nightingale, was the star attraction at the Pony Cart, but more for the size of her generous breasts than the tunefulness of her singing.

"Has he hurt anyone?" Jess said.

"Not yet, as far as I know."

A chattering crowd had gathered outside the saloon, since Mad Dog Rankin, all seven feet of him, was a sight to see when he went off on a whiskey-fueled rampage. Jess didn't want to go in after him, not then, not ever, but there was no one else. He was the sheriff and he had it to do.

"I'll talk to him," Jess said.

"Mind the bowie, Sheriff," Hart said. "He's mighty quick with it."

"Thanks," Jess said. "Those are words of wisdom I ain't likely to forget."

Jess opened the saloon door and from behind him a man jeered, "Go get him, Sheriff!" And the crowd laughed.

Inside, the saloon was filled with a gray light, there being few windows, and the stained sawdust on the timber floor had not been changed in days. Opposite the door several spittoons fronted a pine bar about fifteen feet long. The French mirror behind the bar was covered with protective wood and canvas that only came down on special occasions, Independence Day not being one of them on account of too much festive shooting.

Four people sat at a table, a bottle of whiskey and glasses in front of them. Nancy Nairn wore a demure blue gingham dress, a ribbon of the same color holding back her dark hair. Even as his stomach lurched with apprehension, Jess allowed to himself that the girl had a magnificent shape. The bartender and piano player, looking nervous, filled two other chairs . . . and then there was Mad Dog.

The man looked like an oak tree that had been dragged inside from an ogre's forest. His shoulders were an ax-handle wide and his massive paws resting on the table looked like a pair of Smithfield hams. Dressed in greasy buckskins, he wore two revolvers of the largest kind, and a wicked-looking bowie knife about the size of a cavalry saber was driven into the table. Both his beard and shoulder-length red hair were dirty and tangled and his eyes glowed the greenest hue this side of hell.

Mad Dog heard the chime of Jess's spurs and looked him up and down. "Well, welcome, Sheriff, to our little hoedown. Bring a chair."

"Mr. Rankin," Jess said, "I'm arresting you for disturbing the peace. Let's go."

"And I do not want to be arrested," Mad Dog said. "What do you think of them beans?"

With remarkable speed, a huge Smith & Wesson Russian appeared in the big man's hand. "I said sit down, lawman."

Jess summed things up in his mind and decided to comply with the order. With three people in harm's way sitting so close to Mad Dog a gunfight was the last thing he needed.

After he sat, Mad Dog roared for another bottle of whiskey and a glass. "We'll drink together, Sheriff, and you'll help soothe my troubled soul." The big man nodded. "Yup, that's what you'll do."

"Is that all?" Jess said. "If it's not, then state your intentions."

"My intentions," Mad Dog said as he poured whiskey into Jess's glass, "are to kill everyone here present and then myself. Mad Dog is sad."

"Why?" Jess said.

Tears ran down the man's cheeks. "Because my mother passed away five years ago this very day. Did you know my mother? She was a wonderful woman, a saint. She'd sing to her little Hyacinth when he was a boy until he fell asleep. Mad Dog was afraid of thunder then, way up there on the Kansas plains, but Ma used to kiss him and take all the scare away."

"That's your name? Hyacinth?" Nancy Nairn said.

"Yup, except nobody ever called me by it but Ma. She loved flowers, Ma did, but hyacinths most of all." Mad Dog sobbed. "But now she's gone and I'll soon join her." He glanced at the railroad clock on the wall. "She died at three of an afternoon, and so will we. You'll soon hear her sing in the sweet by-and-by."

The bartender and the piano player exchanged looks. The bartender, a short, thickset man with a broken nose, looked like he was ready to make a play, but Jess glared a warning at him. As soon as he made his move Mad Dog would shoot him. Jess had no doubt about that.

"You suffered a great loss, Mr. Rankin," Jess said. Then putting to use all the time he'd spent comforting sick or injured ranch dogs, he patted the big man on the shoulder and said, "There, there, poor Dog, you must miss Ma terribly."

Mad Dog started to blubber. "I do, oh, I do. Sheriff, you know how deep is my sorrow. Damn it all, you're a good man to the bone and I'm glad you'll come with me when the clock strikes three."

Jess said, "Poor Doggy . . . what song did Ma sing to you when the thunder made you sceered?"

"'Beautiful Dreamer,' it was. She sang it as sweet as an angel, my ma did."

"Nancy"—Jess gave the girl a look—"sing that pretty song for the poor Doggy." He patted his chest and Nancy, as smart as a tree full of owls, scraped her chair over, laid Mad Dog's head on her magnificent breasts, and sang in a thin, plaintive voice the opening verse of Ma Rankin's song.

"Beautiful dreamer, wake unto me . . ."

His head on Nancy Nairn's bust was as cozy a berth as a man could wish and Mad Dog smiled, closed his eyes and settled in like a man does into a feather pillow.

"Starlight and dewdrops are waiting for thee . . ."

Jess rose to his feet and slowly moved behind the big man. "Good Dog . . ." he crooned. "Good Doggy . . ." He drew and slammed his Colt into the side of Mad Dog's head. Nancy screeched and rubbed the top of her left breast. "Damn it! He bit me!"

But Mad Dog Rankin didn't hear. He rolled to his left and fell out of the chair. The bartender didn't hesitate. He stepped into the janitor's closet behind the bar and returned with a rope.

"Hog-tie him good," Jess said. "He's gonna be as mad as a teased rattler when he wakes up."

After he'd trussed the big man, the bartender said, "What you gonna do with him, Sheriff? I suggest you take him out of town and shoot him."

Jess smiled. "Nah, that would be murder. Mad Dog is all right when he's sober."

"When the hell is he ever sober?" Nancy said. "Son of a bitch bit my begonia."

"Is the skin broken?" Jess said.

Nancy pulled out the top of her dress and looked down. "No. It's not."

Jess nodded. "Rub dirt on it. That's what cowboys do for a bite."

"Yeah, Sheriff," Nancy said. "I'll be sure to do that."

Jess, missing the irony, said, "You're quite welcome, ma'am."

Mad Dog Rankin was a load. Jess commandeered a passing wagon and three men helped throw him into the bed and later tossed him into a cell. When the big man woke he called out for his mother, and then, rapidly changing his mind, for Nancy Nairn.

CHAPTER SEVEN

"I'm the city marshal," Kurt Koenig said. "I can't be everywhere."

"How did it happen, Kurt?" Jess Casey said.

"I've only got one eyewitness and she says she saw three ragged men go into Nate Levy's store," Koenig said. "They didn't come out again and she got worried and came looking for you. She didn't find you and sent her son after me."

"At the time I was busy with Mad Dog Rankin," Jess said.

"I know, and damn it, Jess, you don't stay busy with scum like that. He was threatening to kill three captive people. You should have walked into the saloon and shot him dead—no ifs, buts or maybes."

"That's your way, Kurt. It's not mine."

"Your way is to do your best to put me and Luke Short out of business and the hell with everything else," Koenig said, his handsome face flushed.

"Because you didn't kill Rankin, the only friend you got in this town lies at death's door."

"Where is Nate?" Jess said.

"At Dr. Bell's house on 11th Street. He got beaten pretty badly. All they took were clothes and the money Nate had on him, about eighty dollars."

"I'll find them," Jess said.

"And then what, Jess? You'll lock them in a cell for a couple of days? Fine them ten dollars, maybe? In Fort Worth you find them and you kill them. That's how the law works around here."

Jess got up from behind his desk and buckled on his gun belt. "I'll go visit Nate." Then, "See this?" He picked up a massive law book from his desk. "It's the Penal Code and the Code of Criminal Procedure of Texas, revised in 1879. This is the law around here."

"In Texas maybe, not in Hell's Half Acre," Koenig said.

Before Jess could try to stop him Koenig drew his gun and walked rapidly to the door that led to the cells. He kicked it wide, raised his Colt and pumped three bullets into Mad Dog Rankin, smashing him against the far wall of his cell. The big man died without making a sound but he rode Koenig's last bullet into eternity with his eyes wide open in fear and surprise.

"What the hell have you done?" Jess yelled.

"I done what you should have done when you walked into the Pony Cart Saloon today," Koenig said.

"You just committed murder," Jess said.

"No, I executed a prisoner because he could be responsible for the death of a better man than him and for past crimes too many to mention."

"It was cold-blooded murder," Jess said.

"You going to arrest me, Jess? Go ahead, arrest me, and then try to make a murder charge stick. Nate Levy is well liked in this town. Mad Dog Rankin wasn't."

His ears ringing from the gunshots, Jess Casey was too stunned to think clearly. Koenig brushed past him, then said, "If you're looking for me, Jess, come with a gun in your hand. I'll be at the Silver Garter. But first you'd better get Big Sal to remove the carrion from your cell before it stinks."

Jess stared at Mad Dog's bloody body, then walked back to his desk. He poured himself a whiskey from the bottle in his desk and built a cigarette. After a while he rose to his feet. It was time to get Big Sal the undertaker and to visit Nate Levy . . . and ask his forgiveness.

Nate Levy was lying in a makeshift hospital room at the rear of Dr. Arthur Bell's house. The doctor was out on a call but his wife, a pretty blond woman, showed him the way.

"He's resting comfortably," she said. "But he took a terrible beating and my husband fears for his life. Just a few minutes, Sheriff. Don't tire him."

After the woman closed the door behind her, Jess stepped to the bed.

"Nate, can you hear me?" he said. "You're making a habit of this, seems like."

Both the little man's eyes were swollen shut with great purple and black bruises and Jess couldn't tell if he was conscious or not. But then Nate lifted his hand and indicated that Jess should come closer. His split lips moved and in a hoarse whisper he said, "Leon . . . Curtis . . ."

Jess put his ear to Nate's mouth and said, "Are those the men who robbed you?" But Nate had lapsed into unconsciousness and could no longer hear him.

"You look tired, Sheriff Casey," Mrs. Bell said as she showed Jess to the door. "Can I get you a cup of coffee?"

Jess refused, making the excuse of a mountain of official papers back at the office.

"Well, be sure to get some sleep," the woman said. "I declare, you're all used up."

When Jess Casey returned to the sheriff's office it was full dark. He lit the lamps then filled a bucket with water and mopped out his bloody cell. That chore took the best part of two hours and when he finished he sat behind his desk and built a cigarette. He'd just thumbed a match into flame when the door opened and Destiny Durand stepped inside, a frown on her beautiful face.

Destiny was not one to stand on ceremony.

"Jess Casey, you puke, you upset Kurt," she said. "I don't know what to do with him. He says you plan to arrest him, but he likes you and he says that shooting you would make him even more distressed."

"It would distress me, too," Jess said.

"And all over a lowlife like Mad Dog Rankin." Destiny's flame-red dress rustled as she stepped to Jess's desk. "If ever a man needed killing, he did. Everybody knows it was him who broke Rosie St. Pierre's neck at the Pink Kitten last year. But nobody could prove it."

"Destiny, Kurt murdered him," Jess said.

"Listen, mister, if you want to continue as a lawman in this town you'd better learn the difference between a murder and a legal execution. Harry Stout told me that Kurt was in the right." Destiny paused for breath, then said, "How is Nate Levy?"

"He's holding in there," Jess said.

"He's a sweet little man. True-blue, unlike other people I could mention. Another thing, next week Kurt is reopening the Green Buddha in partnership with Luke Short, if Luke's still around. He just thought you should know."

"Is he selling opium?" Jess said.

"That's what the Green Buddha is, an opium den."

"Then I'll close it down," Jess said. "And what's this about Luke Short? Is he leaving town?"

"You don't get out much, do you, Sheriff?" Destiny said. "Right now even as we speak, Banjo Tom Van Meter is in the Alhambra telling anyone who'll listen that he plans to shoot Luke on sight."

Jess glanced at the clock on the wall. "It's after midnight, for heaven's sake."

"I know, way too early to start serious drinking, even for the Acre." Destiny moved to the door then stopped and said, "Sheriff, you're digging a hole for yourself and it's six feet deep. Kurt won't be arrested for killing Mad Dog and he won't allow you to shutter the Green Buddha. And you know all about Luke. He doesn't like you, Custer, so get ready to make your last stand."

CHAPTER EIGHT

Jess Casey saw a way to head off at least one of his troubles. Despite his weariness, he buckled on his gun and headed for the Alhambra, a middle-of-the-road saloon that served a free lunch every day except Sunday.

The moon rode high, lighting up the crowded boardwalks for the jostling sporting crowd. A shabby man wearing a preacher's suit and a prophet's beard yelled that the end of the world was nigh and tried to hand out pamphlets but got few takers. Let the world end when it may, the damned of Hell's Half Acre would keep on partying.

The Alhambra was lit with gas lamps and the place was crowded except for a deserted half circle in the middle of the bar where a lone man stood, a long-barreled Colt in his hand. The fellow was short and flashily dressed, and wore his shiny, slicked-down hair parted in the middle. A pencil-thin mustache, calculated to draw the eye-fluttering attention of the fairer sex, graced his upper lip and was further accentuated by prominent front teeth. Jess pegged him as a nasty piece of work, a dedicated ladies' man suddenly way out of his depth. Such a man should not make death threats against Luke Short.

Jess smiled and stepped toward him. "You must be Banjo Tom Van Meter," he said.

"Stay back," Van Meter said. "I'll kill any man who comes within arm's length of me."

"No, you won't," Jess said.

"You just see if I won't," Van Meter said. He raised the Colt to waist level. "Another step and I'll cut you down." His buckteeth gave him a pronounced lisp.

"Mister, I'm tired, hungry and irritable and I don't need this tonight," Jess said. "Just put the cannon on the bar and we'll talk like kissin' kin."

The little man tensed. Gaslight gleamed on his patent leather hair. "I can drill ya from here," he said.

"And then you'll hang," Jess said. He looked at the men at the bar who were crowded around enjoying the show. "Will you men see to it?"

"You can count on us, Sheriff," a beefy man said, a promise that drew growls of approval.

"You got a decision to make, Banjo Tom," Jess said.

Tears filled Van Meter's eyes. "This is all Luke Short's fault," he said. "I took his woman and now he aims to kill me." More tears fell and the little man was racked by great, shuddering sobs. "I want Lulu. Somebody bring my Lulu here."

"Oh hell," Jess said. He strode to Van Meter and yanked the gun from his hand. "You're out of here. Go home and sleep it off."

He pulled the little man away from the bar, spun him around and gave him an ass-and-collar exit out the door. Then, after a farewell kick to Van Meter's butt, Jess yelled, "And stay the hell away from Luke Short, and send him his woman back."

The crowd spilled outside to see if there was going to be fun, but Banjo Tom, rubbing his butt, vanished into the crowded street. Jess tossed the Colt to the beefy man. "Give him that when he sobers up. Tell him to hang it on the wall and stick to his banjo. He isn't cut out to be a shootist."

That last drew cheers and offers of a drink, but Jess declined and took to the boardwalk. He stopped at a street vendor's cart and bought a meat pie that he ate right there and then returned to his office.

That night Jess dreamed of Mad Dog Rankin and of little Chinese men smoking pipes, all but one who played a banjo. Then Kurt Koenig appeared and his tawny mane made him look like a lion. The big cat opened its great maw of a mouth, its fangs glistening, and stalked toward Jess and it roared and roared . . .

Jess woke up with a start, his heart hammering as fear spiked at him. Dawn light filtered through the office windows and outside two men with tangled wagons roared at each other and threatened imminent fisticuffs.

Jess rose, put on his hat and padded to the door in his underwear. He yelled at the drivers to pipe down and to get their wagons rolling because they were blocking the street.

Later as he built his first cigarette of the day his hands still shook. As visions of Mad Dog, smoking Chinamen, roaring lions and Kurt Koenig cleared his sleep-fogged brain he put his bad dream down to eating a meat pie so late in the day . . .

But deep in his gut he knew that wasn't the reason.

CHAPTER NINE

Ford Talon knew that what was left of the two hundred dollars he'd taken from Herb Coffin's body would not last long. He'd no wish to remain in Fort Worth. In fact he wanted a heap of git between him and Texas, but for that he needed a grubstake.

Raised a gentleman by a doting mother and wealthy father, he had never had to turn his hand to work and was ill suited for manual labor. The only trade he'd learned in Huntsville was how to make little rocks out of big rocks and there wasn't much call for that in Fort Worth.

Talon was eating breakfast in the Ma's Kitchen restaurant when a couple men he knew stepped inside. Lonny Leon and Jeb Curtis had been in the wagons Coffin had brought from Huntsville.

Despite his lack of a beard and new clothes the men recognized him immediately and sat at his table, grinning. Leon, dressed in worn-out duds that were too big for him, said, "You look to be prospering, Ford."

"Doing all right at the moment," Talon said. "It won't last long. Where did you and Jeb find clothes?"

"Stole 'em," Curtis said. "An' got us eighty dollars as well."

"Shut your trap, Jeb," Leon said. "The damned walls have ears." He opened his shabby coat and grinned. "Stole this, too, Ford." The handle of a Remington revolver stuck out of his waistband. "The feller who owned it don't need it no more."

"You boys ate yet?" Talon said.

"Not a bite," Curtis said. "But we're only hungry for coffee. We got big plans, see, an' a man shouldn't eat when he's layin' down plans. Grub makes his brains dull."

"What kind of plans?" Talon said.

"Wouldn't you like to know," Curtis said. He tapped the side of his nose with a forefinger. "It's a secret."

"Damn you fer an idiot, Jeb," Leon said. "It ain't a secret when we're among friends, an' Ford is a friend, ain't you, Major?"

Talon smiled. "We pounded a pile of rock together back in the pen."

Curtis pretended to spit on the floor, drawing a horrified look from a stern matron breakfasting with her husband. "Thirty years for sticking my pizzle into a woman that was married anyway," he said. "Like she even noticed."

"What about you, Lonny?" Talon said.

"Bank robbery," Leon said. "An' I killed a deputy sheriff making my getaway. 'Scum, I sentence you to hard labor for the rest of your natural life,' the judge said. I aim to find that sumbitch one day and kill him."

"You killed three men, huh?" Curtis said to Talon.

"Yes. Herb Coffin was the last of them."

Lonny Leon's face registered surprise. "You done fer Coffin? How the hell did you manage that?"

"It wasn't easy," Talon said.

"Ford don't want to talk about it because he's a gentleman, Lonny," Curtis said. "Ain't that right, Ford?"

Talon smiled. "It's a painful memory. Can I buy you boys coffee?"

"I could use some," Leon said.

The waitress was young and pretty and Jeb leered and grabbed his crotch under the table. This drew a rebuke from Leon, who warned him not to attract attention to himself or he'd ruin everything.

"Ruin what?" Talon said.

"A sure thing," Leon said as he spooned sugar into his coffee. "Do you mind Jasper Dunn, came up the trail with us from Huntsville?"

"I remember," Talon said. He recalled a simian man with carrion-eater eyes and a hairline that came down to his eyebrows. "Murder, wasn't it?"

"Yeah, Jasper killed more 'n his share and enjoyed the doing of it. They were gonna hang him for murdering a sodbuster and his wife up Clay County way," Leon said. "But the governor commuted his sentence to twenty-five years on account of how Jasper got kicked by a mule when he was a younker and ain't quite right in the head. At least that's what his lawyer said."

"A fine man," Talon said.

"Who?" Leon said.

"Your friend Jasper."

"Jasper don't have no friends, but he has big ideas, big plans," Leon said. "He's a thinker, thinking all the time." He leaned closer to Talon. "It's a bank, Ford, a big, fat cattleman's bank on Belknap Street." Leon glanced over his shoulder, then said, "We're gonna take it."

"Who's 'we'?" Talon said.

"Jasper, me, Jeb and five others came up the trail with us, all of them members of the bank-robbing profession."

"Well, are you in, Ford?" Curtis said. "You're smart and we need smart."

"Jeb's right about that," Leon said. "Bank robbers ain't that clever. We want somebody like you, a man used to giving orders."

"When do you hit the bank, Lonny?" Talon said.

"That hasn't been decided yet. We need to steal more horses and guns. What do you say?"

"I say, I'll think about it," Talon said.

"Don't study on it for too long, Ford," Leon said. "There's only room for one more, and I'd sure like it to be you."

* * *

Jasper Dunn was thinking big, bigger than Lonny Leon could ever imagine. Why settle for a bank when he could have it all?

Thirty white men crowded into the basement of an abandoned warehouse on the corner of Houston and 11th Street. Until recently the building had been used for grain storage and was infested by rats, but men who'd endured conditions at Huntsville had no fear of rodents and other vermin.

Most of the men present were still clothed in prison rags, many in bare feet, and all of them were hungry. A few had rolled a drunk or two or picked some pockets and were in better shape, but it was still a tattered, flea-ridden bunch who listened so attentively to Jasper Dunn's voice. Dunn himself was well dressed since he'd taken part in the robbery of Nate Levy's clothing store, and he wore a stolen Colt revolver on his hip.

He stood on a box and pointed in the direction of the street. "Look at you," he yelled at the men squatting on the filthy floor. "You still look like a bunch of prison rats and do you know why? I'll tell you why." His voice rose to a shout. "It's because those people out there don't give a damn about you."

This drew scattered cheers and a cry of "Damn right they don't!"

"But that's all going to change!" Dunn yelled.

"How we gonna change it, Jasper? Tell us how."

The man was a shill planted by Dunn and the reaction was better than he'd expected.

"Yeah, how?" a man yelled and others took up the chorus of "How? How?"

"Because we're taking over Hell's Half Acre," Dunn said. "We'll grab our cut and squeeze this damned town dry, starting with the cathouses and dance halls where the pickings are easy."

"And then what, Jasper?" the shill hollered.

"Then the saloons and the regular businesses and then, moving in one neighborhood at a time, the entire city of Fort Worth."

That was music to the ears of hungry, hopeless men. Suddenly in Jasper Dunn they saw their savior, a man who could give them everything they craved: money, whiskey, women . . . and power.

Murderers, robbers, rapists, the scum of the earth, they cheered Dunn until they were hoarse.

The unholy covenant between the Huntsville cons and Jasper Dunn was further sealed when several black men and Mexicans carried cauldrons of steaming soup into the basement, along with trays of freshly baked bread and bowls and spoons.

"Jasper Dunn looks after his boys," Dunn yelled. "And when you're finished eating there's whiskey and beer for everybody."

As ravenous men fell on the food, Dunn took a man aside who had the scarred face and big-knuckled hands of a street fighter. Their heads close, Dunn said, "Cole, you sure you squared this with the Panther City Boys?" he said. "I don't want any trouble from them. They're organized and there's a lot of them."

"Don't move north of 11th Street, west of Houston or east of Commerce and they'll look the other way," the man called Cole said. "Of course they want their cut. Forty percent of every cent you take in."

"I'll play along for now," Dunn said. "Later I'll settle with the Panther City Boys permanently. Who's in my way, Cole?"

"Kurt Koenig is the big man around town, owns the Silver Garter saloon and the Green Buddha opium den and a lot else besides. He's tough and good with a gun. Luke Short has the White Elephant and he won't be pushed, either. He killed Jim Courtright after he tried to strong-arm him and Jim was nobody's idea of a bargain."

Dunn looked around him. "My God, this rabble eats like pigs," he said. Then, "What about the law?"

"Koenig is the city marshal and there's a green sheriff in the Acre by the name of Jess Casey. He's a stove-up cowboy who won't cause you much trouble."

Dunn absorbed that then said, "I need guns, clothing and horses for these men, and they'll expect wages."

"The Panther City Boys can supply all of that."

"Just mention the name Cole Danvers, huh?" Dunn said.

"Yeah, mention my name and hand over a bagful of money."

"Damn it, I don't have any money."

"I'll ask around, Jasper. Maybe I can find somebody ready to bankroll you for a cut."

"Another cut? Soon I'll have nothing left."

"When you first start out in business you can expect a lot of fingers in your wallet," Danvers said. "That will stop the more successful you become."

"I want to get the ball rolling, Cole. I mean real soon. Look around you. Is this any way for a man to live?"

"Jasper, you saved my life in Huntsville when the guards were planning to kill me to stop my release. I haven't forgotten. I'll do all I can for you."

CHAPTER TEN

Mayor Harry Stout was not in a good mood. He had three problems to solve that morning. One was a personal matter concerning a young lady of his acquaintance who had upped her already expensive rates because of his increasing girth, complaining that he was going to "crush her bones to powder." That sorry situation did not concern Sheriff Jeff Casey but the other two did.

"I want to resolve these irritations this morning, Sheriff Casey," Stout said, scowling. He sat behind a huge polished mahogany desk, his great belly hanging like a sack of grain between his legs. The flag of the United States and the Texas Lone Star stood behind him.

"And they are?" Jess said. His body ached that morning and an old hip injury plagued him.

Stout raised his chubby hand and extended a forefinger. "One. No legal action will be taken against City Marshal Kurt Koenig. He was within his rights to execute Mad Dog Rankin. The man was a damned nuisance." Jess opened his mouth to speak, but the mayor raised a middle finger. "Two. I'm told that there's a wild man running around the town cemetery scaring all the women. You will find that savage creature and arrest or shoot him at your discretion."

Stout leaned back in his chair and linked fingers across his belly as though he had fairly stated his case. "I think I've made myself clear," he said. "Be warned, Sheriff, I will brook no argument over the Rankin business, none whatsoever. If you care to press the matter I will reluctantly dismiss you from your post."

Jess decided to surrender, at least for now. He did not want to make an enemy of Harry, a man who could make or break him.

"Tell me about the wild man," he said.

"Mrs. Anderson and her daughter Mabel, poor things, saw him," Stout said after a quick glance at the clock on the wall. "The creature had a long beard, was dressed in rags, and Mrs. Anderson said he had red, glowing eyes like a demon. Apparently the wild man demanded food, but the two women fled and Mabel, a rather plump young lady, twisted her ankle quite badly. She's now at home under the care of a doctor."

Stout clapped his hands, signaling an end to the meeting. "Do your duty, Sheriff Casey. I look forward to hearing good reports of you."

* * *

Fort Worth's Oakwood Cemetery had been established in 1879, but was already crowded with the notable and notorious. Its spacious, oak-shaded sixty-two acres made the city fathers proud and Harry had approved a sign at the gate that declared:

COME ON IN THERE'S ROOM FOR EVERYBODY

Since the graveyard was relatively new, it had none of the spooky aspects of older boot hills and its marble and granite headstones gleamed in the morning sunlight. There were several mausoleums and one of the largest had been erected under the branches of a spreading oak. But the marble-paneled outer door stood ajar as did the iron security gate behind it.

Jess decided it was as likely a place as any for a wild man to hole up. He drew his Colt and stepped to the door. "Anybody to home?" he said, fully aware how strange that sounded. He moved closer, pushed the door and the gate wider.

"It ain't a graveyard if the gate don't creak, huh?"

The voice came from behind Jess and he swung around, thumbing back the hammer of the Colt. The wild man stood watching him, a smile on his bearded face.

"Don't shoot!" the man yelled. "Don't shoot old Sam Waters. He don't mean no harm."

"You scared the hell out of me," Jess said. "I

should put a bullet into you out of spite. Why are you here scaring white folks?"

"Old Sam's got nowhere else to go, lawman. That's why he sleeps with the dead. They talk to him, tell him secret things."

"You're a crazy old coot," Jess said. "How did you get here?"

"In a wagon. Sam got here in a steel wagon."

"From where? And let me tell you, I'm having a real hard time believing your story."

"Well, I didn't fall out of the sky, sonny." The old man scratched his head, then, "Ah, now my brain is starting to work again. I was brung here from Huntsville. I spent my whole life there, man and boy."

"Who brought you here, Sam?" Jess said. He thought the man looked impossibly old. He was small, thin and wrinkled and when Jess looked into his faded blue eyes there was no one at home.

"Bad men brought Sam here in a wagon"—he shook the iron door of the tomb—"like this. Sam, and a hundred, no, too many, half a hundred. All of them were bad men. When we got to this town they chased Sam away, said he was too old and loco."

"All those bad men were brought here from Huntsville?" Jess said.

The old man nodded. "All of them. Very bad men." He smiled, revealing few teeth and those bad. "Sam was a prisoner for sixty years. He was the oldest of them."

"What did you do to deserve that?" Jess said. "You sure this isn't a big windy you're telling me?"

"I'm telling you the truth. Damn it, boy, they forgot all about me. After years and years passed the guards didn't even know who old Sam Waters was or why he was in jail. They never give Sam no trouble, though."

Jess said, "Do you remember what you did, Sam?"

"Sure I do. When I was twenty years old I stole old man Perkins's chickens and then his milk cow. Sold the milk cow for a jug of whiskey, Sam did, and got three years in jail." The old man shrugged his narrow shoulders. "After I was transferred from the county jail to Huntsville everybody forgot about me. At first I'd say, 'I'm Sam Waters the cow thief. Let me go.' But then some bull would hit him with a stick so Sam stopped saying that an' kept his mouth shut. Prisoners came and went, the deck got shuffled time after time and Sam was the card that got dropped on the floor."

"Sixty years for stealing a cow," Jess said, shaking his head. "That's hard to believe."

"And chickens. Sam stole chickens."

"Sam, think carefully now. Are all those men from Huntsville still here in Fort Worth?"

"Sure are, lawman. Myself included, but they don't want me around."

"They all dressed like you?" Jess said.

"Yeah. Just like me, all in rags."

Jess felt sick, anticipating big trouble coming down. Fifty desperate cons had been dumped on

Fort Worth, by whose authority or for what reason he could not guess. Starving, ragged, their first need would be clothing and food, and that could explain the robbery at Nate Levy's clothing store. It also explained the presence of Ford Talon in the Acre. He was one of them.

And then the old con surprised Jess. He stopped talking about himself as though Sam Waters were a different person and said, "I reckon you're one man agin fifty, lawman. Those Huntsville boys will run riot in this town. Just you wait and see."

"Why did you pretend to be loco, Sam?" Jess said.

"It was my protection in the pen, and I figured it would protect me from you."

"I mean you no harm," Jess said.

Sam nodded. "I finally cottoned to that. You got a good face, Sheriff, like that General Custer everybody talks about. You know, the feller that got massacreed by all them Indians."

"Yeah, I've heard that before," Jess said. "Well, I caught me a wild man. I guess we'd better get back."

"What you going to do with old Sam? I could sure use a bait o' grub. I'm right partial to eggs and bacon and fried bread. You got any of that?"

"Not with me, no," Jess said.

"Am I under arrest?"

"For the moment."

"Then you'll have to feed me."

Jess smiled. "I guess I'll have to at that."

* * *

If Sam Waters expected to eat right away he was sorely disappointed. Like a man washes a muddy dog, Jess held him under the pump behind the office and made him wash all over with lye soap and a scrubbing brush. When the old man was clean enough to pass inspection he was allowed to towel off and Jess frog-marched him into the office, where he tossed him a blanket and ordered him into the cell.

"Stay there until I get back," Jess said. "I'll leave the cell door open."

"What about my grub and where's my duds?" Waters said.

"You didn't have any duds," Jess said. "I'll bring you something to wear."

"And grub," the old man said.

"Yeah, and grub," Jess said.

CHAPTER ELEVEN

"They busted through the back door, Sheriff," Bill Harker said. "Look around you, I'm just about cleaned out. Clothes, shoes, hats, all gone and so is the Colt self-cocker I always keep behind the counter. And look." Harker led the way to a high pile of stinking rags that had been neatly folded and stacked up on the floor. "Their idea of a joke," he said.

Judging by the size of the stack of rags at least a score of men had been involved in the robbery. They'd changed right there in the store and that meant they weren't afraid of much.

The cons Waters had told him about had made their move and Jess had a feeling that worse, much worse, was to come.

"I've a good idea who did this, Mr. Harker," Jess said. "I'll track them down."

"When, track them down?" Harker said.

"It will take time," Jess said. "Can you describe any of the missing clothing?"

"Damn it, Sheriff, I sell rags to people who want better rags than the ones they're wearing. I can't remember . . . wait . . . yeah, I can describe a vest that's missing. A cowboy sold it to me, a black-and-white cowhide vest with fancy horn buttons. It's got a label on the inside that says it was made in El Paso. That's all I can remember."

"It's a good start," Jess said. "A vest like that is hard to miss." Then, an apologetic look on his face, Jess said, "I have to buy some duds for a prisoner, a little feller."

Harker shrugged. "Take what you want, Sheriff, free of charge. I'm out of business. Hell, that little Jewish feller, what's his name?"

"Nate Levy."

"Yeah, him. He's been undercutting me anyway."

"Mr. Harker, Nate's store was robbed just like yours, only he was to home when the thieves arrived and he got badly beaten."

Harker was stunned. "My God, Sheriff, what's happening in this town?"

"Nothing good, Mr. Harker, nothing good."

"Where is Nate?" Harker said. "I'll go visit him and take him grapes. That's what professional courtesy is all about, ain't it? Taking a sick man grapes?"

Jess Casey left the store with an armful of used clothing that was a sight better than the rags Sam Waters had been wearing. He stopped off at the Ma's Kitchen restaurant and got a plate of bacon and beans and a chunk of bread. That too was a sight better than what the old man had been eating.

While Sam Waters, dressed in his new duds, sat in Jess Casey's chair and wolfed down bacon and beans, across town Bruno Cavanni was adjusting the trigger pull of a Colt shopkeeper. "I want that thing to go bang if I even breathe on the trigger," the gambler who owned the piece had told him. Cavanni bent to his task and aimed to please.

He'd learned the gunsmith's trade back in his native Italy at the workshop of the Fabbrica d'Armi Pietro Beretta in Gardone and at the age of seventy-seven was still considered by his contemporaries to be a maestro.

But Jasper Dunn didn't give a hoot about all that, since it was he who beat the old man to death with the gambler's hair-trigger Colt.

"Clean him out, boys," Dunn said, dropping the bloody revolver on the floor beside the dead gunsmith. "Take everything that will fire a bullet and all the ammunition you can find."

"Sporting rifles?" a man asked.

"I said everything," Dunn snapped. "And put the CLOSED sign on the door."

As life went on in the busy street outside, Dunn's men carried the firearms to the horse-drawn wagon waiting in the alley behind the shop's back door. In all, helped by a few of the Panther City Boys, Dunn and his cohorts stole thirty revolvers, seventeen rifles and a dozen shotguns.

Lonny Leon took a fancy to the shopkeeper Colt, wiped off the blood and stuck it in his waistband. He grinned at Dunn. "Now we're rollin', boss."

Dunn shook his head. "We ain't begun to roll yet, Lonny." He pumped his fists and yelled, "Look out, Fort Worth, we're coming to get ya!"

And this drew a cheer from the convicts within earshot.

CHAPTER TWELVE

"Who's that in the cell?" Kurt Koenig said.

"A wild man," Jess Casey said. "And you're not going to shoot him."

"Wild men are not among my usual targets," Koenig said with a faint smile. Then his face settled into grimness. "Jess, you'd better come with me. It's outside your jurisdiction but I think you should be there."

"What happened?" Jess said, fearing the worst.

He was not disappointed.

"Gunsmith's store raided on Elm Street. The owner is . . . was . . . an old man named Bruno Cavanni. He was beaten to death."

"And all his guns were taken," Jess said.

"Yeah, and from what I hear, every last round of ammunition. Get your horse. It's too far for a puncher to walk."

"Crossing the street is too far for a puncher to walk," Jess said. Then to Waters, "Stay right here until I decide what to do with you, Sam."

"Is the big feller aiming to plug me?" Waters said, warily eyeing Koenig.

"Probably," Jess said. "But if you do what you're told I won't let him."

Elm Street was in a quiet area of town, well away from the noise and bustle of the Acre. The gunsmith's shop was a small wooden building set back from the road among a grove of wild oak. A gravel path led to the door, where a number of people had gathered, among them Mayor Stout, an exclamation point of pomposity among the faceless crowd.

An indication of how seriously the mayor took the murder and robbery was the presence of his bodyguard, a seven-foot-tall Irishman named Barry Sullivan, whose enormous breadth of chest was made even wider by the two Remington revolvers he wore in shoulder holsters under his coat. The word going around was that he'd learned the shootist's trade in Ireland and was a dangerous man to cross.

Stout immediately accosted Kurt Koenig. "A bad business, Kurt," he said. "The theft of so many guns and ammunition warns me that there's some threatening game afoot. I say, menacing, sir, menacing. By the Lord, that's the word for it." Then, before Koenig could get a word in, and for the benefit of the crowd, "I demand that something be done, Marshal, and quickly."

Jess left Koenig and the mayor to their cussin'

and discussin' and stepped into the store. The shelves, display cases and gun racks had been stripped bare and Bruno Cavanni's body still lay where he'd fallen. Jess had been told that the Pinkertons were great detectives who could find clues overlooked by other lawmen, but he saw nothing of value. Kurt Koenig stepped inside, his marshal's badge pinned to his coat, and Jess said, "I wish we had a Pinkerton."

"Well, I don't have one of them handy," Koenig said. He looked angry. "Where's the body?"

"Back here. I'm stepping into the alley for a look-see."

The wheel tracks where the wagon had stood were still visible in the alley and many feet had churned the ground where the robbers had loaded the guns into the back. At least a dozen men, Jess reckoned, maybe more.

Kurt Koenig joined him and said, "See anything?"

"Look where they packed away the guns," Jess said. "It took a lot of boots to kick up that much dirt."

Koenig nodded. "There was a bunch of them, all right."

The big man stood deep in thought and Jess said, "It wasn't the Panther City Boys."

"You a mind reader, Jess?" Koenig said.

"No, but I know what you were thinking. This robbery wasn't pulled off by the Panthers."

"I sure hope not," Koenig said. "Most of those boys work for me and I'd hate to hang my own. So who do you think did it?"

"I need more time before I answer that," Jess said. "The thing that troubles me is why the guns? Were they stolen for self-protection or something else? And the beating death of a harmless old gunsmith was the act of a madman. Is that what we're facing, Kurt?"

"A madman with a gun?" Koenig said. "Plenty of those in Fort Worth. Hell, Luke Short could qualify."

Jess allowed himself a smile. "He could, but Luke had nothing to do with this crime."

"Then who did?"

"I told you, give me time," Jess said.

Koenig nodded. "Well, while you're playing for time I'll have my boys round up every suspicious stranger in this town and check his bona fides. I'm not going to mess around with this, Sheriff. If I suspect someone then he's gallows bait unless he can prove otherwise."

"This crime is out of my jurisdiction, Kurt," Jess said.

"Damn right it is, so stay out of my way."

"And you'll be judge, jury and executioner," Jess said.

"That's what I like about you, Jess," Koenig said. "You catch on fast."

CHAPTER THIRTEEN

"He caught on fast, didn't he?" Professor James Carnes said.

"Senator Jennings is not an unintelligent man, unlike the usual run of politicians," said Charles Blair. He was the professor's assistant, an earnest young man with brown hair and eyes and an unruly shock of rusty red hair. "He provided us with a golden opportunity."

Carnes strolled to the hotel room window and stared outside at the traffic on Main Street. Without turning he said, "But do you think I convinced him?"

Blair smiled. "I really think he very much wanted to be convinced."

"How many convicts was it?"

"Fifty-three, I believe."

"Good, then you may take down my letter to Senator Jennings. Start with the usual greetings and about my tedious journey and safe arrival, and then—"

"Excuse me, Professor," Blair said. He removed a piece of lint from the point of his steel pen and then said, "Now I'm ready."

Carnes's frown revealed his irritation. "Right, take this down:

"If fifty-three convicts can be returned to society and cause a minimum of disruption and show every indication that they plan to lead fine, upstanding lives then my theory that long prison sentences are useless and unnecessary will be proven without a doubt. I believe my research will reveal that, in a majority of cases, a custodial sentence of one to two years is enough to show any criminal the error of his ways, especially if our prisons are places of severe physical punishment. Spare not the rod, my dear senator, so that ere the prisoners are released they are already instilled with a horror of ever returning to such a terrible place as a federal penitentiary. Prisoners from Huntsville, where severest punishments are imposed even for minor infractions of discipline, are ideal subjects and I thank you once again for making me familiar with your own bold experiment. Your returning of hardened convicts to be nurtured at the sweet bosom of civilization was, to say the least, a masterstroke."

Professor Carnes waved a hand. "I am, sir, your obedient servant . . . et cetera . . . et cetera. Did you get it all down?"

"Yes, Professor, I did," Blair said. "It was very succinct and to the point."

"Of course it was, my dear fellow. Professor

James Carnes does not waffle. Now come, let us send the letter and then take a promenade around what is called Hell's Half Acre. If there are already Huntsville prisoners at honest employ, that's where we will find them, I'll be bound."

"You must understand, Sheriff . . . ah . . ."

"Casey. Jess Casey."

"Sheriff Casey, you must understand that I have undertaken a most singular task. It is a matter of the greatest moment that I track down the Huntsville prisoners and ascertain how they have reintegrated, if you'll excuse that word, with Fort Worth society."

Jess nodded toward Sam Waters, who stood against the office wall and watched Professor Carnes and his assistant with wary eyes. "That's one of them. But he's a wild man and he bites."

A reluctant smile touched Carnes's thin lips. "You like your little jest, Sheriff." He glared at Waters. "Come now, my good man, do you wish to return to Huntsville? Now? Ever?"

"Sure don't, Perfesser, not now, not ever," Sam said. "That ain't no place for a Christian white man."

Carnes's smile grew. "Good, good, excellent," he said. "And are you seeking honest, gainful employ?"

"If that means do I have a job, the answer is yes. I work for the sheriff."

Carnes clapped his hands, as did his assistant.

"Huzzah!" he said. "Do you have close friends from Huntsville who are also already employed?"

"It's every man for his ownself in the pen, Perfesser. I didn't make any close friends, nor distant ones, either."

"Yes, yes, the dangers of . . . how many years of incarceration?"

"Nigh on sixty year. They forgot about me, like."

"Oh my God," Carnes said. "But nonetheless, Blair, this at least helps prove part of my theory that criminals can once again join society as productive citizens if prisons are made horrendous enough."

"Indeed, Professor," Blair said. "How were conditions in the penitentiary while you were there, Waters?"

Sam said, "I saw men happy to die because they knew hell would be a big improvement on Huntsville."

"Wonderful! Excellent!" Professor Carnes said. "I know I'll find some first-rate subjects here."

"Professor, just what's your game?" Jess said. The man irritated him.

"This is no game, Sheriff," Carnes said. "If I can prove my theory here in Fort Worth it will change our entire penal system. Tell him, Blair."

Blair explained to Jess about his boss's belief in short prison sentences in sadistic hellholes that would terrify even the most hardened criminals back on the straight and narrow.

"It's a revolutionary theory created by Professor

Carnes, a man of destiny, and I'm proud to be associated with his work," Blair said.

"Within one generation, perhaps two, there will be no more criminal class in our great nation," Carnes said. "No one in his right mind will risk a year or two in one of my terror prisons."

Jess glanced up from the makings in his hands. "So you think the convicts dumped here from Huntsville are so scared to go back that they'll all settle down and become church deacons. Is that it?"

"Crudely stated, but that is my belief," Carnes said.

"Not a hope in hell," Jess said. "They're already responsible for three robberies and one, possibly two murders, in this town. And they're just getting started."

"So you say, Sheriff, but I don't believe you," Carnes said.

Jess's face was like stone. "Where are you from, Professor?"

"I hail from the great city of Boston, Massachusetts," Carnes said.

"Out here, if you call a man a liar you better be ready to draw iron to prove it," Jess said.

"I'm sure the professor did not mean to impugn your honesty, Sheriff," Blair said.

"Then let him say it," Jess said.

"Of course I didn't," Carnes said. He wasn't afraid, merely irritated. "All I'm saying is that your own natives could have committed the crimes you mention. This is Hell's Half Acre, after all, and I'm told that such things happen every day." Then, his face severe, Carnes said, "Don't stand in the way of progress, Sheriff."

Jess smiled and said, "Gold watch and chain. Gold ring on your left hand. Diamond stickpin in your cravat and only you know how much money is in your wallet. A lot, I imagine. Go among those convicts and you'll last less than an hour, Professor Carnes. That's how long I give you to live in this town."

"Balderdash! Nonsense! Foolishness! Empty words spoken by an ignorant bumpkin," Carnes said. He turned away from Jess's desk then said, "I wish you good-day, sir."

Blair had the good grace to give Jess a sympathetic smile before he followed his boss out the door.

"That big-city dude has a heap to learn about the West, don't he?" Sam Waters said.

"Yeah, and he'll learn it the hard way," Jess said.

CHAPTER FOURTEEN

"Ride with me, Sheriff," Ford Talon said. "And I'd be obliged if you could loan me a Colt. I will not use Herb Coffin's cursed revolver."

Jess Casey smiled. "You planning to kill somebody?"

"If that's the way the dice roll. Saddle up. We don't have much time."

Jess gave a mocking salute. "Yes, sir, Major."

"You're a general. You outrank me," Talon said, smiling.

Sam Waters stared into Talon's face for long moments, then said, "I'll saddle your hoss, Sheriff."

"Hold on, Sam, first I want to know what's going on here," Jess said.

"He'll tell you on the trail," Sam said. "There's big trouble coming down and this man knows where."

Sam hurried out of the office and Jess rose from his desk. "Talon, the old man saw something in your face that convinced him you're on the level. After sixty years in Huntsville he can read a man and I've come to trust his judgment."

"Trust your own judgment, Sheriff. And trust me enough to give me a gun. We've got lives to save."

"Why should you care, Talon?" Jess said.

"If I didn't care I'd never again be able to hold my head high in the company of men."

The cabin was on Mustang Creek, a few miles south of Fort Worth. The rumor that reached the Acre, carried and embellished by punchers, was that Tom Williamson had struck it rich panning the creek and that now he, his wife and their two teenage daughters had salted away enough gold to keep a man in whiskey and whores for the rest of his life.

There never had been gold in Mustang Creek and most pegged the story as a big windy, but Lonny Leon and Jeb Curtis figured it was worth checking out, especially since the Williamson girls were said to be both pretty and willing.

"Lonny asked me to throw in with them," Talon said as he and Jess Casey rode through rolling cactus and mesquite country under a burning sun. "But I made the excuse that my horse was lame."

"You sure Leon and Curtis are headed to the Williamson place today?" Jess said.

"Yeah, it was all planned for today. They rode out maybe thirty minutes before I sneaked my horse out of Joe Jacobs's livery. I owe for feed and a stall and he expects me to step to the mark and ante up."

"Where is the cabin?" Jess said.

"It's on this bank of the creek overhung by a huge cottonwood and it's got some kind of vegetable garden out front. A mile before we reach the cabin there's the ruin of a stage station and a couple of unmarked graves."

Jess was silent and Talon said, "If there really is any gold Lonny's plan is to find it and then for him and Jeb to ride for Old Mexico and take the Williamson girls with them. They'll kill the parents first, of course, unless the mother is still pretty. If she is, they'll take her along, too."

"And you were offered a share, huh?" Jess said.

"Yeah, a third of the gold and one of the women."

"Lonny couldn't say fairer than that, could he?" Jess said.

"No, I guess not. His original plan was to rob a bank in Fort Worth and then skedaddle. But then he got wind of the Mustang Creek gold."

"Did he offer you a one-third share of the bank money?" Jess said.

"Yes, he did and I considered it," Talon said. "Robbing a bank is clean, but raiding a man's cabin and taking his women is a dirty business."

Jess shook his head. "Talon, don't rob any banks in the Acre, huh?"

"I won't," Talon said. "I don't think I'm cut out for bank robbing, anyway. Nowadays there are too many lowlifes in the profession and they're spoiling it for everybody."

"Major Talon, I hope you're joking," Jess said.

The man grinned. "You'll never know, will you?"

The stage station had been burned in some forgotten Indian attack and the graves held the remains of two nameless souls. In the course of time their bodies would turn to dust and they'd become one with the prairie. Until then, a pair of rectangular mounds of earth stood to remind passing travelers that once upon a time there were people here.

Suddenly hot and weary, Jess took a swig from his canteen. He undid the bandanna from around his neck, soaked it in water and tied it back in place. "We're getting close," he said.

"Seems like," Talon said. Despite the hammering heat of the blazing sun he shivered and said, "Dead folks walking here." He looked around him. "I can sense them watching us. They're afraid."

Jess smiled. "A man like you afraid of ha'ants and sich? I don't believe it."

"My ma was Irish and she saw the dead. I see them, too." Talon kneed his horse into motion. "Let's move on, Sheriff. They don't want us here."

More to take his mind off the gunfight he knew was coming than any other reason, Jess said, "Speaking of ha'ants, take your average puncher now. He's the most superstitious critter on earth. One time when I was working for the old Bar-10 a feller got struck by lightning when he was riding for town one Friday night, killed him and his horse stone dead. Well, the puncher's hat got blown off and landed in the middle of the trail. That hat lay there for three years while everybody that passed rode wide around it. They figured it was a bad-luck hat and nobody would touch it."

"What happened to the hat?" Talon said. His eyes were on the trail ahead and his voice sounded distant.

"One winter a big wind blew up and took it away. All us punchers were relieved when that happened. Let me tell you."

"I wouldn't have touched it," Talon said.

"No, sir, you wouldn't. It was a bad-luck hat," Jess said.

For a while the two men rode without speaking, the only sound the creak of saddle leather and the soft thud of their horses' hooves. A fly droned around Jess's head and he shooed it away a dozen times.

Finally Talon said, "Cabin ahead." Straight as a string, a column of smoke rose into the sky from behind a mesquite-covered rise.

"Seems like," Jess said. He adjusted the lie of his Colt.

Beside him Talon removed his coat, folded it neatly and placed it on the saddle behind him. He'd stuck his borrowed Colt in the right side of his waistband, butt-forward for a cavalry draw. Jess raised a disapproving eyebrow but said nothing.

"Ready?" Talon said.

Jess nodded. "Yeah, let's go save some ladies in distress."

CHAPTER FIFTEEN

"Why the hell did you bring him, Ford?" Lonny Leon said. "We only got three women for us five so he ain't getting a cut."

The women in question huddled together by the cabin door. The oldest, Mrs. Williamson, had a bruised left eye, the result of a blow. Her daughters, pretty and blond, were unhurt but seemed terrified.

Jess's eyes moved to the man who was hanging by his ankles from a limb of the cottonwood. His pants sagged over his calves as he struggled to free himself.

"He tell you where the gold is yet?" Jess said.

"No, not yet, but he will just as soon as Jeb gets the fire lit," Leon said.

Jeb looked up from the smoking kindling he'd piled up under the hanging man's head and grinned. "I'll roast it out of him. Once he feels his hair start to burn he'll squeal like a pig."

A pair of grinning hard cases Jess didn't know stood by the women.

"When does the fun start, Lonny?" one of them said.

"Hell, right now," Leon said. "Why wait? Pull the cork on the sodbuster's jug, Win, and we'll have ourselves a hoedown. Bring one of them womenfolk over here so I can get my mitts on her."

Jess assessed a situation that was rapidly turning ugly and stepped out of the saddle. He walked to the fire that was starting to flame and kicked it over the kneeling Jeb Curtis. Startled, the man cursed and jumped to his feet. His hand reached for his gun and Jess drew and shot him. The distance was five feet. A good man with a Colt doesn't miss at that range. Jess's bullet hit the third button on Curtis's shirt and drove a half inch of horn and a chunk of .45 caliber lead into the man's chest. Jeb's eyes grew as round as silver dollars and he tried to speak, but then death took him by the ear and he fell forward, his face in the embers of the fire.

Meanwhile Ford Talon was entering the fight. A horse soldier by training, he fought from the saddle.

Lonny Leon had retreated to the cover of the well behind him, but Talon caught the hard case named Win out in the open as he dragged one of the young girls by her arm toward his boss. Win pushed the girl away from him and his hand blurred as he went for his gun. He drew and fired in a split second. But Talon was a moving target and Win's hurried shot missed his head by inches. Talon swung his horse broadside to Win and fired. One of his three shots took effect and Win went down on one knee, blood scarlet in his mouth. He tried to raise his gun, but he was lung-shot, coughing frothy blood, and out of the fight.

Jesse saw the danger from Lonny Leon. The man had cleared leather and had stepped away from the well, seeking a target. To his right the second hard case sidled toward him, Colt in hand. Talon was having trouble controlling his horse as the animal reared and fought the bit, unnerved by gunfire and the smell of blood.

Lonny Leon had to be the priority target. The distance between the man and Jess was at least sixty feet, but he two-handed the Colt to eye level, aimed and fired. Somewhere a shotgun roared.

Startled by Jess's shot, Leon swung on him, his gun coming up fast.

Damn! Jess knew then that he'd missed.

As Leon fired Jess was already diving to the ground. The man's bullet hit the rowel of Jess's left spur and set it spinning as he landed hard. Leon advanced on him now, his Colt bucking in his hand. Dirt and pig shit kicked up in Jess's face and a second round plowed across the back of his gun hand, drawing blood.

Fear spiking at his belly, Jess shoved his Colt straight out in front of him and fired. A hit! He shot again and again, both misses. But Leon had been hit hard and blood spread low in his gut.

He staggered back to the well, his eyes on Jess, and began to reload his Colt.

Jess, angry that he'd allowed himself to be frightened, fed shells into his revolver and when all six chambers were loaded he rose to his feet.

Gone was the cabin, the sky, the people, the horses, Pa Williamson kicking and hollering at the end of a rope. Jess Casey saw only a blue-lit tunnel, Lonny Leon standing at the end of it. Like punch-drunk prizefighters the two men advanced on each other, their guns hammering. In a gunfight all the senses but sight close down and neither Jess nor Leon could hear the roar of their guns or smell the acrid bite of powder smoke. Jess took a hit but kept firing, his bullets hitting home. Leon dropped to his knees and Jess moved in on him, unaware that the hammer of his Colt was now clicking on spent cartridges.

But Lonny was out of it . . . until he did the unexpected, an action so bizarre it shook Jess to the core. The man grinned, spat an obscenity at Jess, then put the muzzle of his Colt to his temple and pulled the trigger.

Jess stood stunned, bloodied by his own wound and the scatter from Leon's shattering head. Slowly the tunnel drifted away like smoke in a wind, his hearing returned and he heard someone talk to him, but echoing at a distance.

"Huh?" Jess said.

"I said, you're wounded."

Jess turned his head. His ears rang. Ford Talon stared at him, his eyes troubled. "Come back to the land of the living, Sheriff," he said. "Let me take a look at your misery." Talon pulled up Jess's shirt, stared at the wound for a few moments, then said, "The bullet grazed your side and took a chunk of meat with it. You'll hurt like hell for a few weeks, I reckon."

"Thank you," Jess said. "Just what I needed to hear. What's the butcher's bill?"

"Lonny's dead, all shot to pieces, and so are the other three."

"I thought I heard a shotgun," Jess said.

"You did. Mrs. Williamson damn near cut Dave Driver in half."

"He was the man who was coming after me before I got involved with Lonny. I didn't know him," Jess said.

"Too late to get acquainted now, Sheriff," Talon said. "Some of his body is over there, the rest . . . well, it's around."

Jess walked over to where Tom Williamson was consoling his wife and daughters. The shotgun lay at Mrs. Williamson's feet where she'd thrown it after killing Driver.

Tom Williamson noticed the star on Jess's shirt and said, "You arrived in the nick of time, Sheriff. I'm beholden to you."

"We're all beholden to you, Sheriff," his wife said. Then, distress in her pretty face, she said, "I saw that man kill himself. Why would he do such a thing?"

"I guess because he knew I wasn't about to let him leave here alive, ma'am," Jess said.

Ford Talon said, "Men like Lonny Leon live by the gun, Mrs. Williamson, and they're almighty proud to be called shootists. I believe he shot himself so Sheriff Casey couldn't claim credit for killing him." Then, "This has been most distressing for you, Mrs. Williamson. I suggest you and the young ladies go inside while we make your place habitable again."

"You are most gracious, Mr. . . . ah . . ."

"Talon, ma'am. Formerly Major Talon." He kissed the woman's hand. "Your obedient servant."

Harking back to a better time and place, Mrs. Williamson smiled like a true Southern belle and said, "You are *très galant*, Major."

Talon bowed then said, "Now, if the ladies would care to withdraw . . ."

Despite the horror they'd witnessed in the past few minutes the Williamson girls giggled, blushed and followed their mother into the cabin.

"You, too, Sheriff," Talon said. He picked up the whiskey jug that had been dropped and said to Tom Williamson, "May we?"

"Of course, Major, and there's plenty more where that came from," Williamson said.

Talon passed the jug to Jess and said, "Drink. You need it."

"I'll help you bury the hurting dead," Jess said.

"No, you won't. Not with that hole in your side," Talon said. "Take a good swig and then we'll have the ladies attend to you."

"They'll be happy to," Williamson said. "The girls see you as a hero, like the gallant Custer."

Jess winced, took a pull from the jug and passed it back to Talon. "You should have one yourself. It's good stuff . . . Major."

"I fully intend to," Talon said. "I understand that grave digging is thirsty work."

CHAPTER SIXTEEN

"You weren't here today," Jess told Ford Talon. "You weren't within fifty miles of the Williamson cabin."

Tom Williamson looked at Talon, raised an eyebrow and said, "Sheriff, I don't think Major Talon is catching your drift. Neither am I."

"This might hurt," Susan Williamson said. She had gentle hands but as she bandaged Jess's wound he allowed that she'd been right.

Then Jess said, "Ford—"

"Calling me by my given name now, Sheriff, huh?" Talon said. He had a good smile, one that lit up his entire face.

Jess nodded. "You earned it."

"Well, so did you . . . Jess," Talon said. "Now explain to me why I was here but wasn't here."

"I wish somebody would," Tom Williamson said.

"There, it's finished," his wife said, admiring

her handiwork. "What a brave little soldier you are, Sheriff."

"Thank you, ma'am," Jess said. Then to Talon, "Ford, I want you to be part of the convict crowd. Find out why the guns were stolen and what the cons are planning. Is it a bank? Something else? Pretend you're one of them, but report back to me."

"Go behind the lines as a spy, you mean?" Talon said.

"That's the general idea."

"Mighty dangerous if you ask me," Tom Williamson said.

Jess wanted to snap, "Nobody's asking you!" but he didn't. The man had gone through a terrible ordeal, and he was in his own house and entitled to talk out of turn.

Talon rose and stepped to the cabin window. The day was shading into evening and from horizon to horizon the sky was bannered with pennons of red, gold and jade. Shadows gathered along the creek banks and the tethered horses stomped and snorted as the coyotes sang their hunting songs.

Without turning, Talon said, "What's in it for me, Jess?"

The adoring eyes of the Misses Williamson stared at Jess as though they had asked the question.

"I'll owe you a favor, Ford," Jess said.

It did not occur to Talon to doubt Jess's sincerity. As a Southern gentleman he was well aware that Jess's promise was not given lightly. In Texas a man's word was his bond and men lived and died by it.

Talon turned from the window. "All right, Jess," he said. "I was never here."

"No conditions?"

"The favor is enough."

A silence stretched, then Susan Williamson said, "I have a nice beef stew for dinner and sourdough bread I baked just yesterday."

"We don't want to put you out none, Mrs. Williamson," Jess said.

"You'll be no trouble at all, Sheriff. And you must stay here tonight. It's getting too dark for travel."

For Jess to say that there was not enough room would have been grossly impolite since it implied the Williamson cabin was mean and small. But Talon, with his Old World charm, quickly reassured Susan that he and Jess would be comfortable on the parlor floor.

"We're rough men, ma'am," he said, over the woman's objections. "And much used to harder beds, I assure you."

"Then I will supply you with blankets and pillows," Susan said.

Talon gave a bow. "You are most kind, ma'am."

Mrs. Williamson had been smiling and suddenly her lovely face was serious. "Mr. Talon, we have made light of what happened here today because that's how people like us cope with such things. But I am well aware that if you and the sheriff had not arrived when you did my husband and I would both be dead and our daughters taken into a most dreadful slavery. We can never repay you for what you did."

"If that good smell is the stew, ma'am, then it's payment enough," Jess said.

"Amen to that," Talon said.

The girls clapped wildly and yelled, "Huzzah for General Custer."

And for the first time in years, Jess Casey blushed.

CHAPTER SEVENTEEN

"Nice folks," Ford Talon said as he and Jess Casey rode north through the hazy morning toward Fort Worth. "They sure appreciated the four horses and the rest of the traps."

"Best we let the rest of the cons think that Lonny Leon and the others robbed the cabin and headed for Old Mexico," Jess said. "Bringing in the horses of four dead men would create a heap of suspicion and make your job harder."

"You think Tom Williamson has any gold?" Talon said.

"His place is held together with baling wire and twine and he's plowing an inch of soil on top of bedrock," Jess said. He shook his head and smiled faintly. "No, Tom Williamson doesn't have a poke of gold stashed away somewhere."

"Real pretty wife, though," Talon said. "And shapely with it."

"Now you're starting to sound like a true Huntsville con," Jess said.

"No, sir, not me. Jefferson Davis made me an officer and a gentleman and as far as I know he never changed his mind. I was merely complimenting the lady on her beauty and her husband for his good taste in women."

"I'll take your word for it," Jess said. Then, his gaze reaching out along the trail, "And speaking of women, what's that up ahead?"

"I don't know," Talon said. "But it looks like a job for the law, and you're the only lawman around."

"Is he beating that girl?" Jess said.

"Seems like," Talon said.

Jess kicked his horse into a gallop and headed for the man, a heavy club in his hand, looming over a small, slim girl who lay on her back, her arms trying to fend off more blows. Jess had time to observe behind them a dugout with a wooden door. To one side was a pile of animal pelts and skulls.

When he was within shouting distance he yelled, "You there, back off!"

Jess's leggy horse covered the ground quickly and the man, a huge, bearded brute in greasy buckskins, took a step backward, the mesquite club in his hand ready to swing. Jess did the unexpected. He launched himself from the saddle and landed on top of the bearded man. Jess's wide, bony shoulders hit the top of the man's chest and both of them went down in a cursing tangle of arms and legs.

Now the pain in Jess's side was a living thing.

His wound had opened and he felt a warm gush of blood that seeped under the waistband of his pants. He rolled away from the bearded man, but too slowly. The brute got to his feet, pinpoints of hatred in his black eyes, and he raised the club intent on delivering a skull-crushing blow to Jess's head.

Jess gritted his teeth against the pain and lifted an arm as the girl had done to ward off the club.

Blam!

The shot came from Jess's right. The bullet shattered splinters from the club and drove it from the big man's hand. "Next one goes through your head, pardner," Ford Talon said, smiling, as though having casual words with kin.

"How is the girl, Ford?" Jess said. His eyes raked the bearded man. "I hope I hear good news."

"She's got nothing to do with you," the man said. "She's mine, bought and paid for, and I got a bill of sale to prove it."

"What's your name, mister?" Jess said. Ford Talon was talking with the girl.

"Mort Cooper, like it was any of your business."

"The War between the States is over, Mort," Jess said. "You can't buy and sell people any longer."

"Not in Old Mexico it ain't. That's where I bought her. Cost me eighty dollars and two jugs of whiskey."

Talon stepped beside Jess. "The girl's name is Joselita Juarez. She was born in Chihuahua and she thinks she's fourteen but doesn't know for sure."

"Did he hurt her?" Jess said.

"Yeah, for a long time looks like. She's got bruises all over her and bite scars on her shoulders. There's other stuff. Do you want me to go on?"

"No," Jess said. "I don't reckon I want to hear the other stuff." He glared at Cooper. "I'd like to kill you real bad, Mort."

"For what? Beatin' up on a Mexican slut? I reckon you're as stupid as you look. Now get the hell off my property."

By nature, Jess Casey was not an ill-tempered man, but by times he could be hell on wheels. One of those times was now. He stepped to Cooper, shoved the muzzle of his gun into the man's mouth and thumbed back the hammer. A trickle of blood appeared from Cooper's split lower lip.

"Tell me again that I'm stupid," Jess said. His usually florid face was black with anger. "Am I as stupid as I look? If you can't speak nod your head and then I'll blow it clean off your shoulders."

"Jess, let it go," Talon said. "Don't mess up your gun with that sorry piece of trash. Do you know what blood and brains do to the finish of a twelve-dollar Colt?"

Jess let the anger drain out of him. Cold-blooded murder wasn't his style but he'd come almighty close. "Ford, cover him," he said. "I'll talk to the girl."

"And take her word against the word of a white man?" Cooper said. "I own her and I can do whatever I want to her."

Jess ignored the man and took a knee beside the girl. She was very thin with huge midnight eyes and her black hair had been hacked short with a knife. The dress she wore, if sacking could be called a dress, was holed in several places but it looked as though she'd made an attempt to keep it clean. Her face was dirty and so were her feet and hands.

"You speak English, Joselita?" Jess said. The girl nodded and he said, "Are you hungry?" The girl nodded, but then, her eyes on the glaring Cooper, shook her head.

"I feed her," Cooper said. "When she does her chores and deserves to eat."

Jess rose and got the bulging flour sack from his saddle horn. He kneeled beside Joselita again. Susan Williamson had wrapped up sandwiches made from the meat from last night's stew and a couple of wedges of apple pie.

The girl fell on the food as though starving and quickly demolished a couple of sandwiches and a piece of pie. After she'd eaten, Jess rose to his feet and said, "Ford, we'll take Joselita with us."

"The hell you will," Cooper said. "I'm a trader and the girl is a big part of what I have to sell. Ain't nobody gonna stop by just for a wolf pelt."

"Times are hard all over," Jess said. Joselita stepped beside him.

"You ain't the law here," Cooper said. He stood

with his legs spread, big-bellied and belligerent. "She stays or I'll bring the Rangers down on you."

Joselita moved. It was the last thing Jess, or anybody else, expected.

The girl yanked his Colt from the holster, raised it in both hands and backed away. The gun was pointed at Jess.

Cooper's laughter roared, then, "Kill him! Kill them both!"

But Joselita again did the unexpected. She swung the Colt on Cooper, lowered the front sight . . . and fired.

The man screamed like a gut-shot bobcat. He looked down at the blood spreading over his crotch and quickly shoved his pants down over his thighs. What he saw horrified Cooper, and Jess and Talon exchanged stunned glances.

"She shot it off!" Cooper shrieked. "Oh my God, it's gone."

Appalled, Jess said, "Seems like."

"Damn you!" the girl yelled. "You won't come at me with that anymore."

Cooper fell on his butt to the ground and stared at the bloody ruin of his male parts. He shrieked again and again and Talon said, "If it's any consolation, Mort, I don't think it was a real big loss."

Jess stepped to Joselita and grabbed the gun from her hand. "Give me that!" he said, "You might take a notion to do damage to other folks."

Talon had to raise his voice above Cooper's anguished wails. "What will we do with him? He can't ride a horse. He can't ride anything."

Jess said to the girl, "Does he have a gun in the dugout?"

She nodded. "He keeps a rifle in there."

"Go bring it," Jess said.

The girl returned carrying a beautiful Henry that was in much better shape than Jess's own. He racked it empty then stepped out twenty yards and laid the cartridges and the rifle on the grass. When he returned to Cooper he said, "I don't want you shooting at us as we ride away, Mort. It will take you a while to reach your rifle. What you decide to do with it is up to you."

Cooper screeched, "You can't leave me out here without a—"

"Gun?" Jess said. "It's right over there."

"Bad luck, old fellow," Talon said. "I'm sure the whores will miss you."

Jess and Talon swung into the saddle and Jess beckoned to the girl. "Get up behind me and behave yourself," he said.

But Joselita ignored him, ran to where the moaning Cooper was holding his shattered crotch and said, "All you can do now is blow your brains out, you filthy, disgusting animal." Then she spat on him.

When the girl climbed behind Jess, he said, "Not one to hold a grudge, little lady, are you?"

CHAPTER EIGHTEEN

"What are you planning to do with her?" Ford Talon said.

Jess Casey said, "Hell, I don't know."

"I'll take care of her," Sam Waters said.

"What does an old coot like you know about young girls?" Jess said.

"Because, sonny, I've been around women and I've studied their ways," Sam said. "There's three men in this here sheriff's office and she's scared of all of us. Ain't that right, li'l darlin'?"

"I can take care of myself," Joselita Juarez said.

"Well, you ain't been doin' a real good job o' that so far," Sam said. "And look at you. Grubby as a pup in a mudhole. You need a good scrubbing with soap and water and some decent duds."

"You really do have a way with the ladies, Sam, huh?" Talon said.

"I know what's best for them, if that's what you're saying."

"Yup," Talon said, his face straight. "That's what I'm saying."

The office door flung open and Kurt Koenig barged inside, big as a barn and on the prod. "Sheriff, where the hell were you?" he said.

"On law business, Kurt," Jess said.

"What kind of business?" Koenig said. He was a suspicious man and not inclined to patience.

Jess told him about his shooting scrape at the Williamson cabin and the deaths of Lonny Leon and his three cohorts.

After he'd finished speaking, Koenig pointed at Joselita. "What the hell is that?" he said.

"That's another story, Kurt," Jess said.

Koenig's handsome face settled into exaggerated repose. "Oh, do tell me about it, Sheriff Casey," he said. "I'm simply dying to hear." His polite words notwithstanding, the big man's anger was on the simmer.

Jess said, "Well, see, this is how it happened . . ."

He recounted what had happened at the dugout, his rescue of Joselita and the wounding of Mort Cooper by the girl.

Koenig shook his head. "Jess, what the hell are you? Some kind of knight in shining armor riding around Texas saving maidens in distress?" He looked at Joselita and made a face, not liking what he saw. "And what are you going to do with that?"

Sam Waters said, "She'll scrub up real nice, Mr. Koenig."

"Impossible, like trying to sweep sunshine off the porch," Koenig said. He again directed his ire at Jess. "Your job is to uphold the law in Hell's Half Acre. What happens beyond its boundaries is a job for the Texas Rangers or a United States marshal. What happened to the Williamsons and this girl was none of your concern."

"You sound out of sorts, Kurt," Jess said, holding back a smile.

"Damn right I'm out of sorts." Then, with heavy emphasis, "After you deserted your post, Luke Short and Banjo Tom Van Meter got into it. You know that there's been bad blood between them? Well, not any longer. Last night Van Meter walked into the White Elephant, guns blazing, vowing to punch Luke's ticket. Luke was bartending that night and grabbed the shotgun behind the bar and cut loose. Van Meter took both barrels in the belly and was carried out, cursing Luke and the mother that bore him. Banjo Tom died three hours later in mortal agony, or so I was told."

"You could handle that," Jess said. "Luke is always real sorrowful after a killing."

"I did handle it. But that wasn't the worst of what happened last night in your absence," Koenig said. "There was blackhearted deviltry to come." He removed his wallet, thumbed out some bills and said to Sam Waters, "Here, take this. For God's sake get that . . . person . . . to the bathhouse and then buy her some clothes at the New York Hat Shop. Tell Adelaide Collins that Kurt Koenig sent you. She'll know what to do."

He shook his head. "Damned sheriff's office is turning into an orphanage."

Waters touched the money to his forehead. "Thankee, Mr. Koenig. I'll do what you say straightaway."

As Joselita stepped past Koenig, she said, "Thank you, mister. I didn't always look like this."

The big man waved a dismissive hand then said, "Jess, the devil's work is afoot. Have you met Herm Porter, one of the Panther City Boys who works for me?"

"I haven't had that pleasure," Jess said.

"Well, you'll never have it now. Last night around midnight his body was thrown through the front window of the Silver Garter. Herm had been all shot to pieces and this"—Koenig reached inside his coat—"was pinned to his forehead. Yeah, you heard right, his damned forehead."

The piece of bloody paper he passed to Jess read:

KOENIG GET OUT OF FORT
WORTH OR YOU'LL BE NEXT

"It isn't signed," Jess said.

"Of course it isn't signed," Koenig said. "If I had a name I would've killed him by now instead of sitting here cussin' and discussin' with you. I swear you get a long Yankee face on you when you don't know what to say next."

"What can I say, Kurt?" Jess said. "I'll look into it."

"Good. That sets my mind at rest," Koenig said, scowling. "Destiny says she's out of her own mind with worry and Luke Short thinks I plan to hang him. So how did you enjoy your ride in the country, Jess?"

Jess passed the note to Ford Talon. "Anything suggest itself to you?"

"*Koenig* and *you'll* are spelled properly," Talon said. "Whoever wrote this has been taught his ciphers."

"Who the hell are you?" Koenig said.

"Name's Ford Talon. I know who you are."

Koenig glared at Jess. "Are you collecting people now? What the hell is this?"

"Ford is a friend of mine passing through," Jess said.

Koenig nodded, then, "Any friend of Jess's . . . you know the rest." The big man stepped to the door, stopped as though in thought, then turned, his face troubled. "What's happening in the Acre, Jess? You know something. Tell me what it is."

Jess and Talon exchanged glances, then Jess said, "The governor dumped fifty-three prisoners from Huntsville on us, Kurt. Most of them killers. I think at least some of the cons are responsible for what happened to Nate Levy and Bruno Cavanni, and maybe to your boy Herm Porter."

"Where the hell are they?" Koenig said.

"Right here in the Acre," Jess said. "Ford Talon here is one of them."

Koenig didn't like that one bit. Perhaps subconsciously his hand dropped toward his holstered Colt. Jess saw and said, "The men Ford killed needed killing. He saved my life yesterday."

"An exaggeration," Talon said. "You were doing all right."

Jess said, "Ford served the South as a major of cavalry, Kurt. I consider him a friend."

"Did you have anything to do with the murder of Herm Porter?" Koenig said. Dropping the Lost Cause into the conversation had softened him a little.

"I wasn't here, remember?" Talon said. "Besides, I don't normally go around killing people I don't know."

"So that leaves fifty-two," Koenig said. "Where are they?"

"Fifty-one, actually," Jess said. "Sam Waters is a convict."

"Damn it, Jess, are you staffing the sheriff's office with criminals?" Koenig said.

"Only Ford and Sam, and that's just temporary."

Jess rose to his feet. "I'll go talk with Luke Short, ease his mind," he said. "That should help Destiny sleep better."

"Hell, I'll take care of Luke," Koenig said.

"No, you won't," Jess said. "What the Acre doesn't need is another killing."

CHAPTER NINETEEN

"Banjo Tom came in with a gun in each hand, hunting trouble," Luke Short said. "Everybody saw it."

"Kurt Koenig says that's how it happened, Luke," Jess said.

"Then why the hell are you here, all dressed up in your sheriff's suit?" Luke said.

Luke was hardly in a position to criticize Jess's mode of dress, since he sat at a table in the White Elephant in a shabby robe worn over a long nightgown that showed coffee stains. Not one to go unheeled, a blue Colt lay on the table in front of him, reflected in the silver coffeepot.

"Kurt says you think he's planning to hang you," Jess says. "He says Destiny can't sleep worrying about it."

"Worrying about him or me?"

"About Kurt. Destiny doesn't want you to go off half-cocked and call him out."

"Hell, she knows that even on my best day Kurt can shade me," Luke said.

"Maybe she recollects Jim Courtright," Jess said.

"Jim made a mistake. If you stand belly to belly with a man, look out for his watch chain. When he brought up his gun the hammer got tangled in my chain and then I done for him." Luke allowed a ghost of a smile to touch his lips. "Long-Haired Jim could shade me. I was lucky that night."

"Well, Kurt has no intention of hanging you," Jess said. "He knows you shot Van Meter in self-defense. Besides, aren't you two business partners?"

"Only in the Green Buddha, but I buy his opium for my place."

Luke poured himself coffee with a rock-steady left hand. When he put the pot down he said, "I may not be the fastest gun in Hell's Half Acre, Sheriff, but by God I'm sneaky, and sneaky wins gunfights."

Jess smiled. "Is that a warning, Luke?"

"Damn right it is. I'm warning you to stay away from the Green Buddha." Luke's blue eyes turned the shade of hardened steel. "Don't cross me on this, Casey."

"I want opium and morphine out of the Acre, Luke. And I heard that there's already been a couple of deaths. I won't let that stand."

Luke's face didn't change. "You heard what I

told you," he said. "I have big money invested in the Green Buddha and I don't intend to lose it."

Jess rose to his feet. "That's a fight for another day, Luke."

"I got a feeling that day will come mighty soon," Luke Short said.

Despite the wound in his side, his stiff-kneed cowboy gait and the punishment his feet took in high-heeled boots, Jess Casey had walked to the White Elephant, figuring that he should show his star around town.

When he reached the New York Hat and Dress Shop he stepped inside, a welcome chance to rest his barking dogs. The snooty shopgirl was most helpful.

Yes, she had served modome.

Yes, modome had bought some clothes and shoes.

And she was so sorry that the sheriff had missed modome. She had left with an older gentleman not twenty minutes before.

Jess thanked the lady and continued on his way. He walked past an alley named McKenna's Close and stopped when he heard a woman cry out, her voice muffled quickly as though someone had put a hand over her mouth.

A laughing urchin ran out of the alley and almost collided with Jess. "Why the hurry?" he said.

The boy, all red hair and freckles, said, "Three

big fellers caught a girl and they have her back there. I'm gettin' my buddies so they can watch the show."

Jess cuffed the boy's head and said. "Get away from here, you little pervert, and don't come back."

The urchin rubbed the back of his head, shot Jess a frightened glance and took off running.

Whores entertaining men in alleyways was a common occurrence in the Acre and normally Jess would have walked on by. But something about the woman's cry troubled him . . . maybe the ring of her voice.

Ignored by the passing crowds and rumbling wagons, Jess drew his gun and stepped into the alley. He stood still for a few moments to let his eyes adjust to the gloom and then walked forward on cat feet. He heard a man laugh and another said something that made him laugh again.

The alley was clear and Jess recalled that it opened up into the rear of a tenement block where there were usually stacks of stored packing cases and sawn lumber. He stopped to allow a little calico cat to walk between his feet and then stepped to the end of the alley. Coming from his left he heard the woman's muffled cries and the husky voices of men. For a moment Jess stood still, his feet apart, his eyes wary and alert. Behind him the street sounds were subdued, coming from the far end of a tunnel. Jess knew what he faced. There were three of them and they wouldn't hesitate to kill him without qualm or conscience. They must know that rape was a hanging offense in the Acre and that City Marshal Koenig would string them up without the inconvenience of a trial. That knowledge would make them desperate, and when he intervened his life and the woman's would not be worth a plug nickel. But he had it to do.

Jess stepped into the open.

The three men had their backs to him, concentrating on the woman, who was struggling fiercely. Her dress had been torn from her shoulders and Jess caught a glimpse of the frightened, peaked face of Joselita Juarez.

The devout will tell you that God provides. That day He provided for Sheriff Jess Casey all right. Jess knew that if he opened the ball with a six-gun quadrille the girl was sure to take a bullet. But lying at his feet was what looked like a broken table leg more than two feet long. He holstered his gun and picked up the leg. It was heavy— mahogany, he figured— and square in shape.

The man in the middle was pushing up Joselita's dress and didn't hear Jess cat-foot up on him. During his struggle with the girl the man's hat had fallen off and his bullet head made a perfect target. Jess swung the table leg, crashing it into the side of the would-be rapist's skull. Jess didn't wait to see him drop. The man on his left, small and thin with the face of a hungry rodent, stepped back, his lust-fogged brain momentarily unable to comprehend what had happened. He paid for that lapse. A corner of the table leg crashed into the bridge of his nose and the man screamed and staggered back, his hands to his bloody face. The third fellow was bigger, meaner, and a fighter. His hand dropped for his gun but he was one step too close to Jess. The back of the sheriff's work-hardened hand slapped the man across the mouth, drawing blood, staggering him. Giving him no time to recover, Jess moved in, swung the table leg and slammed it into the left side of the man's head. For a moment the man swayed on his feet and Jess thought he might need to hit him again, but the fellow dropped like a felled oak and hit the ground hard.

The bloody table leg in his hand, his wounded side aching, Jess looked around at the carnage he'd caused. Two men down and the third, his nose smashed and his eyes swollen shut, whimpered like a snake-bit pup. When Jess glared in his direction the man unbuckled his gun belt and let it fall to his feet. His voice thick, he said, "I'm out of it. Leave me the hell alone."

"Did the girl say that same thing?" Jess said.

The man wiped blood from his chin and said nothing.

Joselita stared down at the torn remnants of her dress. She looked at Jess and said, "It's the only pretty thing I ever owned and now it's ruined."

"I'll get you another one," Jess said as he stripped the two unconscious men of their gun belts. "Did they . . ."

"No. They didn't. I fought them."

"Where the hell is Sam Waters?" Jess said.

"He wanted to go for a drink, said the experience of being in a shop full of women's fixin's had aged him a ten year. I told him he should go to the saloon and I'd walk back to the sheriff's office. I was passing the alley when these animals jumped me."

"Sam left you to walk alone in the Acre?" Jess said.

"I told him it would be all right," the girl said. Her hair was trimmed and clean and she looked almost pretty.

Jess was mad clean through. "When I find Sam Waters I'm gonna kill him. No, I'll tear his guts out. I'll—"

"Don't blame Sam," Joselita said. "It was all my fault."

"He should've known better," Jess said. He kicked the man closer to him in the rib. "You, on your feet." The man got up on his hands and knees and Jess kicked him again. "I said on your feet." He'd already thrown away the table leg and now he pulled his gun. Jess motioned to the other fallen man and said. "And haul that piece of garbage upright."

It took a while for Jess to get his three dazed prisoners shuffling in the same direction. But when he reached the entrance to McKenna's Close he halted them and said, "Listen up. We're walking to the sheriff's office. On the way a man gives me sass or back talk I'll shoot him in the balls. A man tries to escape I'll shoot him in the head. Any questions?"

There were none.

CHAPTER TWENTY

Destiny Durand stepped into Jess Casey's office like a breath of fresh air. She was one of those women so spectacularly beautiful that the dogs get out from under the porch to look at her. And she was all smiles. Jess took that as a warning.

He rose to his feet and said, "What can I do for you, Miss Durand?"

"I've come to see the prisoners, Sheriff Casey," Destiny said. She smiled sweetly. "I've never seen three rapists before."

"They didn't . . . I mean . . ."

"Attempted rape is the same thing as rape as far as I'm concerned," Destiny said. "I'm going to give those three a piece of my mind." She looked around. "Where is the girl?" Then, "Kurt told me what happened to her and how she got here."

"She's out back at the pump, for I swear the seventh time," Jess said. "She says even lye soap can't get her clean."

"I'll go talk to her," Destiny said.

"I guess it would be good if she could talk to another woman," Jess said.

"Really, General Custer?" Destiny said, an eyebrow rising. "You are an expert on the subject?"

"No. I mean . . . yes . . . no, I mean no."

Destiny smiled. "You blush like a schoolboy, Sheriff. I find it most refreshing."

Jess decided to keep his mouth shut as the woman rustled to the door, her French perfume scenting the air like a breeze in a wildflower meadow. He sat in his chair and wondered if the valiant Custer had ever blushed.

Unlike the sporting crowd, the respectable citizens of the Acre considered Jess the law and had no qualms about barging into his office at any time of the day or night.

Destiny had just stepped out the door when it opened again to admit the huge form of a scowling man in a bloodstained apron. But what alarmed Jess was the gleaming curve of the massive butcher's cleaver he held in his right hand and the sniveling, trembling wretch he grasped in the other.

"Do you know me?" the man demanded. He had high, Slavic cheekbones, a huge blue chin and a great handlebar mustache set off by a pair of magnificent side-whiskers. Jess calculated he stood four inches over six feet.

"I'm afraid not," Jess said. The shivering

wretch looked like he'd been eating nothing but birdseed for a month.

"My name is Ivan Baranov," the man said. He had a strong Russian accent. "They call me Butcher Baranov."

"What can I do for you, Mr. Baranov?" Jess said.

The big man shook the wretch so violently Jess could swear he heard his skinny bones rattle. "Sausages, sir!" Baranov roared. "I'm here to accuse this man of the attempted theft of two cold-smoked sausages. By God, sir, it's a hanging offense."

Jess tried to be stern. "What's your name?" he said to the wretch.

"Wilkins, sir. Lem Wilkins." His voice was small, timid and trembling.

"Lem Wilkins by name, Lem Wilkins by nature, I'll be bound," Baranov said. "I've been victimized by his kind before."

"Why did you steal the sausage?" Jess said.

"Russian sausage, don't forget," Baranov said. His fist on the ragged collar of Wilkins's coat was as big as an anvil and looked like it could crush Wilkins's skull like an eggshell.

"My children and my wife are hungry," Wilkins said.

Baranov shook Wilkins again and said, "That's no excuse for stealing food out of another man's mouth to feed your own starving brood. Why don't you work?"

"Sir, I do. I'm the swamper at the First Chance saloon."

"And don't they pay you?" Jess said.

Wilkins said, "It's not enough. I have six children and two bits a day is never enough. Sir, if you lock me up I can't work and my children will starve. Have mercy."

"Mr. Baranov, do you still want me to hang this man?" Jess said.

The huge butcher shook Wilkins again until the little man's teeth chattered, then stared into his eyes. "I want to cut off your head," he said. "I want to crush your bones to powder." Then, after a terrible wail from the depths of his melancholy Russian soul that made Jess jump, he said, "But I can't. I can't. I see the faces of starving little children and my heart is melted." He lifted Wilkins by the scruff of his neck and shook him again, even harder this time, and the man danced in the air like a puppet on a string.

"You will come with me," Baranov said. "I will give you meat for your family." Then he growled like a slavering mastiff, "But I still want to crush your bones."

"I'm sorry, Mr. Baranov," Wilkins said in his small, mousy voice.

"Sorry!" the butcher bellowed. He waved the cleaver in the little fellow's face. "A taste of this medicine will make you sorry." Baranov wailed again. "No, no, no. Not that. Never that. Come with me. I will give you meat and sausage."

Without another word to Jess, Baranov

marched Wilkins outside. As they passed his window he saw the big Russian brandishing the meat cleaver over the little man's head and Wilkins looked like a scared rabbit.

For a moment Jess thought about following the pair but decided that the big Russian wouldn't chop Wilkins into cutlets. At least he hoped he wouldn't.

But then Destiny Durand stormed inside, Joselita Juarez in tow, and laid another problem on his desk. "Did you do this?" she said.

Jess was alarmed. "Do what?"

Destiny tugged at the shoulder of the girl's dress. "Buy her this rag?" Before Jess could answer, Destiny lifted the hem of the dress, revealing Joselita's thin legs. "And she has no undergarments."

"I sent Sam Waters with her," Jess said. "He said he knew everything about women's fixings."

"Sam Waters! You mean that crazy old buzzard who's been working around here?"

"Sam said—"

"I don't care what Sam said," Destiny snapped. "The way this child has been treated is a disgrace, Sheriff, and I'm holding you responsible. Why didn't you escort her to and from the dress shop?"

"Sam Waters—"

"Is Sam Waters the new sheriff of the Acre?"

Jess clutched at a straw. "Well, at least nothing real bad happened."

Destiny was outraged, a green-eyed tigress. "Nothing real bad happened. The child had to fight off a gang of rapists and you say nothing real bad happened? Look at the bruise on her cheek. That's nothing bad?"

"I meant—"

"I know what you meant, Sheriff Casey. And I think you're a disgrace to the star you wear." Destiny laid down her purse and it clunked . . . a thing Jess would later remember with regret.

"Sheriff, Joselita is coming to live with me, and I don't wish to hear any objections," Destiny said. "Do I make myself clear on that point?"

Jess had no intention of raising an objection. A peace officer's office was no place for a young girl, especially one who'd been abused her entire life.

Wary of Destiny's wrath, Jess picked his words carefully. "That sounds just fine, Miss Durand."

"And I should hope so. Now I want to see the prisoners. I wish to familiarize myself with the inhuman faces of rapists."

"Do you think that's a good idea?" Jess said.

"Yes, I do. And I'll also watch them hang." Destiny's smile was dazzling. "Besides, I may be able to identify them. All kinds of trash find their way into the Silver Garter."

"I see no need for that," Jess said. "I'll find out who they are."

"Sheriff, do I have to send for the city marshal to overrule you?"

"I think Kurt would agree with me." He

thumbed over his shoulder. "Back there is no place for ladies."

"Just a quick look. Afterward I may be willing to overlook the fact that you're a child abuser."

Jess sighed. "If I allow you to see the prisoners will you leave and hopefully never come back?"

"Yes. I know where I'm not welcome," Destiny said, her back stiff.

Jess rose and got the key for the locked door that separated the cell area from the rest of the office. "This way," he said. "Step carefully." Then to Joselita, "You stay there, girl."

Destiny picked up her purse and followed him.

Late afternoon sun angled through the jail's two small windows and made dust motes dance. But shadows had already gathered in the corners where the spiders lived. There were two cells. One was reserved as Jess's sleeping quarters, the other held the three prisoners. When they caught sight of Destiny they crowded to the bars, their eyes moving over her voluptuous curves and luxuriant, upswept hair. One of them whispered something and another laughed.

"Seen enough?" Jess said.

Destiny surprised him. In a clear, ringing voice she said, "I'm a friend of Joselita Juarez, the little girl you tried to rape today." Then she really surprised him.

Her right hand went into her purse and she came up with a Smith & Wesson .32. She aimed at the cell and cut loose. Three shots. Very fast.

As the prisoners dived for the floor, Jess stood

stunned for a moment. Then he reached out and wrestled the little revolver from Destiny's hand. "Damn it, woman!" he yelled. "Get out of here,"

He pushed Destiny out the door and crossed the floor to the cell. "Anybody get hurt?" he said.

There was only one casualty. The man with the broken nose had yet another misery. A bullet had burned across the meat of his left shoulder, spilling more blood than the shallow wound merited. "I need a doctor," he said. "The crazy whore tried to kill me."

"Yeah, I know," Jess said. "Pity she missed."

When Jess closed the door behind him and walked into the office, Destiny Durand shoved out her bared wrists in a dramatic fashion and said, "Yes, put me in manacles, Sheriff Casey. Chain me. I hope I killed all three of them."

As patiently as he could, Jess said, "Two of your shots went wild, the third winged one of them but it's not serious."

"Then charge me with attempted murder," Destiny said. "I want my day in court. I want to tell the men of this town what women think of the rapists in our midst and the stubborn refusal of the law to do anything about it."

"Miss Durand, I'm charging you with disorderly conduct and plan to release you into the custody of Kurt Koenig once he pays your ten-dollar fine," Jess said. "I'm also confiscating your gun."

"But . . . but I tried to kill those men . . . those monsters," Destiny said as Joselita put a comforting arm around her shoulders.

"I don't think the prisoners were ever in much danger," Jess said. "Two of your shots went into the ceiling and as far as I can tell the third bounced off the floor and burned one of them."

Destiny's beautiful face was crestfallen. "Then you won't shackle me, subject me to the chains."

Jess smiled and shook his head. "Nope. Not a hope in hell."

CHAPTER TWENTY-ONE

The edge of the knife blade dug deep enough into the left side of Ben Hoard's neck to draw a trickle of blood. "Perhaps I didn't make myself understood," Jasper Dunn said. "I want thirty percent off the top."

Cole Danvers of the Panther City Boys stood at the closed office door to prevent anyone from walking in. He wore two guns that evening, more for intimidation than need. "Listen to Mr. Dunn," he said. "For the kind of protection he can supply, thirty percent is a bargain."

"Damn you, I already pay protection money to Kurt Koenig," Hoard said. "I can't afford two of you."

"In a few days Koenig won't be around anymore," Dunn said. "Then your only business partner will be me."

Hoard said, "Big talk, mister. On your best day you can't take Koenig. Just being here makes you a dead man. Kurt will kill you."

The knife dug deeper. Blood seeped over the white collar of Hoard's frilled shirt. "I said thirty percent," Dunn said.

"Go to hell."

Dunn removed his knife from Hoard's neck and stepped back from the overstuffed chair where the man sat. He turned to Danvers. "Cole, bring me a whore, a pretty one," he said.

Danvers nodded and left.

"What are you going to do?" Hoard said. He was a fat man, the founder of the Gentleman's Retreat cathouse, and his completely bald head glistened with sweat.

Dunn smiled. "You'll see. I think after the little demonstration I plan you'll agree to my business proposition." He shrugged. "Of course it may take more than one. Demonstration, I mean." His thumb tested the edge of his knife. "Ah, it's very sharp, the way I like it."

"Kurt Koenig will kill you," Hoard said.

Dunn's anger flared. "Stop saying that! I hate it when you say that. You've no idea how it irritates me. Makes me want to kill somebody."

Wisely, Hoard decided to keep his mouth shut.

A few moments later Danvers stepped into the office with a pretty blond girl. She looked around and smiled uncertainly, but the presence of her boss in the room seemed to reassure her. Her reassurance quickly evaporated, though, when Danvers forced her arms behind her back and shoved her into a straight-backed chair. Dunn quickly gagged the girl with a bright red bandanna and then stripped her chemise from her shoulders and breasts.

"Very pretty," Dunn said. "What a pity to ruin such a pair." The girl's blue eyes were wide open, terrified. The man placed the blade of his knife at the top of the girl's chest and said, "Take your pick, Mr. Hoard. Left or right?"

"Leave the girl alone, you sorry piece of trash," Hoard said.

He attempted to rise from his chair but Danvers shook his head and said, "I wouldn't do that. Mr. Dunn might decide to go for the throat."

Dunn smiled and said, "No preference? Then I'll choose for you." He stood back and rubbed his chin and he studied the girl's breasts. "The right one, I think. It's so pretty."

Dunn placed the blade at the top of the girl's breast and drew blood. Her struggles against Danvers's hold were futile and she whimpered deep in her throat.

"Wait!" Hoard yelled. "Thirty percent! I agree to thirty percent."

"I thought you might," Dunn said. His voice was silken, like the purr of a contented cat, but his eyes were demonic. "Mind you, Mr. Hoard, I would very much have enjoyed the cutting." He looked at Danvers and said, "Take off the gag and let her go." And then to the girl, "If you tell anyone about this . . . ah . . . demonstration, I'll come back here looking for you." He held up the knife and let gaslight ripple on its blade. "And I'll bring my little friend with me."

"I won't tell anybody," the girl said. "I swear I won't."

"There speaks a wise young lady," Dunn said. "But just remember, my dear, I'm a creature of the dark and I bring death with me."

The girl fled in horror and Dunn said to Hoard, "Now, let's take a look at the books, shall we?"

"A fair night's work, I'd say. Three hundred dollars on a slow evening is not to be sneezed at," Jasper Dunn said. "And we're only getting started."

Cole Danvers nodded. "When we're making thousands a night we'll look back on our three hundred and laugh."

"There's no doubt about that," Dunn said.

"Would you really have cut the whore?" Danvers said.

"Of course. She came very close. As I told Hoard, I was rather looking forward to it." Dunn's eyes shifted. "You, Mr. Talon, please step over here."

The stifling warehouse basement at Houston and 11th was crowded with men and smelled of sweat, gun oil and leather. Most of the cons were now well dressed and armed and had lost Huntsville's lean and hungry look. Talon had shed his coat and wore only his shirt and pants. He had a Colt holstered butt-forward at his waist.

"Obviously Herb Coffin didn't kill you, Mr. Talon," Dunn said.

"He tried," Talon said.

"Ah, then I won't trouble you for the details, but I assume Mr. Coffin is no longer with us."

"No, he's not," Talon said.

Dunn said, "I hated that man. Sooner or later I would have killed him myself." He studied Talon's face for a moment, then said, "Where have you been since then?"

"Around," Talon said.

"You look like you're prospering," Dunn said.

Talon forced a smile. "Prospering on the money I took from Coffin's pocket. But it's running out and that's why I'm here. I heard you're looking for men."

"I'm looking for gunmen, Mr. Talon. Do you qualify?"

"I can skin iron with the best of them," Talon said.

"Hmm . . . I wonder." Dunn snapped his fingers and smiled. "I know. Here's a jolly lark." He waved a hand at a couple of men standing close to the table where he sat. "Bring the black and stand him against the wall over yonder."

A few moments later a badly beaten black man was dragged from a corner and shoved against the far basement wall. Unlike the others he still wore rags and he was unarmed. Like the girl at the cathouse, he was terrified.

"This creature's name is Paris Berry and he undercut my authority," Dunn said. "Without my permission he rolled a drunk on Main Street, it doesn't matter where, and then put the knife to him. He spent the money on whiskey and then had the audacity to return here and boast of it. Naturally his was an act of defiance and a danger to all of us and I sentenced him to death."

This drew a roar of approval from two score throats, and Jasper Dunn smiled and waved a dismissive hand as though he did not deserve such an accolade. "Silas Topper, Mr. Topper, are you there?" he said.

"Right here, boss." This from a small, lean man with wicked eyes who packed one of Bruno Cavanni's engraved Colts in an ornate gun belt and holster. Ford Talon recalled seeing the little man around Huntsville but knew nothing of his background. Jasper Dunn set him straight.

"Mr. Talon, or should I say Major Talon, may I present Mr. Silas Topper, probably the fastest man with a gun in the great state of Texas."

Talon nodded to the man but made no attempt to shake hands.

But Topper didn't seem to notice. "There ain't no probably, boss," he said. "I am the fastest gun in Texas and everywhere else."

"Huzzah!" Dunn said, clapping his hands. "Your skills didn't deteriorate while you were in Huntsville, did they?"

"Sure didn't," Topper said. "I'm faster now nor I was ten years ago."

"Excellent," Dunn said. "Now gather around, everybody and listen up. Major Talon—yes, he was a major in the war—wishes to join our merry band of thieves. But ere I grant him that favor he must prove that he is worthy. I told him that I need a man of courage—which he undoubtedly is—but who is good with a gun. Now he must demonstrate his shooting skill that we may judge."

This brought a cheer, and Jasper Dunn got to his feet. "Follow me, gentlemen," he said. When he stood opposite the black man, he said, "Now one of you men step off fifteen paces between us and the condemned."

When that was accomplished Dunn said, "Here's how it will work. On my command, Mr. Topper and Mr. Talon will each draw and fire one shot at Paris Berry. Of course, Mr. Topper, a shootist of renown—"

"Seventeen kills," Topper said, grinning.

"Yes, yes, quite," Dunn said. "As I was about to say, Mr. Talon's quickness on the draw and shoot will be measured against Mr. Topper's skill and accuracy. If Mr. Talon comes close, he will be invited to become one of us."

"Suppose he's as slow as molasses and misses?" Topper said.

"Why, then you will kill him, Mr. Topper," Dunn said.

Talon looked at Berry. Tears ran down the man's cheeks but he stood where he was against the wall and made no plea for mercy. He knew his death was inevitable and he'd be appealing to merciless men.

This would be cold-blooded murder but Berry

was already a dead man. Talon knew that he had to go through with the killing or his usefulness as a spy would be over before it even began. He took comfort in the fact that the black was a killer and had knifed a man after taking his wallet. But it didn't help much.

"Are we ready, gentlemen?" Dunn said. "You will wait on my command to fire . . . Fire!"

Two shots sounded as one.

Jasper Dunn ripped the dead man's shirt apart and studied his wounds. After a moment he whooped then yelled, "Two bullets to the chest not two inches apart. Crackerjack!"

"Let me see that, boss," Silas Topper said. He peered closely at the wounds and said, "Yeah. I can only get two fingers between them. But I was faster."

"Yes, but not by much," Dunn said. He rose to his feet. "Take a look see at your handiwork, Mr. Talon. Superb shooting!"

Ford Talon forced himself to look at the dead man. He decided to play the tough guy. "I hurried the shot, pulled a little to the left."

"You done good," Topper said. "Almost as good as me."

Now Talon changed roles, going from tough to humble. "I'll never be as good as you, Silas." Topper grinned and slapped him on the back and Talon knew he'd been accepted into Dunn's den of thieves and killers.

"Let's celebrate," Dunn said. "Cole, break out the whiskey."

Everybody cheered but Talon remained silent. He felt sick to his stomach.

CHAPTER TWENTY-TWO

As soon as Jess Casey saw Kurt Koenig's face he knew he bore bad news. The sight of the stern professor James Carnes, his assistant and what looked like a lawyer walking behind him confirmed that impression.

Koenig tossed a telegraph wire on the desk. "Read it and weep," he said. "It came in this morning."

"No need to read it, Sheriff," Carnes said. "It's an order from Senator Jennings to release your prisoners immediately."

Jess ignored the professor and picked up the wire. It confirmed what the man had said. "Those men are charged with the attempted rape of a fourteen-year-old girl," Jess said. "I'm keeping them locked up until they stand trial."

"It appears that attempted rape is not the case," the lawyerly-looking man said. He laid a card on the desk. "My name is Jethro Tull, attorney-at-law."

Jess stared at the lawyer and made no answer, and Tull said, "We have two witnesses who will swear that they heard the girl try to sell sexual favors to the three men you have in custody. When you arrived, Sheriff, and laid about you with a vicious club, the girl became frightened and changed her story."

"Who are these men you claim as witnesses?" Jess said.

Professor Carnes answered that question. "Like the men in your cell, they are former Huntsville prisoners who are trying to make an honest living and tread a straight path."

"Who are they?" Jess said, his anger growing.

"At this stage their names should not matter, but I will give them to you anyway," Tull said. "They are Mr. Deke O'Conner and Mr. Jasper Dunn. At the moment both gentlemen perform odd jobs but are actively seeking gainful, full-time employment. Mr. Dunn is seriously considering becoming a member of the clergy and is already studying to that end."

"Sheriff Casey, did anyone beside yourself witness the alleged assault on the girl?" Tull said.

Jess felt the walls closing in. "No."

"Mr. O'Connor and Mr. Dunn will swear that the female—one Joselita Juarez, a Mexican of no fixed abode—was laughing and giggling as she led the men into McKenna's Close and Mr. Dunn will say with one hundred percent certainty that he heard the girl repeatedly mention the sum of two dollars."

Carnes said, "Sheriff, your harassment of the Huntsville prisoners must stop instanter. Senator Jennings is most anxious that this experiment succeed, as am I and attorney-at-law Tull."

Tull said, "You will release the accused into the professor's custody now, and I will arrange for a federal judge to conduct a trial, probably in Houston. And may I ask you to curb your victimization of men who are desperately trying to turn their lives around? Professor Carnes says they know that they've been given a unique opportunity and are grasping it with both hands."

Jess looked at Koenig and said, "Do you believe this rubbish?"

"No, I don't. But we haven't got a choice, Jess," he said. "An order from a senator bears weight and he has the support of the governor."

"You mean I have to hand them over?"

"That's exactly what the marshal means," Tull said. His voice took on an authoritarian tone. "Sheriff Jess Casey, you are required and commanded to release the following prisoners into the custody of Professor James Carnes: William Looper, aged twenty-six."

"You mean Loco Looper," Jess said. "Thirty years for rape and murder."

"Adam Gavin, aged thirty."

"They call him Gorilla Gavin," Jess said. "Thirty years for rape and murder."

Tull was irritated, but he pressed on. "James Turner, aged twenty-eight."

"Otherwise known as Dark Alley Jim," Jess

said. "Twenty-three years for the knife murder of a parson."

Tull gritted his teeth in rage. "Do your duty, Sheriff. Release those men immediately."

Jess rose to his feet. "You know you gentlemen are signing your own death warrants, don't you?" he said.

"That sir, is an impertinence," Carnes said. "Now obey Mr. Tull's order and do your duty."

"If I was you I'd watch my back, Jess," Kurt Koenig said. "Those three boys didn't look like the kind to forgive and forget."

"Can you believe what just happened?" Jess said.

"Of course I can believe it. Senator Jennings released dangerous criminals into an established community, if you want to call the Acre that. Don't you think the government is interested and so are prison authorities up and down the country? If this works, other states will follow Texas's lead and release long-term convicts that have become a burden on their nickel-squeezing budgets."

"And since Jennings was the first to do it, he'll become a big man in Washington," Jess said.

"He has an election coming up," Koenig said. "He's got to make this harebrained scheme of his work, or at least be seen to work."

"And Carnes and Tull?" Jess said.

"The way I figure is that Carnes is a do-gooder who wants to be famous and Jethro Tull, well, he's a lawyer and he'll work for anyone who'll pay him. I suspect the money is coming through Carnes from Jennings and there's probably a pile of it."

"I feel like I'm butting my head against a brick wall," Jess said.

"Get used to it," Koenig said. "This is Hell's Half Acre, normal law doesn't apply here. And don't expect any help from our esteemed Mayor Stout. Harry isn't about to butt heads with a United States senator."

"I will not butt heads with a United States senator," Mayor Harry Stout said. "Sheriff Casey, I'm surprised you'd even ask. Besides, Professor Carnes said the convicts are settling down nicely and fast becoming model citizens of our fair city."

"Does that include the three who tried to rape Joselita Juarez?" Jess said.

Stout sat back in his chair and waved a ringed hand. "Boys will be boys, Sheriff. No harm was done."

Jess said, "Why don't you ask Joselita Juarez that?"

Stout sighed. "Sheriff Casey, I have never doubted your dedication to duty but by times you can be a most tiresome man. Did you read the newspaper this morning?"

"No, not yet," Jess said.

"Look." He held up the paper and the head-lines read:

Mex Jezebel Tempts Three to Their Doom

WHITE MEN FACE THE NOOSE

"Is there no justice in this town?"

The GAZETTEER Demands the Release of the McKenna's Close Three.

"Hardly an unbiased account," Jess said. "And the would-be rapists have already been released."

"White men languishing in a jail over the accusations of a Mexican whore makes better copy," Stout said. "And the *Gazetteer*'s publisher needs a new printing press. It's just a matter of business."

"Joselita Juarez is a child," Jess said. "She is by no stretch of the imagination a whore."

Stout raised his hands and wailed, "Sheriff, what do you want me to do?"

"For starters, give me the authorization to hire six deputies at seventy dollars a month and I'll clamp down on both convicts and the opium trade."

Stout was appalled. "I will do no such thing. Fort Worth can't afford six deputies and I will not butt heads with a senator, I told you that already. And in addition I've fallen in line with the rest of the country and the sale of opium is now perfectly legal in this town. I just yesterday signed the new law into effect. I thought you knew that."

"I didn't until now. The new law was at the urging of Kurt Koenig and Luke Short, no doubt."

"At the urging of two prominent, taxpaying citizens of this town. I can say no more than that." He smiled. "Dare I tell the fair sex that they can no longer purchase laudanum for their female problems and to soothe fussy children? I think not."

"I need those deputies, Harry."

"Very well, I will consider the matter and then take it to committee."

"When will that be?"

"Soon, Sheriff Casey. No later than Christmas or shortly afterward."

"But this is only July," Jess said.

"I know it is and that reminds me that I have work to do. My, how time flies," Stout said. He smiled. "You're doing a crackerjack job, Sheriff Casey. Keep up the good work."

CHAPTER TWENTY-THREE

"I think the place is shaping up nicely," Kurt Koenig said. "What do you think, Luke?"

"Looks good to me," Luke said. "Maybe we could add an extra tier of bunks. Three high should be manageable for the attendants."

"I'll mention that to the builder tomorrow," Koenig said. The unfinished interior of the Green Buddha was lit by only one oil lamp and Koenig pointed through the shifting gloom to a curtained area at the rear.

"That's what I call the 'top hat and tails' section, reserved for the high rollers. No bunks, just cushions, and I plan to staff it with the prettiest Chinese girls I can find," he said.

Luke Short nodded. "And a couple of guns."

"I've taken care of that. Cole Danvers, one of my Panther City Boys, will be a full-time guard, him and a friend of his, a draw fighter out of Tennessee by the name of Silas Topper."

Luke's face stilled in thought, then, "Seems like I heard that name before, years ago. Topper . . . Topper . . ." He shook his head. "No, I can't recollect, but it will come back to me."

"We should be ready to open next week," Koenig said. Then, "No hard feelings, Luke?"

"You mean about Banjo Tom? I thought you'd hang me for sure, get rid of a partner and move in on his business."

"I don't work that way," Koenig said. "We shook on our deal and a man can't go back on that."

Luke nodded and said, "No hard feelings."

Koenig carried the oil lamp to the door and blew it out before he and Luke stepped outside and locked the door. "Hey, you got to see this," he said.

Two torches, almost as tall as a man, stood on each side of the Green Buddha entryway, held upright by iron sconces. "They're fueled by oil," Koenig said. "Watch this." He reached into his pocket, found a match and thumbed it into flame.

The bullet hit a split second later.

As Koenig and Luke dived for the dirt the lead *spuuuunged!* off one of the sconces and set it ringing. Koenig's Colt was in his hand. "See anything?" he said.

"Not a damn thing. It's as dark as the inside of a boot."

Another shot. A probing bullet that kicked up dirt and grass a few feet from where Koenig lay.

Luke, not a long-fused man, got up on one knee and yelled, "Show yourself and fight like a man, you damned yellow-bellied son of a bitch."

A derisive laugh sounded from somewhere in the gloom, followed by another bullet that drove Luke to the ground again.

Koenig fired, then dusted two shots to the left and right of his target.

"I saw his gun flare," he said.

"Did you hit him?" Luke said.

"Hell, I don't know," Koenig said.

"Maybe we can Injun over there."

"Better than lying here. Let's do it."

The two men began a slow crawl across bottle-strewn waste ground. Then Luke cursed softly. "Damn, I think I bellied over a dog shit."

"Good," Koenig said. "You'll smell better."

After ten yards Koenig stopped and said, "See anything?"

"No, and I've had enough of this Injun crap. I'd rather die on my feet like a man."

Luke pushed himself erect just as a woman screamed and a man yelled, "What the hell?"

"Your bullet didn't do much for his looks, but do you recognize him?" Luke Short said.

"Yeah, I recognize him," Kurt Koenig said, his face bitter. "It's Cole Danvers."

"I thought he was one of your boys," Luke said.

"So did I," Koenig said.

"One of your bullets went right through our

house, Mr. Koenig," the man who'd called out said. His dark-haired wife clung to him and she looked dumbly at the corpse's bloody face.

"I didn't hurt anybody, did I?" Koenig said.

The man shook his head. "No, my two youngest sleep in dresser drawers in the bedroom but the bullet hit the ceiling above them."

Koenig reached into his pocket, brought out some coins and handed the man a double eagle. "This will pay for the damages," he said. He knew twenty dollars was probably more than this working man earned in a month, but he felt guilty about the young 'uns in the drawers.

And he was devastated by Cole Danvers's treachery.

"He was in the Silver Garter and heard me tell Destiny I was headed to the Green Buddha to meet you," Koenig said to Luke. "And he heard me say I was planning to light the lamps."

"He should have waited a couple of minutes, then he could've nailed you for sure," Luke said.

"Yeah, he hurried the shot—nerves, I guess—and it done for him," Koenig said. He shook his head, his handsome face bleak. "Hell, Luke, I liked the man."

"I know. That always makes a killing harder, when you're shooting at a feller you like. I felt that way about Jim Courtright, thought he was just fine. But he was a tad excitable, like your dead man."

"This way, Sheriff," a woman's voice said. The dark-haired wife stepped out of the door and Jess

Casey followed her. To Koenig she said, "I was out front talking to the neighbors when he asked me if I heard the shooting. I hope I done right, Mr. Koenig."

"You did just fine," Luke said.

"I heard the shooting, figured that it came from the direction of the Green Buddha and knew you two must be involved," Jess said.

He kneeled and studied the dead man. "I don't know him," he said.

"His name is Cole Danvers," Koenig said. "He worked for me. At least I thought he did up until tonight."

"Who killed him?" Jess said.

"I did. He didn't give me any choice," Koenig said. "He took a pot at me from out of the darkness and I fired back."

"Middle of the forehead," Jess said. "That's good shooting."

"I got lucky," Koenig said.

"Damn, what's that smell?" Jess said.

"I crawled through dog shit," Luke said.

"You're gonna be real popular in the street," Jess said. Then to Koenig, "If Danvers was one of your boys, why did he try to kill you?"

"Did you put him up to it, Jess?" Koenig said.

"I sure didn't."

"Then I don't know."

"I'll send somebody for Big Sal," Jess said. "Get the body out of here."

A shooting star burned a scarlet scar across the face of the night sky and reflected in Jess's eyes. "Unlucky for somebody," he said.

CHAPTER TWENTY-FOUR

A hansom cab drawn by a gray horse splashed through a rare midsummer rain and stopped outside the forbidding bulk of an abandoned warehouse.

For a moment the cab stood motionless but then rocked on its springs as a tall man wearing a canvas slicker and a plug hat alighted, followed by a second figure dressed in a long black coat with a velvet collar. Like his companion he wore a bowler.

The man in black said something to the cabbie that made the man nod and then the tall man stepped beside him, his gun hand inside his slicker. "This must be the place, Mr. Thurgood," he said. "I don't see any other warehouses around."

"This is the place, all right," Gideon Thurgood said. "Stay close."

Somewhere a clock struck midnight and the rain chattered to a gusting south wind. The warehouse was constructed of corrugated iron and had once been given a coat of orange paint to cover rust.

Thurgood stepped to the door. It was closed with a crude, hand-forged shutter bolt, and he said to the tall man, "Open it, Gabe."

The man drew the bolt then pushed the metal door open. The hinges screeched as the door moved several feet then stopped, leaning inward on its hinges. "Let me, Mr. Thurgood," Gabe said. "It's as dark as hell in there." He reached into his slicker, pulled his Colt from a shoulder holster and stepped inside.

Thurgood followed. "I can't see a damned thing, Mr. Steel," he said.

"Maybe they're all gone," Gabe Steel said.

"No, I was assured that they're here, all right. But I thought they'd be easier to find. Let us proceed with caution."

Steel took one cautious step, his eyes searching a wall of darkness, then another . . .

A clattering, clanging, clashing clamor rang around the warehouse followed by the hoarse shout of a man and the thud of feet pounding on wooden stairs.

"Trip wire," Steel said. "Damn, I walked right into it."

"Who goes there?" a man's voice from Steel's right said.

"We're friends," Thurgood yelled quickly.

Lantern light bobbed and several men came into view, half hidden in the gloom. "Who are you? And state your intentions," a man said.

"My name is Gideon Thurgood. My intention is to talk business with Mr. Jasper Dunn."

"Who sent you here?" the man said.

"Attorney-at-law Mr. Jethro Tull. We have a mutual friend, it seems."

"I'm Dunn," the man said. "Walk this way and tell the gun to holster his iron."

"Do as he says, Gabe," Thurgood said. "At this early stage of the game we can't afford any unpleasantness."

Thurgood and Steel followed Jasper Dunn down a flight of rickety wooden steps to the shadowy basement area, lit by a few oil lamps. Stepping over the recumbent bodies of sleeping men, he led the way to a corner where a cot was set up and a desk and chairs.

"Sit," Dunn said. He was flanked by a couple of armed men, one of them the fast gun Silas Topper and the other Ford Talon holding a sawed-off scattergun. Dunn waited until the two visitors were seated, then said, "Proceed, and I hope for your sake I like what I hear."

Thurgood's face looked as though yellowed parchment had been stretched tight over his skull. His eyes were as gray as a sea mist and were without warmth. He took a silver cigar case from his pocket, selected a thin cheroot and placed it between his lips. Steel quickly lit it for him. Behind a haze of blue smoke he introduced himself, then said, "A new drug, Mr. Dunn. Come now, have you not heard about it?"

"Can't say as I have," Dunn said.

"It's made from opium and was first produced in Germany as a medicine and like opium and morphine is perfectly legal in the United States. But it is easy to make and the craving it causes is intense. Once the opium hounds get a taste for it, you can charge what you want," Thurgood said. He clenched his white, bony hand into a fist. "Mr. Dunn, you can squeeze them dry and make a fortune."

Jasper Dunn was wary. "Why are you telling me this?" he said, his eyes guarded.

"Because the smart money is on you to become the new big auger in this town. Or have I been wrongly informed?"

"Who is the informer?" Dunn said.

"Why, Jethro Tull, of course. I understand he liberated three of your men from jail yesterday. He's a very sharp fellow, knows where all the bodies are buried."

"Where can I get this stuff?" Dunn said.

"The short answer is from me," Thurgood said. "I will not reveal my sources at this time. Let me just say they are located west of the Mississippi and are eager to get started."

"Who are you, mister?" Dunn said. "What are you?"

"You already know my name. By profession I'm an itinerant hangman, but I grow weary of travel. I just hanged a poisoner in Houston who'd recently toured Europe and in exchange for a clean drop, he told me about his use of this new drug and how it was made."

"So you came to Fort Worth looking for me," Dunn said.

"Not immediately," Thurgood said. "Fort Worth was recommended to me as a wide-open town. I wrote to my friend Mr. Tull and he confirmed that fact, especially the area named Hell's Half Acre, and he told me about you and your convict army." The hangman's wide mouth stretched in a smile, revealing teeth like yellowed ivory piano keys. "How could I resist? Mr. Dunn, you're poised to walk a wide path and I want to be a part of it."

"How much a part of it?" Dunn said.

"I come with a guarantee," Thurgood said. "After the first shipment of merchandise arrives by rail, I will stay in Fort Worth for three months. If you don't realize a considerable profit by that time I will leave and no hard feelings."

"And if there is a big profit, what's your take?" Dunn said.

"Fifty percent of all sales."

Dunn slammed back in his chair. "That's not a go." He glanced at Ford Talon. "What do you think?"

"Fifty percent of something is better than fifty percent of nothing," Talon said. "He may be right. Your initial cash outlay will be relatively small and the profit margin in the Acre alone could be huge."

"If after three months there is no profit just walk away from it, Mr. Dunn," Thurgood said. "You have nothing to lose."

"If there is no profit you have everything to

lose, Thurgood," Dunn said. "Starting with your life."

Gabe Steel stiffened, then pushed back from the desk.

Dunn smiled. "The gun is nervous."

Thurgood smiled. "Mr. Steel is overly protective. It's his job. Do we have a deal?"

"All right, a deal," Dunn said. "And remember, if this doesn't work out like you say it will, it's your neck, hangman."

"Walk with me, Major Talon," Jasper Dunn said after Thurgood left.

Preceded by Talon, he walked up the stairs into the dark warehouse. Dunn stepped to the door and pulled it open. "I've always loved the rain," he said, gazing out at the downpour. "Though it's rare enough in Texas."

"You didn't bring me up here to discuss the weather," Talon said.

"No, I didn't." Dunn didn't take his eyes off the rain. "Cole Danvers is dead."

"Yeah, I heard."

"I sent him to kill Kurt Koenig and he failed."

"Koenig is not an easy man to kill."

Dunn ignored that and said, "Things are shaping up, Talon. What do you think about Thurgood?"

"He means what he says."

Dunn nodded. "Seems like." Then, "Koenig

and Luke Short still stand in my way. One way or another they have to go."

"With Koenig and Short there's only one way—you have to kill them."

"Then we must make that a priority. What about the sheriff . . . what's his name?"

"Jess Casey." Talon treaded carefully. "He can keep."

Dunn nodded. "Good. So long as he doesn't get in my way he can live for a while longer. Leave me now."

Jasper Dunn stepped outside, spread his arms and turned his face to the falling rain.

CHAPTER TWENTY-FIVE

At fifteen minutes past midnight as Jasper Dunn plotted with Gideon Thurgood, fate brought three people together on a rainy, pitch-black night at a most unlikely place, the city's Oakwood Cemetery.

It had not been Sheriff Jess Casey's intention to wander far from Main Street. Despite the foul night and the late hour the stalwarts of the Acre's sporting crowd and those who preyed on them were very much in evidence and the Acre still showed snap.

The rain glistening on his slicker, Jess did his appointed rounds, walking as far north as the White Elephant, where Luke Short, smelling better, gave him a cool welcome. "Hell, why don't you stay home," he said. "There's a better lawman than you on duty tonight."

"Rain slowing business, huh?" Jess said.

"Look around you," Luke said. "I couldn't give booze away."

Jess stepped outside where a woman in a rain cape had apparently been waiting for him. "Sheriff, this may be nothing," she said.

"But," Jess said, smiling.

"Well, I saw Flora Lynch carrying her lantern and start toward the cemetery like she does," the woman said.

"She does that often?" Jess said.

"No, not often." The woman was older and had tired brown eyes. "She's been tetched in the head this five year since her husband and two young 'uns were taken by the cholera. On the anniversary of their deaths she visits their graves at night and kneels and prays and cries until sunup."

"Why at night?" Jess said.

"God help us, all three died at the midnight hour."

"You want me to bring her back . . . ah . . ."

"Mrs. Baggerly, Sheriff. Edith Baggerly. My old man, Mr. Baggerly, delivers firewood. Do you know him?" She saw the lack of recognition in Jess's face and said, "Ah well, never mind, but the thing is Mrs. Lynch was being followed by a man, and real sneaky he was, keeping to the shadows, like."

"Can you describe him?"

"Big man. Wearing a cowboy coat like yours and a bowler hat, Sheriff."

"Maybe it was just a feller going home in the

same direction, trying to stay out of the rain," Jess said.

"Maybe so. But Flora Lynch is still a fine-looking woman and I worry about her so. If you ask me, that man was up to no good."

Mrs. Baggerly's concern was real and Jess decided to take her seriously. "I'll take a walk up that way and make sure she's all right," he said.

"Bless you, Sheriff," Mrs. Baggerly said. "I feel so much safer now with a lawman around who listens to ordinary people like me."

"You're very welcome, ma'am," Jess said. "You can depend on me."

In fact the last thing in the world Jess wanted was to walk up to a dark graveyard after midnight in a teeming rain to rescue a crazy lady.

When Jess Casey stepped through the cemetery gates he loosened the Colt in his holster and his eyes probed the darkness. He saw nothing but the looming branches of the wild oaks and the steel needles of the slanting rain. There was no wind to speak of and the only sound was the snake hiss of the downpour . . . and a woman's sobs.

Jess looked around him in an attempt to pinpoint the direction of Flora Lynch. It could be no one else. He walked into the cemetery and passed a small aboveground tomb flanked by grieving angels. Rain poured down the cheeks of the angels like tears, as though their sorrow at the death of a child was too much to bear.

"Mrs. Lynch! Are you there?" Jess called out.

No answer. But the sobbing continued, a woman in such terrible distress it made Jess's skin crawl. He walked on, his eyes and ears reaching out into the rain-torn night. He walked under oaks that ticked water onto the shoulders of his slicker and the air smelled of leaf mold and rotten vegetation, and gibbering things crawled in the grass but Jess couldn't see them.

"Mrs. Lynch!"

No answer.

The rain hissed like a baby dragon revealed by an upturned rock. Jess came to a wide, graveled path that left the main route through the cemetery at a right angle. He stopped and looked along the footpath, a tunnel of blackness with a dim pinpoint of light in the distance. His boots crunching on gravel, Jess walked toward the light, rain falling around him. The sobs, heart-wrenching and prolonged, grew louder with his every step.

"Mrs. Lynch!"

The woman's crying stopped for a moment then began again.

Jess had seen no sign of another man in the cemetery and he reckoned he'd been correct when he told Mrs. Baggerly the fellow she'd seen had probably been making his way home. He decided to check on Flora Lynch anyway. Maybe he could convince her to call it a night.

When he finally saw her, he walked close to the woman and stopped. She kneeled in front of a single headstone, her head bowed. Mrs. Lynch's black mourning dress was soaked and her hair spilled over her shoulders and ashen face in lank, brown tendrils. Her long, thin fingers clutched a soaked Bible and her wedding ring gleamed dully in the dim lantern light. Jess thought she may have been pretty but in the rain and darkness it was impossible to tell.

"I'm Sheriff Casey, ma'am," Jess said. He waited for a response, got none and said, "I was worried about you, Mrs. Lynch. Mrs. Baggerly said she saw a man following you."

The woman's head turned slowly to Jess. Her eyes were hidden in shadow and her lips were white as chalk. "He did," she said. She pointed into darkness. "He's over there."

Jess drew his gun and followed the woman's pointing finger. He passed a grave and saw the man stretched out across another. He lay on his back and the handle of a knife stuck out of his chest. Jess holstered his Colt and took a knee beside the man. The look of horror frozen on the dead man's face distorted his features but Jess recognized him. He was Adam "Gorilla" Gavin, one of the three ex-convicts Jess had arrested for the attack on Joselita Juarez.

The ground around the grave was torn up, as though there had been a violent struggle before somebody had summed it up with a knife.

Jess stepped back to the woman. For a moment

he and Flora Lynch were wrapped in silence and rain and then Jess said, "Who killed him, Mrs. Lynch?"

"I did," the woman said. "He grabbed me and tried to drag me to the ground." Her fingers strayed to her cheek. "He struck me here and then I used my husband's bowie knife on him." Her smile was one of incredible sweetness. "I was going to use the knife to free my husband and the children from the grave, but I can't, can I? They are buried too deep and that's why they will never, ever, come home, will they, Sheriff?"

"I'm afraid not, Mrs. Lynch," Jess said. "I reckon they're with God now. Let me take you away from here and I'll get someone to look after you."

Flora got to her feet and then surprised Jess. She spun away from him and performed a strange, leaping, dervish dance as she chanted, "Never coming home . . . never coming home . . . never coming . . ."

Jess stepped to the woman and put his right arm around her shoulder. "Easy, Mrs. Lynch, easy." He opened his slicker and tried to share its meager shelter. That's when he discovered that Flora Lynch was left-handed.

She did it so easily, so effortlessly, so thought-lessly.

Her hand went down to Jess's holstered Colt, she pulled it free of the holster and then she danced away from him. "If my family can't come to me, I will go to them," she said.

She put the muzzle of the Colt to her temple, thumbed back the hammer and pulled the trigger. She dropped like a rag doll.

"No!" Jess yelled. "No, no, no."

He kneeled beside Flora Lynch's dead body. Rain fell on her upturned face. She was smiling like a bride in church.

Jess Casey kneeled by the woman's body for the rest of the long night. Come dawn the rain stopped and two of the cemetery's workers arrived. They said soothing words to Jess, lifted him to his feet and helped him back to the sheriff's office.

Jess slumped into his chair, still wearing his wet slicker, and buried his face in his hands. He was done. All used up. After a while he removed the star from his shirt and threw it across the floor.

CHAPTER TWENTY-SIX

"Where the hell have you been, Sam?" Jess said. He tightened the saddle cinch then slapped the neck of his horse.

"Been on a drunk, Sheriff," Sam Waters said. "It happens to me now and again. I start, then can't stop drinking and nothing on God's earth can stop me until I decide it's over."

"You look like hell," Jess said.

"Beggin' your pardon, sonny, but so do you," Waters said. "Where you headed?"

"Sam, pick a direction and I'll take it. North, south, east or west, I don't particularly care so long as it's out of Fort Worth."

"It's gonna look bad, Sheriff. The word is out all over town and lawyer Tull says you done it."

"Done what?" Jess said.

"You left it too late. You should've saddled on your hoss and rode out hours ago afore sunup."

"Done what, Sam?"

"Word is that you shot the widder woman Flora

Lynch and stabbed some feller who was with her," Waters said. "Lawyer Tull says you were jealous that the widder was seeing another man so you done fer them both."

"The lovers met after midnight at a graveyard in a pouring rain, is that it?" Jess said.

"That's the word, Sheriff," Sam said. He looked down at his feet. "I heard about what happened to Joselita. I'm right sorry about that."

"What's done is done, Sam, and it doesn't matter a damn any longer." Jess swung into the saddle. "I'm getting the hell out of here."

"Can't say as I blame you, Sheriff, but I wish you'd change your mind," Sam said.

"I'm not the sheriff here any longer," Jess said. He looked down at Sam. "As to Flora Lynch, yeah, I killed her. I killed her by my own carelessness because I've learned nothing a lawman should know. She was left-handed, Sam. I should have been ready for that." He touched his hat. "So long, Sam."

Jess kneed his horse into motion and rode through the alley beside the sheriff's office. When he reached the street Kurt Koenig greeted him with a scowl and a Greener shotgun.

"Going somewhere, Jess?" he said.

"Away from here, Kurt. It's all yours."

"That's not going to happen, Jess. Harry sent me to arrest you."

"You really think I murdered Adam Gavin and Flora Lynch?" Jess said.

"Of course not," Koenig said. "You're not the

kind to kill a woman and why stick a man when you can shoot him? It doesn't make much sense."

"I'm riding out of here, Kurt," Jess said.

"I can't let you do that," Koenig said. "I like you, Jess, but if I have to I'll blow you right out of the saddle."

Jess looked into Koenig's eyes. The man meant exactly what he said.

"Don't even think about it, Jess," Koenig said. "You can't outdraw a finger on a trigger. Pull the Colt with your left hand and let it drop."

"Do as he says, Sheriff," Sam Waters said. His face was worried as he stood beside Jess's horse. "Mr. Koenig is a determined man and quick on the shoot."

"The old coot speaks sense," Koenig said.

"Take my gun, Sam," Jess said. "It's easy enough to do."

"Where do you want me, Kurt? In the cell?" Jess Casey said.

"I won't subject you to the indignity of that," Koenig said. He tossed the star onto the desk. "And pin that to your shirt. You're still sheriff of Hell's Half Acre."

Jess picked up the badge, stared at it for a few moments, then said, "I couldn't even stop Flora Lynch killing herself. I wasn't lawman enough to figure that she was left-handed."

"You're not a Pinkerton, you're a lawman in a mighty rough town," Koenig said. "Left hand, right hand, it doesn't matter a damn. If the woman wanted to blow her brains out she would have found some way to do it."

"Could you have prevented it, Kurt?" Jess said.

"After I found Gavin's body I would have grabbed the grieving widow by the hair and dragged her kicking and screaming all the way to the sheriff's office," Koenig said. "Does that answer your question?"

Jess managed a smile. "You're a hard man, Kurt."

"Damn right I am. Pin on the star, Jess. Here comes the hanging posse."

Led by the rotund Harry Stout, who smelled of his morning bourbon, three men barged into the office. With His Honor were Professor James Carnes and the shifty-eyed Jethro Tull.

Stout's gaze immediately fell on Koenig and he said, "Glad to see you here, Marshal." He shook his head. "A dastardly deed, yes, I say dastardly, has been perpetrated in our fair city." He didn't look at Jess.

"Come now, Marshal Koenig, has he confessed?" Tull said.

"Are you talking about me?" Jess said.

"Yes, you. And I'm also talking about an honorable young man cut down in his prime and the savage murder of a grieving young widow."

"Mrs. Lynch stabbed Gorilla Gavin when he

tried to force himself on her," Jess said. "Then she shot herself."

"A bowie knife?" Tull looked from Carnes to the mayor and both men smiled knowingly. "Are you trying to tell us, Casey, that Mrs. Lynch's frail hand had the strength to thrust that instrument of destruction into the brawny chest of a grown man?"

"It's amazing how much strength a woman can muster when she's fighting for her life," Koenig said. "Or her honor."

"And you are an expert on such things, Marshal?" Tull said.

"Yes," Koenig said.

Tull stared at him, expecting more, but when Koenig added nothing further he again turned on Jess. "Explain the murder of Mrs. Lynch, at least your version of the facts."

"I wanted to share my slicker with Mrs. Lynch because it was raining so hard," Jess said.

"Very gallant of you, I'm sure," Tull said. "And an ideal way to get close to a shapely young woman."

Jess didn't rise to the bait. "Mrs. Lynch was left-handed and she easily grabbed my gun from the holster. Then she stepped back and shot herself. If you've examined the body you've seen the wound is in her left temple. I should have been able to stop her, but I could not."

"That's a small admission of guilt, at least," Tull said. "It still doesn't explain how a woman could kill a grown man with a bowie knife."

"I don't know," Jess said. "I wasn't there."

"No, he wasn't," Koenig said. "Tull, your case is so thin it's transparent. I think it's an obvious ploy to get Sheriff Casey out of the way."

"A serious accusation, sir," Carnes said. "Be wary how you tread. Mr. Gavin was under my personal protection and it's well known that Sheriff Casey hates all convicts, even those who have reformed. I can bring great senatorial power to bear on Fort Worth." Then a barb. "Mr. Mayor, I trust that you are fully aware of that fact."

"Indeed I am, sir," Stout said. Then to Jess's surprise Harry showed game. "But I will not be threatened, sir, nor hear threats leveled at my city."

"Merely a statement of fact," Carnes said. He looked as shocked as Jess had been.

"Then perhaps they should be left unsaid," Stout said. He glared at Koenig. "Why are you so sure Sheriff Casey was not the one who killed this . . . what's his name?"

"Gorilla Gavin," Jess said, to Tull's obvious irritation.

"Yes, him," Stout said.

"A respectable lady of this town named Mrs. Edith Baggerly approached me this morning as I was walking here," Koenig said. "She said she was deeply distressed when she heard that Sheriff Casey was being accused of a double murder."

"How could she possibly know that?" Tull said. "I didn't know until this morning and I at once informed the mayor."

"Fort Worth is a small, close-knit community," Koenig said. "If City Hall knows it, a minute later so does the whole town."

Stout harrumphed, but said nothing. Then he placed his open hands across his great belly and nodded, as though Koenig had fairly stated the case.

"Mrs. Baggerly says she was the one who told Jess Casey that Flora Lynch was being followed by a man," Koenig said. "That was at least fifteen minutes after she first spotted him. And answer me this, Tull—why was Gorilla in the cemetery in the first place? I mean, well after midnight, in pouring rain?"

Tull was a seasoned lawyer and seldom lost for an answer. "Mr. Gavin went there to protect . . . to save . . ." His voice petered out. Even he couldn't bring himself to say that Gorilla Gavin had Flora Lynch's well-being in mind.

"All this changes nothing," Professor Carnes said. "One of my charges has been brutally murdered and I want to get to the bottom of this."

"You heard the sheriff," Harry Stout said. "He was killed by Mrs. Lynch. As far as I'm concerned that is where the matter will rest, pending further inquiry. Now, gentlemen, it is almost noon and I am a man who needs his lunch. I bid you good-day."

The mayor stopped at the door and said to Jess, "Under the circumstance you did all a man could do, Sheriff. I had not heard your side of the story until I got here. Mrs. Lynch, God rest her soul, was a crazy woman who killed Adam Gavin and then took her own life. For the time being, there's an end to it."

After the mayor huffed and puffed his way onto the boardwalk, Carnes said, "You have not heard the end of this, Sheriff Casey. You are trying to kill off my convicts one by one."

"Professor, I think they're doing a good job of that all by themselves," Jess said.

CHAPTER TWENTY-SEVEN

In the long-shadowed late afternoon, Gideon Thurgood and his shadow, Gabe Steel, stood on the platform of the Texas and Pacific railroad depot awaiting the arrival of a package and a person.

The package was a first shipment of the new drug, from Germany, since Thurgood's manufacturing plant west of the Mississippi had hit delays and was not yet in operation. The person was Hiram Hartline, better known to lawmen in Texas and the New Mexico Territory as the Second Horseman.

Thurgood welcomed both his acquisitions with enthusiasm, but the Horseman most of all. Though he knew Hartline only by reputation and had hired him sight unseen, he was most impressed by his visitor. Hartline was a tall man, well over six feet, and lean as a lobo wolf. He habitually wore the costume of the frontier gambler, black frock coat and pants, frilled white shirt and string tie. His long face was adorned by a well-cared-for imperial and a patch made of red silk covered his left eye. Like Wild Bill Hickok he carried a pair of ivory-handled Colts tucked into a scarlet sash around his middle, the fringed ends falling to his knees. A black, low-crowned hat completed his apparel and he wore an ornate silver ring on his left hand, the mark of the professional gambler. Hiram Hartline had killed ninety-three men and had always gone out of his way to piss on their graves. He always sent red roses to the widows.

"I can't tell you what an honor it is to meet you, Mr. Hartline," Thurgood said. The gunman had refused his proffered hand. Hartline never shook hands with anyone. "You and I are destined for great things."

Hartline acted as though he hadn't listened. His cold gray eyes were fixed on Gabe Steel, the man he pegged as a gun. Hartline looked Steel up and down for long moments then dismissed him.

"My horse," he said.

A black porter was passing and Thurgood said, "Boy, bring this gentleman his horse from the boxcar."

"No," Hartline said. He stared at Steel. "You get it. Big red sorrel."

Steel, already irritated that Thurgood had hired another gun without his knowledge, was taken aback. Then his anger flared. "You go to hell," he said.

Hartline was fast, faster than any mortal man should be. He pulled a Colt and slammed the barrel across Steel's face. Blood erupting from his right cheekbone, Steel dropped, but his hand clawed for his holstered gun. He froze as the muzzle of Hartline's Colt pushed into the bridge of his nose. "Try it," the gunman said. "You're a twitch of my finger away from death."

Gideon Thurgood was stunned. The assault on Steel had happened so quickly and without warning. The porter saved the situation and possibly Steel's life. "Should I get the hoss?" he said.

Thurgood nodded then helped the unsteady Steel to his feet. "That was unnecessary, Mr. Hartline," he said.

The gunman turned eyes to Thurgood that had a hundred different kinds of hell in their depths. "When I tell a man to do something, he jumps to it," he said. Then a viper smile. "Or I shoot him."

Hartline shoved his Colt back into the sash. "Now you can buy me a steak, Thurgood," he said. "And I eat it bloody."

In that moment Thurgood realized he'd made a terrible mistake. He'd not hired a man . . . he'd hired a monster.

Luke Short brought the word to Kurt Koenig.

"Why would Hiram Hartline be in town?" he said.

"He isn't." Koenig pushed a glass of bourbon

across the bar to Luke. "He isn't because he doesn't exist. He's a boogerman parents use to scare naughty children."

Luke reached into his pocket and tossed a cardboard label tag onto the bar. "It says 'Property of H. Hartline' and it was attached to a silver saddle that came down in the afternoon train. That and a big red stud."

"Some rooster pretending to be Hartline, probably," Koenig said.

"He buffaloed a man on the depot platform and then was going to kill him until another feller intervened," Luke said.

"All kinds of men get buffaloed in this town," Koenig said. He watched a couple of punchers who were playing cards and getting loud.

"They say Hartline sold his soul to the devil in exchange for a fast draw," Luke said. "They say he's killed a hundred men."

"Folks say lots of things," Koenig said. He took his eyes off the card players and went back to polishing glasses. "Who told you all this?"

"A railroad porter who comes into my place. He says he saw Hartline with his own eyes, a big man who carried two guns in a red sash."

Koenig smiled. "Like Hickok did. I tell you, Luke, whoever he is he's a would-be badman. If he comes in here on the boast, all horns and rattles, I'll take care of him."

No one ever doubted Luke's sand, but his eyes were haunted as he said, "Just suppose it is him, Kurt. Suppose Hiram Hartline really exists. They say the devil took his soul early and told him he'd store it in the lowest pit of hell for fifty years. They say Hartline is now just a shell of a man without a soul. But he's still the fastest gun that ever lived or ever will live."

Now Koenig was irritated and slightly spooked. "They say . . . they say . . . who says?"

"Folks around," Luke said.

"Folks around are talking out of their butts." Koenig laid down the glass he'd been polishing and said, "If Hartline is real, which I doubt, he's come to the wrong town. He won't leave here alive."

Lukc tossed down his whiskey, then said, "Kurt, how can you kill a man who's already dead?"

CHAPTER TWENTY-EIGHT

The realization that he hadn't eaten a square meal in days drove Jess Casey to the restaurant for an early dinner. But even as he opened the door and stepped inside he wasn't hungry.

Jess walked into an atmosphere as tense as a fiddle string. A dozen people, including a couple of women, sat in silence at their tables, and the usual kitchen noises were subdued.

"Did somebody just die in here?" Jess asked the waitress. He smiled when he said it.

The girl didn't smile in return. Nervous as a whore in a confessional, she nodded in the direction of the window that looked out onto the street. Two men sat at a table, one of them older, austere, respectable-looking, the other a flamboyant creature in gambler's frilly duds, ivory-handled Colts stuck into a scarlet sash around his waist, and falling over his shoulders was long, chestnut hair as thick and luxuriant as a woman's. Jess had seen his kind before and they tended to be a touchy, dangerous breed. A frontier dandy who grew his hair that long and dressed like an effeminate dude had to be mighty good with a gun.

What drew the attention of the other diners was how the man ate. He forked chunks of bloody meat into his toothy, cavernous mouth, gulping them down without chewing, like a hungry wolf. He didn't eat. He devoured.

Jess was as fascinated as the rest of the customers, but turned his attention to the eggs and bacon on his plate and discovered he was hungry after all. He completed his meal with bread spread thick with butter and honey then sat back, a satisfied man, and started to build a cigarette.

When he looked up from the makings, the ravenous wolf—for that was how Jess thought of him—was staring at him, a slight smile on his thin lips. But it was not a good smile. It was a contemptuous smirk, as though the man had looked deep into Jess's soul and found him wanting.

Then he spoke. "You can smoke when I leave," he said.

Every eye in the place was turned in Jess's direction. He shrugged, thumbed a match into flame with his left hand and lit the cigarette.

It seemed that the man regarded Jess's action as an act of defiance. He rose to his feet, tall, elegant and significant, and stepped to Jess's table. "Put out your tongue and use it to douse that quirley," he said. "Do it now or I'll kill you."

"Sheriff, that's Hiram Hartline talking to you,"

Gideon Thurgood said. "Be very afraid and do like he says. Wet your tongue and it won't hurt so bad."

"Wise advice," Hartline said. "If I was you I'd take it."

Jess smiled. "I've heard of you, but I thought it was just a big campfire story. I heard you sold your soul to the devil and you're as fast as a demon with the iron."

Hartline's hands were on the butts of his revolvers. "You heard right, little man. And who are you? I like to be introduced to the wretch I'm about to kill."

"Why, my name is Old Scratch," Jess said. "And I'm here to collect my score."

Hartline's eyes narrowed at this affront but then opened wide as Jess's bullet smashed into his right kneecap. The man screamed and fell. Jess rose to his feet, his Colt ready. Hartline, face twisted in pain, shrieked his rage and went for his guns and Jess shot him in the chest and then, to further discourage the man's aggression, in the middle of his forehead.

Gideon Thurgood hurried across the floor and saw Jess's gun swing on him. "Don't shoot!" he yelled. Aghast, he looked at Hartline and then at Jess. "You killed him. He was . . . he was . . ."

"A piece of garbage," Jess said. "I reckon he was a damned bully who made a reputation killing rubes and desk clerks."

"You didn't call him out. Your gun was under the table and you shot him."

"I figured I should do that before he shot me," Jess said.

"But he was the best . . . the best there ever was," Thurgood said. "I can't believe this. Nobody will believe this."

"It just goes to show you that a man who's sold his soul shouldn't visit Hell, even a half acre of it," Jess said.

"But . . . but you weren't afraid," Thurgood said. "Any man would have been afraid of Hiram Hartline."

"Mister, I'm the sheriff of Hell's Half Acre," Jess said. "If this place has taught me anything it's that I don't scare worth a damn, especially when a loudmouth braggart is trying to do the scaring."

"Sheriff? But I was told you'd quit." This from the grease-spattered owner of the restaurant.

"I had. But now I've changed my mind," Jess said.

Luke Short was the first to pay homage.

He stepped into the sheriff's office that evening with a bottle of champagne and two glasses. "For the hero of the hour!" he declared as he laid the bottle on the table.

"You heard, huh?" Jess said.

"Heard? The whole town is buzzing," Luke said. "You done for the most feared gunman the West has ever known. Here, let me open this." He popped the champagne cork and then filled two fizzing glasses, one of which he passed to Jess. He raised his own and said, "To the man who killed Hiram Hartline!"

Jess left his glass untasted. "Luke, I'm not going to celebrate the taking of a man's life."

Luke was puzzled. "Hell, Casey, this will make you famous, the cock o' the walk in Fort Worth. The big-city newspapers will want your story and Buffalo Bill will come calling, and he'll pay plenty. Hickok and that Bill Bonney kid became famous and they never came up against a shootist like Hiram Hartline." He raised his glass again. "Enjoy the champagne because you'll never drink water again. Damn it all, you're the baddest man in the West and from now on every ranny who wears a gun will step around you and touch his hat and call you sir."

"Let it go, Luke. Let me be," Jess said. "And take the champagne with you."

Luke tried to wrap his brain around that, then, "I don't understand you," he said.

"That makes two of us, Luke," Jess said. "I don't understand me, either."

CHAPTER TWENTY-NINE

"This changes nothing," Jasper Dunn said. "I'm almost ready to make my move and a two-bit sheriff won't stand in my way."

"You aren't hearing me, Mr. Dunn," Gideon Thurgood said. "He killed Hiram Hartline."

"I'm hearing you real well," Dunn said. "So the lawman got lucky once. It won't happen a second time." Dunn sat back in his chair. "Why did you bring in a second gun?"

"For my personal protection, Mr. Dunn. We're in a dangerous business. In my capacity as a circuit hangman, I made many acquaintances among the law profession and Hartline was recommended to me."

"He didn't do a very good job of it, did he?" Dunn said.

"As you said, the sheriff got lucky."

Dunn tapped the box that Thurgood had laid on his desk. "That's the merchandise?"

"Yes, the first shipment."

"When will there be another?"

"Soon. I can assure you of that."

"Are you burying Hartline?"

"Yes, but the Oakwood Cemetery authorities say he can't be laid to rest in consecrated ground, so I've arranged for a burial outside the town."

Dunn smiled. "You believe Hartline sold his soul to the devil?"

"No."

"Everybody else seems to."

"He was a cold-blooded killer with a fast draw, that's all," Thurgood said. He laid a burlap sack on the table. "I brought you his Colts as a gift."

Dunn looked around at his men. "Any of you boys want the devil's guns?" He got no takers and men close to his desk stepped away, their horrified eyes on the sack.

"I don't want them, either," Dunn said. "Bury him with them." Then, "Oh, by the way, I found customers already at a brothel on 11th Street. Whores will try anything that promises to ease the pain of their lives. If all goes as I expect it will, I'll want more supplies in a hurry."

"You'll get them, Mr. Dunn, I assure you," Thurgood said.

"Good, then I'll be in touch. Now go bury the devil's dead and take his guns with you."

"Tell me about it, Jess," Kurt Koenig said. He wore his city marshal shield on the front of his frock coat and he looked worried.

"You're talking about what happened in the restaurant yesterday evening?" Jess said.

"I'm not here to listen to your life story, am I?" Koenig said. "This is official business."

"Hiram Hartline was going to kill me just for the hell of it, so I killed him first."

"Tell me about it," Koenig said.

After Jess finished talking, the big man said, "I saw Hartline in action once. He put down four men in a saloon in the Arizona Territory, holding his gun in one hand, a whiskey in the other. He was hellfire that day, all right."

"I heard he sold his soul to the devil," Jess said.

"Heard that my ownself," Koenig said. "Maybe it's true." He studied a wanted dodger on the wall and without taking his eyes off it said, "Somebody is moving in on me, Jess."

"Is this anything to do with Hartline?"

"Maybe nothing, maybe everything. Who was the man with him?"

"I don't know. Tall, thin, dressed in black, looked like an undertaker to me or a parson."

"Is he a gun?"

"I don't think so. Too old for that."

"Three of my accounts quit on me," Koenig said. "Said they're buying their protection from somebody else, a man who scares them."

Jess smiled. "Since forcing merchants to pay for protection is against the law, you can hardly expect me to be sympathetic."

"This is the Acre. Everybody needs protection," Koenig said. "I'm a businessman who provides that service. I also sell opium, a perfectly legal product." The big man stepped to the window and looked into the busy, dust-churned street. "Somebody pushes me, I push back harder."

"What are you telling me, Kurt?" Jess said.

"Suddenly I'm in the prophesying business, Jess. I see blood in the streets and I hear the cries of dying men. Somehow I think that your killing of Hartline marked the beginning of something . . . something bad . . . something ugly." Koenig smiled. "There's an old German saying that goes: *Ein Unglück kommt selten allein.* It means 'One disaster comes rarely alone.'"

"When it rains it pours, huh?" Jess said.

"Exactly that," Koenig said. "But when it rains trouble in the Acre it pours blood."

The wagon creaked through the darkness and the lanterns on each side of the driver's seat pooled light on the grass like spilled orange paint. Big Sal, dressed in a man's shirt and overalls, a battered hat on her shorn head, urged on the reluctant Morgan in the shafts. Beside her, silent and morose, her assistant glanced back at Hartline's rocking, sheet-wrapped body and shook his head.

"He's got no soul, Sal," he said. "A man with no soul can't die."

Sal spat tobacco juice over the side of the wagon, close to where Gideon Thurgood walked. "He's got three .45 bullets in him. He's dead, all right." She said to Thurgood, "What do you think, hangman. Is he dead?"

Thurgood trudged on, his head bent. He said nothing.

"Then I'll take that as a you don't know," Big Sal said. "Well, I've buried all kinds and none have ever come back to haunt me."

"This one will," the assistant said. He was a small, spare man and his high cheekbones and coarse straw-colored hair hinted at an Eastern European ancestry. "Bullets can't kill a man who has no soul."

The wind had picked up and black, silver-edged clouds scudded across the face of the moon. Coyotes had yipped earlier but had fallen strangely quiet and the air smelled of dampness and the odor of wormy earth.

Thurgood spoke for the first time since they left Fort Worth. "The wagon tracks are getting deeper," he said. "The ground seems soft enough for the shovel."

"Where do you want to plant him, hangman?" Big Sal said.

"Pull off to the side, closer to the trees," Thurgood said. "He doesn't need to be too deep."

After the wagon lurched to a halt, Big Sal and her assistant climbed down from the seat. "We'll dig the hole first," she said to the little man. "Bring the lanterns."

As the undertakers dug, their sweaty bodies outlined by bronze light, Thurgood stood by the wagon. Now the motion had ceased and Hartline's body lay still, yet Thurgood had the feeling that he was being watched, that under the sheet the dead man's eyes were open, aware. He shivered and stepped closer to the deepening, yawning chasm of the grave and the smell of dank earth.

The wind grew stronger and the trees shook their branches and moaned. The night seemed to grow darker, held back only by the lanterns, their flames dancing.

Big Sal climbed out of the grave and said to Thurgood, "I'll get him." She stepped to the back of the wagon, dragged out the body by its feet and then tucked the corpse under one massive arm. The woman carried the dead man to the grave and let him drop. "Well, he's planted," she said. "Now we can cover him, Stefan."

"No!" the little man yelled. "We must destroy him. He is *vampyr.*"

"Hell, he's just a dead man like any other," Big Sal said. "Get your shovel."

"He has no soul," Stefan said. "He will rise from the grave and kill us."

"Go on with the burial and we'll get out of this infernal wind," Thurgood said. "It seems like the whole world is about to blow down."

"I will destroy him," Stefan said.

He rooted around in the back of the wagon and rushed to the grave with a hammer and a sharpened piece of wood. The wind howled and the trees shook. Stefan yelled and jumped into the grave.

"Stop him," Thurgood yelled above the gale. "He's gone crazy!"

But Big Sal was strong, not nimble, and she was too late.

Stefan raised the hammer and pounded the stake into the corpse's unbeating heart. Immediately a terrible, drawn-out groan rose from the grave.

Thurgood was horrified and lurched back, his arms up in a defensive gesture, and Stefan jumped out of the hole, shrieking in terror.

"Fools, it's nothing!" Big Sal yelled to make herself heard above the wind. "Dead bodies do that all the time. It's escaping gas caused by corruption."

"He wasn't dead long enough to corrupt," Thurgood said. He tried desperately to hold on to his jangling nerves. "For God's sake throw the dirt on him."

As strong as any two men, Big Sal grabbed a shovel and got to work. Within minutes the grave was filled. Without a word she picked up the lantern, ran to the wagon and tossed the shovel into the back. She climbed into the seat beside the gibbering Stefan and cursed him for a pansy.

"Wait!" Thurgood yelled. He jumped into the wagon and roared, "Get the hell away from here!"

Big Sal needed no second urging and the old Morgan seemed to sense something was badly amiss, got the wind under her tail and lurched into a shambling canter.

Thurgood looked back at the grave. Was it Hiram Hartline standing on his grave or a trick of the fleeting moonlight? He didn't know and had no wish to guess.

"Faster!" he yelled at Big Sal. "Damn you, faster!"

CHAPTER THIRTY

A shaken Gideon Thurgood jumped the next train out of Forth Worth and left Gabe Steel to look after his interests. Jasper Dunn was not pleased by this arrangement.

"Can I depend on the hangman to deliver as he promised?" he asked Steel.

"He told me to assure you that the shipments will arrive on time," Steel said. "He'll wire ahead to let you know."

"I've sold all the product he sent me," Dunn said. "I need more."

"It will be forthcoming in the next day or two," Steel said. His right cheek was bandaged where it had been laid open by the front sight of Hartline's Colt. "When you move against Kurt Koenig and Luke Short I'm to give you any assistance I can."

"You mean gun assistance?" Dunn said.

"Just that," Steel said.

Dunn's forefinger flicked to the man's bandage, "You didn't do much good against Hartline."

"Had he lived, I would have killed him," Steel said.

Loco Looper, who was standing close to Dunn's desk, sneered, "Big talk is easy."

"I can back it up," Steel said. "Maybe you'd like to try me sometime."

"No cross talk. Time for that after we take this town," Dunn said. "Real or not, legend or not, Hartline was a big loss. We needed his gun."

"He was fast on the draw," Steel said, with grudging admiration from one draw fighter for another. Then, "Have you put together a plan yet, Mr. Dunn?"

Ford Talon had been sitting on the edge of his cot, but now he got to his feet and stepped closer to Dunn's desk.

"Kurt Koenig will be a tough nut to crack," Dunn said. "He's fast with a gun and he's got the backing of the Panther City Boys and probably the sheriff." He took time to light a cigar then said, "Luke Short is the easier target. Apart from a couple of Irish bouncers he's on his own."

"How do we play it, boss?" Talon lashed.

"We move in on him, demand ninety percent of his business, he refuses and we run him out of town or kill him, whatever is the more convenient at the time."

"When?" Talon said.

Dunn frowned. "A questioning man, aren't you, Talon?"

"I like to be ready," Talon said.

"The walls have ears," Dunn said. "When the time is right, I'll tell you. But it will be soon. I mean within the next couple of days soon."

"He was a pimp, ran maybe three or four girls," the landlady said. Her name was Mrs. Orpha Brown. "This is how I found him this morning."

"What was his name?" Jess Casey said.

"Archie somebody or other. He kept to himself, paid his rent on time and I never asked for his last name." She crossed her arms under her plump bust and said, "Well, I'll leave you gentlemen to it."

The late Archie, dressed in pants and a shirt, sprawled across his bed. There was no sign of a struggle and nothing to suggest that the man had committed suicide.

Jess was visiting Nate Levy in his hotel room and Dr. Arthur Bell was in attendance when Mrs. Brown came looking for him. Nate, declaring that he was no longer an invalid, insisted on accompanying Jess "to keep him out of trouble."

"He's been dead for at least eight hours," Dr. Bell said. "Hello, what have we here?" The physician examined the inside of Archie's forearms. "Looks like he used morphine."

"Is that what killed him?" Jess said.

"It's not out of the question. Too much morphine and the breathing slows and eventually stops."

Nate Levy, who had been poking around the

shabby room, picked up some items off the wood floor. "What's this stuff, Doc?" he said.

"Lay it on the table there," Bell said. One by one he examined a syringe, a soupspoon and a candle. He sniffed. "Smells like vinegar."

"He was injecting vinegar?" Nate said. He was pale but looked well.

"Unlikely," the doctor said. "I believe he melted something in the spoon, then used the syringe to inject it into his arm. It wasn't morphine, but something else."

"Any idea what it was?" Jess said, ice in his belly.

Dr. Bell shook his head. "No, Sheriff Casey, I have no idea. A drug, certainly, but not one I'm familiar with."

"It's a *new* drug, Doctor," Jess said.

"Certainly a new one on me."

"Made from opium."

"It could be that, I suppose, but I can't make an informed guess if that's the case."

"I believe this is the first overdose in Fort Worth," Jess said. "And I don't think it will be the last."

Dr. Bell dropped his wooden tube stethoscope into his bag and snapped it shut with an air of finality. "Well, keep me informed, Sheriff," he said. "If a new drug is involved this might turn out to be an interesting case."

* * *

Dr. Bell's footsteps had no sooner faded on the staircase when another, lighter tread took their place. A dark-haired girl wearing a demure day dress of pink cotton stepped into the room and glanced at the body on the bed. "Is he dead?" she said.

"I'm afraid so," Jess said. "And you are?"

"Julia Grimes, but they call me Alaska on account of my cold feet."

"Did you know the deceased?" Jess said.

"Know him? I was married to him. Was he shot?"

"I think he died from an overdose of a new drug," Jess said. "Have you heard about it?"

"Archie told me he was trying something new—that's all I know," the girl said.

"Any idea who sold it to him?" Jess said.

"Mister, this is the Acre. Any number of people could've sold it to him." The girl walked around the room, looking in dresser drawers and a cigar humidor and a number of jars and boxes. "Nothing. Not a red cent. Just like Archie to die penniless."

Nate, always the gentleman, said, "Mrs. Grimes, if you need a few dollars . . ."

"No thanks, Pops," the girl said. "I have gentlemen friends who'll take care of me." She smiled. "Ah . . ." She stepped to the bed, put her hand under the pillow and produced a Remington derringer. "I figured it would be there. It's worth a few dollars, huh?"

"Will you take custody of your husband's body, Mrs. Grimes?" Jess said.

"Hell no. Archie never took care of me when he was alive, why should I take care of him now he's dead? And he is dead, isn't he? He was always such a lying piece of—"

"He's as dead as he's ever going to be," Jess said.

"Good," the girl said. She stood at the bottom of the bed, joined her hands and bowed her head. "Dear God, please rest Archie's double-dealing, tinhorn soul. Amen." She smiled. "There, I've done my duty as a good wife." She stepped to the door, sang out, "So long, gents," and then was gone.

"Nice lady," Nate said with a straight face.

"She has cold feet, though," Jess said.

CHAPTER THIRTY-ONE

Silas Topper's instructions from Jasper Dunn were simple: "Look around the White Elephant, gauge the opposition and don't be afraid to kill somebody if you can make it look good."

"You can depend on me, boss," Topper said, his reptilian eyes gleaming. "I always let the rubes go for their gun first."

Ford Talon wondered if now was the time to play his hand. He could report to Jess Casey and head this thing off at the pass, but he immediately dismissed the idea. Luke Short was more than capable of taking care of himself and Talon decided he had to stand pat until something bigger came down.

He watched Topper swagger to the stairs, his hand resting on his gun. Earlier Talon had gone outside to smoke a cigar and saw blood on the moon. At the time he considered it a bad omen, but now he wondered . . . for whom?

* * *

As surely as night follows day, a man with a gun rep will be tested. And the man who killed a living legend most of all.

Silas Topper decided to disobey Jasper Dunn's orders. He'd no intention of visiting the White Elephant. Luke Short was of little importance and he could wait. Besides, what fame was there in picking a white-faced rube from the crowd and gunning him? The answer was none, none at all.

But gunning the man who killed Hiram Hartline was . . . what was the saying? . . . ah yes, a different kettle o' fish. Topper smiled to himself as he took to the boardwalk. Soon he'd be the most famous gun in the entire West. He'd walk with a swagger and cut a wide path and the rubes in their one-horse towns would doff their hats to him, and the women . . . well, he'd have his pick.

Topper was feeling good, so good he decided to dally and savor what was to come. A bottle of whiskey and a willing whore. That's what a man like him needed before entering a gun battle.

The whore's name was Elsie, pretty enough, but she seemed bored and Topper took no pleasure in her. As for the whiskey, it tasted sour in his mouth and he cut his bed session short. He badly needed a kill and it had been foolish of him to postpone it. To watch a man die, to see the horror in his eyes at the time and manner of his death, was better than convulsing on top of a woman, better than the raw burn of whiskey . . . better than anything.

"You know what's better than anything, Sheriff?" Sam Waters said.

"No," Jess Casey said. "But I'm sure you're going to tell me."

"It's what I got right here in this glass. Three fingers of Old Crow with just a . . . leetle . . . drop of water to bring out the flavor, like."

"Is that a natural fact?" Jess said. "Well, I'll give it a try."

"Just a smidgen now," Sam said. He picked up the water glass and let a drop fall into Jess's whiskey. "There. Now, take a taste o' that."

Jess tested his bourbon, tried it again and said, "You know, Sam, I think you're right. It does taste better."

Sam smiled and nodded. "See, when it comes to drinkin' whiskey I'm what they call a connoisseur."

"Where did you learn a ten-dollar word like that? Con . . . con . . ."

"Connoisseur. Feller teached me that word in Huntsville. He was an eddicated feller and was gonna learn me other big words but then they hung him. *Connoisseur* was the only one I ever learned."

"It's a crackerjack word," Jess said." A man who knew a word like that could've gone far and made his mark."

"Well, they hung him for poisoning his wife, so that's as far as he went."

"Pity," Jess said. "They should have kept him alive to teach them big, important words."

"Ah hell, what do prison guards know?" Sam said.

"I'll drink to that," Jess said, raising his glass.

This had to be done out in the open with as many witnesses as possible and Silas Topper considered the conditions excellent. The day was just beginning its fade into evening and most of the goods wagon traffic was gone from Main Street. But there were many pedestrians about, mostly of the respectable merchant sort, and street vendors plying their wares.

If a man wanted to enhance his rep as a revolver fighter this was the time and the place.

Silas Topper's wide-legged stance outside the sheriff's office almost immediately drew attention. He waited awhile and let the curiosity build. People stopped in the street, whispered to one another and already he felt like the big man in town. He glanced around, grinning, and was satisfied. It was time. Confident of his blinding speed on the draw and shoot, Topper felt invincible.

"Casey!" he yelled. "I'm calling you out. You killed a friend of mine and I'm here to even the score."

* * *

Jess Casey doused the oil lamp then stepped to the window. "Who the hell is that?" he said.

Sam Waters joined him and peered outside. "That there is Silas Topper. In Huntsville I was told he's the fastest, deadliest gun in Texas. A thing I was told by the kinda folks who never lie about important stuff like that."

"He must have been a friend of Hiram Hartline," Jess said. "Or even kinfolk."

"Sheriff, you stay in here and lock the door," Sam said. "I'll go get Mr. Koenig."

"You stay put, Sam," Jess said. "I can't show yellow in front of all those folks out there."

"You can't shade him, sonny," Sam said. "He's a demon with a gun."

Then, from outside, "Casey, are you coming out or do I have to go in there after you?"

"He's making it clear, Sheriff," Sam said. "He's stated his intentions."

"Then let him make it clear to my friend Mr. Greener," Jess said. He took down a shotgun from the rack, opened it and inserted two bright red shells into the chambers. He stuck two more in his pocket.

"Sam," Jess said, "if he cuts my suspenders out there, could you see your way clear to gunning him first chance you get?"

"You bet, Sheriff. An' I'll use the very scatter-gun you got in your hands." Sam grinned. "I ain't been here long, but already I know all the dark alleys in town."

"Thank you kindly, Sam," Jess said. "Makes a

man feel better knowing his friends are looking out for him."

"Ah, hogwash," Sam said. "No thanks needed. I'll be glad to do it, Sheriff, and I'll see you buried decent as well."

"If I don't come back, you can finish the rest of the Old Crow," Jess said.

Sam knuckled his forehead. "Thankee, Sheriff. By God, you're a white man through and through."

Jess stepped to the door and behind him he heard Sam say, "So long, Sheriff."

"Yeah, you, too, Sam. So long."

"Well, about time." Topper grinned when Jess stepped onto the boardwalk. His carrion-eater's eyes flicked to the shotgun pointed right at his belly, both its hammers eared back. "This is a draw fight," he said. He looked around him and played to the crowd. "This here is a draw fight."

"This here is any kind of fight I care to make of it," Jess said. He smiled. "It's a scattergun fight, Topper, and you don't have a scattergun."

Topper considered that and one question flashed into his mind: Could he draw and fire faster than it took Casey to pull the Greener's triggers? He'd never tried it before and had no answer. But he had an odd, sickly sensation in his belly and was surprised when he realized it was fear.

Jess gave him an out.

"Unbuckle the gun belt, Topper, and then step

away from it," he said. "I want to see those hands move as slow as a hound dog in August."

A large crowd had gathered and people watched in silence as the drama played out. "Here, this won't do," a strict-looking man said. But nobody paid him any heed.

"Damn you, Casey," Topper said through gritted teeth. "Damn you to hell."

"I got the drop on you, Topper," Jess said. "Make your play or shuck the gun belt." He looked over the crowd. "You folks move on now. This here is over." His eyes flicked to the gunman. "Ain't it, Topper?"

The man stood, his primitive brain trying to grasp what was happening to him. He'd been cut down to size by a man he could outdraw any hour of the day, any day of the week and it seemed that his humiliation was witnessed by the whole population of the Acre.

Jess was not a particularly patient man and his experiences in the Acre had shortened his fuse. "Oh for heaven's sake," he said.

He stepped off the boardwalk, covered the distance between him and the hesitant Topper in a few long strides and then slammed the butt of the heavy shotgun into the gunman's face.

Topper went down leaking blood and after the man hit the ground, Jess removed his gun belt. His eyes lingered for a few moments on the fancy Colt in the holster and it made him wonder.

As the crowd still gaped, Jess grabbed the little gunman by the back of his shirt and dragged him onto the boardwalk through the sheriff's office and into a jail cell. Topper lay on the floor and didn't stir.

After he locked up Topper, Jess stepped to the front again and laid the Colt on the desk. Sam had already lit the oil lamp and he said, "Whiskey, Sheriff?"

"Yeah. Three fingers with a drop of water," Jess said.

CHAPTER THIRTY-TWO

"What do you think about this?" Jess Casey said, holding up the fancy Colt.

"I don't know guns, Sheriff, but it sure looks purty," Sam Waters said.

"Too purty to be a working gun," Jess said. "This looks like something a dude on a Wild West show would use. The engraving is still sharp, like it was done recently."

"Well, maybe ol' Silas had it fancied up," Sam said.

"You said Topper is a famous draw fighter. This revolver hasn't spent much time in gun leather." Jess shook his head, talking to himself, not Sam. "Who would own a Colt like this?"

"Somebody with money to spend. That's fer sure," Sam said.

Jess unloaded the Colt and walked back to the cells. Silas Topper sat on the cot, his head in his hands. When he heard Jess's boot steps he looked up. There was blood across the bridge of his nose and more had dried black on his upper lip.

It seemed that Topper was not a man to mince words. "Next time I see you with a gun in my hand I'll kill you, Casey," he said.

Jess held up the long-barreled Colt. "Where did you get this?" he said.

Topper gave the revolver a cursory glance. "Go to hell," he said.

"I reckon you stole it from Bruno Cavanni's gunsmith shop," Jess said. "If I can find its rightful owner and he confirms that he left it with the old man I can hang you, Topper."

"You ain't hanging nobody, cowboy," the little gunman said. "By first light tomorrow I'll be out of here and you'll be dead."

"Save your neck," Jess said. "Tell me who else was in on the robbery."

"I'm telling you nothing," Topper said. "If I was you I'd spend the rest of my time making peace with my God. Now get the hell away from me."

Jess stepped to the door, then said, "You ever put a drop of water in your whiskey, Topper?"

"What the hell kind of question is that to ask a man?" the gunman said.

"On the morning I hang you, that's how I'll fix it. Sound good to you?"

"I'm gonna kill you, cowboy," Topper said through gritted teeth. "I'm gonna shoot you in the belly and listen to you scream."

"All right, if that's your attitude you don't get any water," Jess said.

* * *

Jess left Sam Waters at the sheriff's office and walked along the thronging street to the Silver Garter, the fancy Colt shoved into his waistband. The sporting crowd was out and Jess followed a bartender's nod and made his way across the packed dance floor to Kurt Koenig's table. Destiny Durand, breathtakingly beautiful in a dress of white silk, sat with him. A bottle of champagne sat in an ice bucket at Koenig's elbow.

"Howdy, Jess," Koenig said. "Is this business or pleasure?"

"Business, though it's always a pleasure to see your lovely companion," Jess said with a little bow to Destiny.

"You're learning, Sheriff Casey," the woman said with a dazzling smile. "Now you should inquire about my ward."

"Very well then," Jess said. "How is Joselita?"

"I think her life is in danger," Destiny said. "A couple of nights ago we were followed here to the saloon. Fortunately I met a Panther City Boy I knew and he scared them off."

"It could have been Loco Looper and Dark Alley Jim Turner," Jess said. "I still intend to bring them to trial."

"Forget that," Koenig said. "A circuit judge dismissed the case last week. No doubt he was paid handsomely."

"Why wasn't I told?" Jess said.

"Jethro Tull told me in my capacity as city

marshal," Koenig said. He smiled. "In the grand scheme of things, Jess, you don't count."

"Since the case was dismissed, why was Joselita followed?" Jess said.

"I don't know," Koenig said.

"Where is Joselita?"

"She's upstairs in her room and there's a guard at the door," Destiny said. "She'll be down shortly."

"Is that wise?" Jess said.

"Sheriff, the girl is not a prisoner," Destiny said. "We'll keep an eye on her, and she's very wary around men."

Koenig grinned. "Except for Red Stark."

"Who's he?" Jess said. Suddenly he felt protective.

"He's a young puncher, rides for the Lazy-T," Destiny said. "He comes in every Friday night and makes moon eyes at her."

"And what about Joselita?" Jess said.

"She makes moon eyes back at him," Koenig said. He nodded to the gun in Jess's waistband. "You planning to shoot me with that there hogleg?"

"No," Jess said. "It's not loaded." He passed it to Koenig. "Don't drop it," he said.

"What am I looking for?" Koenig said.

"Have you ever seen that Colt before?" Jess said.

"I've seen a hundred just like it," Koenig said.

"Look closely at the engraving and the fit of the ivory handles," Jess said. "That revolver is a work of art."

Koenig nodded. "The work has been well done," Koenig said. "And its balance is near perfect. Now, let me guess. You took this off a feller earlier tonight and you think it's one of the guns stolen from Bruno Cavanni's workshop."

"How did you know about Silas Topper?" Jess said.

"Is that his name? The word I heard is that he's a draw fighter but you put the crawl on him with a scattergun and then coldcocked him with the butt as a way of saying howdy."

"Why didn't you come talk to me?" Jess said.

"Jess, you're a big boy now," Koenig said. "You're the man who killed a legend and a man who kills a legend becomes a legend himself. You don't need my help to enforce the law in the Acre any longer. Now folks are scared of you. You catching my drift?"

"Hell, I don't want folks to be afraid of me," Jess said. "I need them to stand behind me."

"Kurt meant bad folks, Custer," Destiny said. "All them mean Injuns out there on the street who dearly want to take your scalp."

"Destiny, don't tease Jess," Koenig said. "When he isn't shooting folks or bashing them over the head with clubs he's a sensitive soul." He passed Jess the Colt. "There's a man named Pleasant Woodis, lives just outside of town with a Lipan woman. Don't let his name fool you, he hates everybody but he often spent time with Bruno Cavanni."

"Then this could be his gun?" Jess said.

"Maybe, but it's a long shot. I know he has an interest in English hunting rifles." Koenig pushed away a drunk who'd bumped into his chair, then said, "There's only one problem: Pleasant has a tendency to shoot trespassers on sight."

"How do I get to his place?" Jess said.

"Easy. Take 12th Street and head west. After a couple of miles you'll come across a cabin and a warning sign. After that, proceed at your own risk."

"I'll go talk to him tomorrow," Jess said.

"Your funeral, Jess," Koenig said. "If I was you . . . Good Lord, what have we here? The belle of the ball has arrived."

Jess turned and did a double take. A few startled moments passed before he recognized a transformed Joselita Juarez. She wore a dress of pink organdy and her hair was brushed back and secured with ornate silver combs. Destiny or one of the other girls had obviously made up her face, transforming what had been an abused, homely fourteen-year-old into a lovely young woman.

As she'd been taught, Joselita said, "It's nice to see you again, Sheriff Casey." She offered her hand and Jess took it in his own, bowed and kissed it and would forever wonder why he'd done such a foolish thing.

"You're becoming quite the *galant* gentleman, Sheriff," Destiny said. Then, her eyebrow lifting, "Did you read an instruction book?"

Joselita sat beside Destiny and soon their heads

were together, whispering. Koenig was in deep conversation with a bartender and Jess shuffled to his feet and said, "Well, I guess I should be going."

But nobody paid him the slightest mind.

CHAPTER THIRTY-THREE

It felt good to be riding again across rough, sun-scorched country as empty and lonely as a crater on the moon. Jess Casey smelled air made sweet by pine and wildflowers and allowed the vast silence to settle on him, so different from the constant racket and ever-present odors of horse dung, crowded bodies and cattle pens of the city.

Jess, for the present in a lighthearted frame of mind, was about to launch into song, a thing that would have pleased him and irritated his horse, when he noticed a recent grave near a stand of mixed pine and hardwoods.

He drew rein and studied the tree line. Nothing moved but the wind.

After a few moments Jess rode closer then swung out of the saddle. The grave showed signs that the occupant had been buried in a hurry and Jess counted three sets of footprints.

"A friend of your'n?"

The voice came from behind him and Jess

turned slowly, then his line of vision dropped to the tiny man who now faced him, the double-barreled rifle in his hands pointed right at Jess's belly. Staring into the black eyes of a Holland & Holland 4-bore aimed at your guts is a conversation stopper and it took Jess quite a while before he found his tongue.

Finally he said, "No, he wasn't a friend of mine."

"Don't matter now who he was," the man said. "Friend or foe, he's dead."

The little man wore pants, miner's boots and an elaborately beaded buckskin shirt that must have taken an Indian woman a long time to make. His thin gray hair was long and he had blue eyes that were faded almost to gray, as though he'd seen too much in his life and worn them out. He looked Jess up and down then said, "Got a star on your shirt. You must be some kind of a lawman."

"Name's Jess Casey and I'm the sheriff of"— Jess decided to exaggerate—"Fort Worth."

"And you boast of it?" Jess made no answer to that and the little man said, "Name's Pleasant Woodis. I live hereabouts."

Jess grinned. "The very man I want to see. I'm here—"

The huge gun came up quick and Woodis's eyes were suspicious. "For why are you here?" he said.

To his considerable discomfort Jess saw that both hammers of the elephant gun were cocked.

His words tumbled out in a hurry. "I thought you might be able to identify a Colt revolver."

"If it says Colt on it, then it's a Colt revolver," Woodis said.

"I think the one in my saddlebag may have belonged to you," Jess said.

"Who told you that?"

"Man named Kurt Koenig."

"Damned scoundrel. He hasn't been hung yet?"

"Not yet, but he's working on it," Jess said.

Woodis nodded, then said, "Come with me. My cabin isn't far."

"We can do it right here," Jess said. "As I said, I brought the revolver with me."

"Mister, I ain't inclined to be friendly, so do as I say," Woodis said.

"Sure," Jess said. "Your cabin will be just fine."

"It better be," Woodis said. "Catch up your horse and come."

The Woodis cabin was well built and set close to a running stream. The interior was comfortable, furnished in wood, leather and soft rugs. It smelled of Woodis's pipe, gun oil and baking bread. One wall was hung with rifles of all kinds, fine weapons that must have come with hefty price tags. Woodis unloaded the Holland & Holland, extracting cartridges that looked as big as howitzer shells, and hung the rifle back on the wall.

"Coffee," he said to his woman.

Tall, stately and silent, the Lipan woman

nodded and stepped into a small kitchen. She wore a severe black dress with white collar and cuffs and her glossy black hair was pulled back in a tight bun. Jess thought she was a fine-looking woman but there seemed to be no joy in her.

As the woman poured coffee, Pleasant Woodis identified the Colt almost immediately. "It started as a plain, twelve-dollar Colt and then I had it engraved by Bruno Cavanni. You can see for yourself that he did an excellent job. I took the Colt back to be fitted with ivory. Then I heard that he'd been murdered and his store robbed. I figured this was among the stolen guns. I never thought I'd see it again."

"I took that from a man I now have in custody, Mr. Woodis," Jess said. "Are you prepared to stand up in court and state that the revolver is yours?"

"If I will put a noose around the neck of a man who murdered my friend, then, yes, I will," Woodis said.

"I will have to take the Colt back though," Jess said. "It has to be entered into evidence."

"It's a fine weapon, a revolver a man can be proud of," Woodis said. "But you can take it back. Once the murderer is hanged, I'll reclaim it." Woodis took time to light his pipe, then said, "Kurt Koenig tell you that I shoot trespassers?"

Jess said, "He did, but I didn't believe him."

"Is that so," Woodis said. "Well, it's just as well because it ain't true. I've been here nigh on twenty year and in all that time only shot but two."

He pointed with his pipe. "Know why I didn't shoot you?"

"No, but I'm glad you didn't. That cannon you carried could put a big hole in a man."

As though he hadn't heard, Woodis said, "I didn't shoot you because you reminded me of a friend of mine, General George Armstrong Custer. You ever hear of him?"

"Of course," Jess said. "Everybody's heard of Custer and his gallant last stand."

"I was supposed to be with him as a scout, but a week before the 7th rode out of Fort Lincoln I came down with the rheumatisms. I missed the whole shebang," Woodis said.

"Well, you saved your scalp," Jess said.

"That's one way of looking at it, I guess. But I would rather have died with Custer, standing under the flag in one moment of hell-firing glory than grow old and rot away like I'm doing now."

Woodis buried his face in his hands.

The Lipan woman spoke for the first time. "You've upset him. He won't speak again. Go away now."

Jess got to his feet, shoved the fancy Colt into his waistband and said, "I'll be in touch, Mr. Woodis."

The little man didn't answer.

CHAPTER THIRTY-FOUR

Sam Waters hung by his feet from a ceiling beam, a wooden bucket filled with water under his head. As a refinement in torture, the only way he could prevent himself from drowning was to hold up his head and place an intolerable strain on his neck and back muscles.

Jess Casey opened his Barlow, cut the rope as he walked past and stepped quickly to the cells. As he'd expected, the cell door hung open and Silas Topper was gone.

A thud of a falling body, the clang of the bucket and Sam's curses reassured him that the old man was unhurt, and indeed that was the case.

"Only my pride is hurt, Sheriff," he said, drying his hair with a towel. "They jumped me and I didn't have a chance."

"How many?" Jess said.

"Five. All of them big fellers."

"How many?" Jess said.

"Two. But they were big, all right, and strong."

"Recognize either of them?"

"Sure. I was in Huntsville with them, wasn't I? One was Loco Looper. He's a crazy man and it was his idea to put the water bucket under my head. The other was Dark Alley Jim Turner. Mean as a teased rattler that one."

"When did it happen?" Jess said.

"Right after you rode out of town. You talk with that crazy Woodis feller?"

"Yeah. He says it's his Colt and he's willing to testify that in court if it can put a noose around Silas Topper's neck."

Sam looked uncomfortable, as though he held something back, then he said, "Sheriff, ol' Silas told me a message to give to you."

"Yeah, I know. He says the next time he sees me he'll kill me."

Sam looked surprised. "You spoke to him?"

"No, but what else kind of message should I expect from a lowlife like Topper?"

"He's quick on the draw an' shoot, Jess."

"I know, but he doesn't like shotguns, none of his breed do."

"Ain't much fun carrying around a Greener scattergun everywhere you go," Sam said.

"I know. Seems like I'll have to put my trust in Sam Colt, huh?" Jess said.

"If you need me, I'll be at your side, Sheriff."

"Thanks, Sam," Jess said. Then, because the old man was hurting, blaming himself for Topper's escape, "I can't think of a man I'd rather have at my side when the chips are down."

Pleased, Sam Waters grinned and said, "Damn right."

"Topper, you stay away from the sheriff, you hear?" Jasper Dunn said. "You'll have time enough to kill him later."

"He cut me down to size in front of the whole damn town," Topper said. "I can't let that go."

"Nor will you," Dunn said. "But you must bide your time."

A man named Ed Lacey, who seemed to have been born with a permanent sneer, had been hovering near Dunn's desk. Now he smirked and said, "You ain't the first man that turned yeller at the sight of a shotgun." Then he made a mistake. He took a step closer to Topper.

In one fluid motion, the little gunman rose from his chair, swept a whiskey bottle from the desk and swung it fast and hard against the side of Lacey's head. The glass shattered and the man went down, landing solidly on his butt.

"You want in?" Topper said. "Go for the iron and we'll see who's yeller."

Dunn jumped to his feet. "That's enough, Topper!" he yelled. "I don't want us fighting among ourselves."

Topper listened, but Ed Lacey didn't.

A man of reputation who'd killed more than his share, he had never, even in Huntsville, had anyone put hands on him. To be struck by a bottle was an insult he could neither abide nor forgive.

His face livid, eyes devilish, Lacey grabbed for his gun.

He didn't even come close. Topper put two bullets into Lacey's chest before he cleared leather, then, an aimed shot, a third between his eyes. It later became a matter of discussion in Hell's Half Acre if that last shot was necessary. The consensus of the graybeards huddled around their winter stoves, was that it was not needed but a grandstand play on Topper's part.

Either way, it didn't matter a damn to Ed Lacey. He kicked his legs a time or two then sprawled on the floor, dead as a bearskin rug.

His smoking gun in his hand, Topper glared around the room. "Anybody else want to say I'm yellow and make their play?" He got no takers, but his gaze spiked at Ford Talon with all the warmth of an ice pick. "Maybe you, soldier boy?"

Talon shrugged and looked at the dead man. "Doesn't seem to be much future in it, Silas."

Jasper Dunn said, "Mr. Topper, come and have a drink. Let's have no more unpleasantness. You, too, Mr. Talon."

Dunn smiled but secretly he was worried. His dependence on violent cons, a few like Topper treading the ragged edge of insanity, was a double-edged sword. They might kill off one another before he could take over the town. Ford Talon was a cool customer, but Dunn couldn't bring himself to trust him. There was something about the man that didn't ring right, a crack in the bell. He'd bear watching.

The bottom line was that Jasper Dunn realized he had to make his move against Luke Short sooner than he'd planned . . . like tonight.

CHAPTER THIRTY-FIVE

It was Luke Short's habit of a late evening to step outside the White Elephant and take a stroll to get the saloon smoke out of his lungs and the smell of booze from his nose. Not that Luke minded those things, but in strict moderation fresh air was good for a man.

His usual route was to walk south into the Acre, stopping every now and then to ease his swollen feet that a doctor had told him were caused by dropsy.

A dandy by inclination, the night that Dunn decided to make his move, Luke was dressed to the nines in a pearl gray frock coat and top hat of the same shade and he sported spats and a silver-headed cane. A short-barreled Colt resided in the leather-lined back pocket of his pants. He was well known to the ladies of the evening who called out to him as he passed on his promenade and inquired if he desired a little female companionship. It was a familiar ritual and Luke's reply never varied: "Not tonight, ladies, but perhaps tomorrow."

But that night he exchanged words with an Irish whore named Mary Kelly, who two years year later on her return to London would become Jack the Ripper's fifth victim. Mary tucked a large-denomination note into her décolletage and Luke continued on his way, handing out silver dollars to the poor and destitute, kissing the odd baby now and then.

Thus, as he entered the Acre, people who met him on the boardwalks considered Luke Short a likable-enough gentleman, generous and good-natured . . . all but two, that is: Len Crawford and Kirk Graham considered him a target.

Crawford and Graham figured they had the perfect location for an ambush and assassination. Acting on instructions from Jasper Dunn, they positioned themselves in an alley named Tam's Wynd. Even in daytime the towering tenements on each side made the narrow passageway as black as mortal sin. Directly across Main Street, its two front windows aglow with bright gaslight, stood Lottie Lambert's Corset, Collar & Cuff Shoppe. Anyone passing the alley would be silhouetted against the light for several seconds, an easy target for a couple of shotgun blasts. And Luke Short's stovepipe hat, a rarity in the Acre, was the mark of Cain that would identify him.

Kirk Graham, a murderous brute who'd killed his grandparents with a mattock for the seventeen dollars in savings they kept in a tin box, fingered his Greener and whispered, "Len, I'll let him have both barrels in the head and then you cut loose as he falls."

Len Crawford nodded. "Make it good. The sawn-off son of a bitch is a demon with a six-gun."

"I won't miss," Graham said. He grinned. "I'm already thinking about how I'll spend the fifty dollars Dunn give us."

"You think he'll come this far?" Crawford said. "Maybe he'll stop and go back."

"Dunn said he always passes this alley on his walk. Why should tonight be any different?"

Crawford touched his tongue to his dry top lip. "Hell, just don't miss, Kirk. If you do we're dead men."

"I won't miss," Graham said. "And neither will you."

Minutes passed and the two assassins grew anxious. Worse, the rising moon spilled wan light into Tam's Wynd so that Graham's and Crawford's jailhouse-pale faces were visible in the gloom.

"Damn him, he ain't coming," Crawford said.

"Wait here," Graham said. "I'll take a look."

He propped his shotgun against the wall to his right and walked on cat feet toward the mouth of the alley. Later Luke would say it was a mistake that cost Graham his life.

"Are you gentlemen looking for me?" Luke appeared from the end of the alley, parting the

gloom like a sable curtain. He held a Colt in his
gun hand, the silver-topped cane in the other.
"Well, here I am, as large as life and ready to
open the ball."

Crawford, a rapist and woman beater, was not
a gunman. He'd never even met a gunman and
all he knew about draw fighters he'd read in the
dime novels. A cool gun hand would have deployed the Greener very quickly, but Crawford
lacked sand and took time to shriek for Graham's
help. That was all the time Luke Short needed.

Luke, shooting at a distance of five feet,
slammed two bullets into Crawford's belly, figuring the shock of getting gut-shot would immediately cause him to drop the scattergun and put
him out of the fight. He was right. Crawford
screamed, slammed against the wall and slid to a
sitting position. He yelped and wailed and the
Greener fell from his bloody hands.

Graham was a tougher proposition. In his time
he'd fought men. Separated from his shotgun, he
skinned iron and shot at Luke, who took a hit.
Luke returned fire, aiming for the white blur of
Graham's face. A miss. His legs in danger of
giving out, Luke reeled a little as he and Graham
exchanged shots. He staggered a few steps forward, steadied himself against a wall and emptied
his revolver at Graham. In the darkness, Graham
a bobbing, weaving target, his remaining two
shots went wild and the hammer of his Colt
clicked on an empty chamber.

Graham roared in triumph and advanced on

Luke. "I've got ye now, you damned runt," he said.

Luke saw the shotgun propped against the wall, but he knew he'd never reach it. Graham would gun him for sure. But for some reason the man held his fire, shuffling forward, his revolver at the ready, getting close. Then grinning, showing a rotten mouth, he stated his intentions. "Between the eyes, Short. You get it right between the eyes."

Luke Short was a small, well-coordinated man and almighty sudden. Steel sang from a scabbard and Graham cried out in pain as a two-foot-long blade ran him through. Luke jerked the sword free of the man's chest and the blade dripped blood as he watched Graham collapse to the ground.

Luke saw the agonized question on the dying man's face and he smiled and raised the blade in a salute. "Sword cane, a gentleman's weapon. Something you know nothing about."

Graham's pained eyes lifted to Luke. "Well, I'll be damned," he said.

"You most certainly will," Luke said. But he was talking to a dead man. He turned his attention to Crawford, who was dying in considerable pain. "Have you made your peace with your Maker?" he said.

"Get it over with," Crawford said. His teeth were gritted and there was black blood in his mouth.

Luke nodded. "Good-bye, old fellow," he said.

He shoved the sword into Crawford's heart and watched as all the life in him fled.

When Jess Casey reached the alley, Luke was unconscious, overcome by the bullet wound in his lower chest.

CHAPTER THIRTY-SIX

"Luke Short will not die young of a bullet wound," Dr. Arthur Bell said. "He'll die young of something else." He saw concern in Jess's face and added, "He'll be up and about in a few days."

"The men who tried to kill him?" Jess said.

"Both dead of bullet and sword wounds," Dr. Bell said. "First time I've written that on an Acre death certificate." His gaze moved to the woman in Jess's office. "How are you keeping, Mary?"

"I'm just peachy, doc," Mary Kelly said, her eyes bold. Born in Ireland, she'd lived most of her life in Wales and her speech had a Welsh lilt. "I'm going back to Britain, to London town, to see if I can make a new life for myself."

"Stay off the streets and avoid the gin, Mary," Dr. Bell said. "Before you leave come and talk with me. I have a colleague in London who's a fine surgeon. I'll give you a letter of introduction and perhaps he can help you find a situation. I think you might prosper in service, start as a scullery maid and work yourself up. Many have done it before you."

"You're very kind, Doctor, but I have a friend in the East End who promises to be ever so helpful. Catherine Eddowes is her name. She's a very happy woman, always singing like a lark."

"Is she turning tricks, Mary?" Dr. Bell said.

"Yes, and I will, too, but only until I get on my feet, like," Mary said. "Oh, that was funny . . . only until I get on my feet."

Jess smiled, but Dr. Bell remained stern. "If you change your mind, remember my letter. If you don't, well, take care of yourself."

After the physician left, Jess said, "Miss Kelly, did Luke Short tell you he was going to seek out the two men in the alley and kill them?"

"Yes, before they killed him," Mary said. She glared at Jess. "Sheriff, you're not going to put Luke's head in a noose for defending himself."

"That is not my intention," Jess said.

"I'll swear on a stack of Bibles that they planned to murder Luke then or later."

"I'm sure you will," Jess said. "You may go now, Miss Kelly."

The woman flounced to the door, but her dress caught in the bolt and Jess heard a tearing sound.

"Look at that!" Mary Kelly said. "I'm all ripped to shreds."

* * *

"I swear that man has more lives than a cat," Jasper Dunn said. "Two of my best men gone and Short is still kicking."

"You want I should go deal with him, boss?" Silas Topper said.

Dunn ignored that and said to Loco Looper, "He's wounded and in bed under doctor's orders, you say?"

"That's what I heard," Looper said.

"Then it's time to make our move," Dunn said. "Mr. Talon, you and six other men come with me. Mr. Topper will be one of them. Mr. Looper, you will stay here and guard this building."

"What's your plan?" Ford Talon said.

"We'll break the weakest link in the chain thrown around the Acre," Dunn said. "That link is Luke Short."

"You plan to kill him?" Talon said.

"It would have been the more simple way, but no, Mr. Talon, I won't kill him, at least tonight," Dunn said. "Mr. Short will sign a contract and all will be well."

Dunn rose, strapped on his gun belt and said, "Let us be on our way. The game begins."

Despite the late hour the White Elephant was still thronged, though the girls had their high-heeled shoes off to rest their aching feet and the sporting crowd showed signs of the wear and tear of whiskey and the gambling tables.

Dunn stood just inside the door with his men,

then said, "Mr. Topper, you will circulate and talk to the bartenders and other staff. Sound them out, Mr. Topper. See how they feel about a change in ownership."

Topper nodded. "They'll feel good about it or answer to me."

Dunn said, "No gunplay if it can be avoided." Then, "Come, Mr. Talon, it's our Christian duty to visit the sick."

The pretty young woman who answered Luke's door shook her head when she saw two men standing in the gloom of the upstairs hallway.

"Mr. Short is resting comfortably," she said. "But he is not seeing visitors."

Dunn said, "He'll see me." He pushed the girl aside and stepped into the room. Then, a quick turn of his head and, "Mr. Talon, don't let her leave. If she screams cut her throat." He stepped to the bed. Luke lay on his back, his face pale. His eyes were closed and his breathing was ragged. Dunn removed the Colt from the bedside table.

"Mr. Short, can you hear me?" he said.

A man who lives by the gun wakes instantly. "Who the hell are you?" Luke said. His hand reached out to the table.

"Is this what you're looking for, Mr. Short?" Dunn said, holding up the Colt. Then, his face full of mock concern, he said, "Are you wounded very badly? Is it fatal, perchance?"

Luke struggled to rise but the effort was too much for him and he sank back onto the pillow.

His voice weaker this time, he said, "Who are you?"

"Why, my name is Jasper Dunn, Mr. Short. I'm your new partner."

"I don't need a new partner," Luke said. "Now get the hell out of here."

Dunn reached into the inside pocket of his coat and produced what looked like a legal document. "I've drawn up the contract and I'm sure you'll agree it's quite straightforward, Mr. Short. We split the White Elephant right down the middle. Ninety percent for me, and the remaining ten percent is your share. Generous of me, don't you think?"

Luke's face was black with anger and he tried to rise from the bed, but Dunn pushed him back and said, "Sign it, Mr. Short." He nodded to Talon. "Bring pen and ink from the desk over there. Take the girl with you. She'll witness the signature." The woman was terrified and Dunn grinned. "She'll give us no trouble, will you, little darling?"

"Dunn? Is that your name?" Luke said.

"Yes. Jasper Dunn. Your partner."

"I'll kill you, Dunn," Luke said. "I swear to God I'll kill you for this."

Talon laid the pen and inkwell on the desk. He was tearing himself apart. Was this the time to intervene? Should he pull his gun and shoot Dunn down? Something told him that it wasn't a good idea. Once Topper and the rest of them heard the shot they'd come running and Talon knew he'd be a dead man. Talon had bigger plans in the making and the voice of reason in his head whispered, *Bide your time . . . bide your time.* And he heeded it.

Dunn dipped the pen into the inkwell and held it out to Luke. "Sign the contract. Make it legal."

"Go to hell," Luke said, fighting to rise from the bed.

His struggle revealed the thick, bloodstained bandage that covered his wound. Dunn saw it and, his face filled with a fiendish rage, he slammed his fist into the wound.

And Luke Short screamed in pain.

"Sign it, sign it, sign it," Dunn screeched. Talon saw that Luke Short was barely holding on to consciousness, his face an agonized white mask. Dunn shoved the pen into Luke's hand. Black ink splattered over the white pillow and sheets. "Sign it," he said. "Damn you, sign it." He forced Luke's hand across the page and the sputtering pen scrawled what looked like the signature of a demented mental patient.

"It's signed!" Dunn yelled. And to the horrified girl, he said, "Can you write your name?" The girl nodded and he pointed with the wooden end of the pen and said, "Sign your name down there where it says 'Witnessed by.' Do it now or by God I'll kill you."

The girl's hand trembled, but her signature was legible. "Sally Boyd," Dunn said. "You did very well, Sally. Now, Sally, sweet Sally, go pull the curtains aside and open the window. I'm the new owner of the White Elephant and Mr. Short is leaving us."

The girl did as she was told and Dunn got Luke by the shoulders and dragged him out of the bed. Groaning in pain, Luke was semiconscious, unaware of the full enormity of what was happening to him. Dunn hauled him to the open window. Sounds of mirth, the clink of glasses and the tinkling of a piano could be heard from the saloon below.

Dunn manhandled Luke's head and shoulders into the open window.

"Dunn, I want no part in this," Talon said. "That's no way to treat a man."

"Who the hell cares what you think?" Jasper Dunn said. He pushed Luke out the window and then glanced down at the alley below. When he pulled his head back he grinned. "He fell very well, I think. Landed on his thick head."

"Is he dead?" Sally Boyd said, the tips of her fingers straying to her lips.

"Probably," Dunn said. "Or close to it." He scowled at the girl. "You mention this to anybody, sweet Sally, and I'll throw you to my men. They won't treat you nice."

The girl shook her head. "I promise I won't say a word."

Dunn's cold eyes shifted to Talon. "And what about you, Major? Will you keep your mouth shut?"

"For now, yes," Talon said.

"For now? I don't like that answer."

"It's the only one you're going to get, Dunn," Talon said.

Dunn's cold gaze raked him, as though his eyes had claws.

CHAPTER THIRTY-SEVEN

Luke Short was in a hell of a fix and he knew it. Weak from loss of blood, hurting badly from his wound, his options were few. He could stay where he was and hope someone found him or he could crawl out of the alley and seek help.

The coyotes made up his mind for him.

A big male stepped through the darkness and stopped, his nose high, scenting blood. In the time it took Luke to blink, two more appeared and advanced on him, their heads low. But it was the huge dog that attacked first. The animal growled then lunged at Luke's face and he threw up a hand to protect himself. The coyote bit hard on Luke's hand and he cried out in pain. Startled, the big dog backed off, but not for long. Crazed by the blood smell, the two smaller coyotes went for Luke's ankles where they showed under his nightgown. The big male went for the face again and Luke felt its breath on his cheek. He punched out at the dog and connected with a right hook to the left side of the animal's head. The coyote yelped and stepped back and Luke kicked away the two that were worrying his ankles bloody.

But his strength was waning fast and the coyotes sensed weakness and grew bolder.

In an instant all three were on top of him and Luke fought desperately, kicking and punching in a snarling tangle of legs, jaws and flashing fangs. Now he was getting bitten badly and the unequal struggle slammed Luke's back into the timber wall of the White Elephant. His right hand hit something hard. An empty wine bottle. Luke's fingers closed on the neck of the bottle and he swung hard at the big male. But his hand was slick, covered in blood, and the bottle flew out of his grasp and thudded harmlessly into the wall opposite. At that moment, Luke Short knew he was done for. The coyotes were finding openings in his guard and were in a frenzy to make the kill.

"God forgive me," he whispered, a three-word atonement for a lifetime of sin. Then he dropped his arms and let the coyotes take him.

Ford Talon stepped out of the White Elephant while Jasper Dunn was busy inside organizing his takeover of Luke Short's business. Talon told himself he needed a cigar, but his real purpose was to check on Short and find out if he was still alive. No doubt the fall from the window had broken his neck, but there was also the chance that the little man was still alive and suffering.

Talon stepped off the boardwalk and heard a growling, snarling commotion in the alley. A man cursed loudly, then came the thud of a heavy object hitting a wall. The snarling rose to a crescendo, but the man's voice was now silent. Talon drew his gun and stepped into the darkness.

Luke's nightgown was a bundle of white to his right and he saw the dark shapes of three large coyotes as they frenziedly nipped and tore at Luke.

Talon charged, kicked the big dog away and then fell on the other two. But the fight went out of them quickly. The human wasn't wounded prey but was on his feet and ready for a fight. The three coyotes melted into darkness and left the bloody field to Talon.

Luke Short was in a bad way. He was unconscious and his breathing was ragged and it looked to Talon that he wasn't going to make it. He thought about it. Was Luke Short any concern of his? Apart from one meeting in Jess Casey's office he didn't even know the man. Best to leave him where he was and let nature take its course. But even as he considered that, Talon knew he couldn't do it. Luke was a human being and he needed help. That was the open and shut of it.

Luke was a small man and Talon had strong arms. He picked up the little gambler and carried him to the mouth of the alley. Out in the darkness the City Hall clock struck three and people had all but vanished from the street, though inside the White Elephant there was a hubbub of voices as Dunn laid down the law to his new employees.

Talon had no idea where the doctors were located in this town and he knew no one who would take Luke in and care for him. No one, that is, but Sheriff Jess Casey.

It was a fair walk from the White Elephant to the sheriff's office, but Luke was a light burden and Talon wasn't even breathing hard when he kicked on the office door with the toe of his ankle boot.

After a couple of minutes a lamp was lit inside and Jess Casey, wearing only his long underwear and hat, padded on bare feet to the door. He didn't open it, but said, "This better be good or I'll shoot you down right where you stand."

Talon raised his voice, "Sheriff, it's me, Ford Talon. I've got Luke Short with me and he's damn near knocking on death's door."

The key turned in the lock and Jess allowed Talon inside. "Put him on my cot back there. I'll bring the oil lamp."

All Talon said was that Luke had been shot and then attacked by coyotes. Jess kept his questions for later, examined Luke's cut and battered body, then said, "The coyote bites look worse than they are. If the bullet wound doesn't kill him he'll survive."

"He looks like he was run over by a Texas and Pacific cannonball," Talon said.

"I'll bring in Dr. Bell to take a look at him in the morning," Jess said. "Now do you want to tell me how a man lying in his sickbed gets savaged by a pack of brush wolves?"

"I don't want to reveal too much," Talon said. "That is, if you still want me to be a spy. As it is, I think the convicts are growing suspicious."

"Yes, I want you to pretend to be one of them. Just tell me what you can."

Talon sat on the corner of Jess's desk. "The cons have organized and the top dog is a man named Jasper Dunn, one of the Huntsville fifty. He was serving two score and five for a double murder before he got paroled. Dunn's aim is to take over Hell's Half Acre, especially the alcohol and opium trade. He's pushing morphine users to try a new German drug."

Jess opened the desk drawer, gauged the level of the Old Crow bottle, then poured a drink for Talon and himself. "And that brings us to Luke Short, huh?"

"Yeah, earlier tonight Dunn forced Short to sign a contract granting him a ninety percent share in the White Elephant. Then he threw him out of a window. Later I found him in the alley playing with his puppy dog friends."

Jess was stunned. "Luke let himself be railroaded like that? That's hard to believe."

"Believe it, Sheriff. After Dunn threw a punch into Short's bullet wound, the little man wasn't in any shape to fight back. Dunn grabbed Luke's limp hand and guided the pen across the bottom of the contract."

"That won't stand up in court," Jess said. "You were there, you can testify to what happened."

"There was someone else present, a girl. She witnessed Luke's signature and she's scared enough to say it was legal and aboveboard. Who is a jury going to believe? A pretty girl or a Huntsville convict? Sheriff, Dunn's next target will be Kurt Koenig and the Silver Garter. If I testify against him in court, I'm out. I can't find out when and how the takeover is coming down."

Jess said, "Kurt Koenig can fend for himself. It's this new drug worries the hell out of me. That's why I want you to stay close to Dunn. I have to stop it before it gets out of hand. Who is his supplier?"

"A man named Gideon Thurgood. You met him in the restaurant the day you killed the immortal Hiram Hartline, his hired gun."

Jess felt the need for a gulp of whiskey. He drank deep, then said, "Where is this Thurgood now?"

"The short answer is back East somewhere," Talon said. "The long answer is that he had to bury Hartline in unhallowed ground, on account of him being the Second Horseman of the Apocalypse and all. Then after he planted him Thurgood saw Hartline's ghost and hightailed it out of Texas."

"I saw that grave," Jess said. "I didn't see any boogerman."

"I guess Thurgood wishes he hadn't."

Talon drained his glass. "I have to get going. I'll be missed."

"Tell me where Dunn is located," Jess said.

"Not yet, Sheriff. Go barging into his headquarters he'll gun you for sure."

"Then I'll close down the White Elephant in the morning and cut off the supply at its source," Jess said. "I'm sure I can come up with some city code violation. If Dunn is there I won't arrest him just yet. Later, when I have more proof of his guilt, I'll teach him that he can't get away with attempted murder and theft of property in the Acre."

Talon stood. "You think closing down Luke Short's saloon is a good idea?"

"No, it's a terrible idea, but it's the law," Jess said.

CHAPTER THIRTY-EIGHT

Jess Casey would not sleep in the cell he reserved for lawbreakers, preferring the discomfort of his chair to a smelly, flea-ridden cot.

At first light he got to his feet, stretched the kinks out of his battered body and checked on Luke Short. He shook the little gambler and said, "Mr. Short, how are you feeling?"

Luke groaned, opened one startled eye and said, "You! Oh God, I've died and gone to hell."

"Close, Luke," Jess said. "You're still in Texas."

"What happened to me?"

"How much do you remember?"

"Big feller made me sign a contract . . . tossed me out the window . . ." Luke wearily shook his head. "I don't remember anything after that."

"You were attacked by coyotes," Jess said

Luke was surprised. "Coyotes?"

"Yeah, then Ford Talon saved you and brought you here."

"The convict?"

"He saved your life, Mr. Short. I reckon you owe him."

"There isn't much life left in me to save," Luke said. "But I'm beholden to him, all right."

"The man who made you sign the contract and then tossed you out of the window goes by the name of Jasper Dunn," Jess said. "He now owns ninety percent of the White Elephant"—then a line right out of the law book he'd been studying—"and all properties pertaining thereto."

"In other words, I've been thrown out of my own place," Luke said.

"Seems like," Jess said.

"Then I'll go take it back," Luke said.

He struggled to get out of bed but Jess, a bigger, stronger man than he, pushed him back into the pillow. "The law will handle it," he said.

"What law?" Luke said, angry now at his own weakness. "Koenig, the city marshal, would like nothing better than to see me out of business. More for him. And as for you, Casey, well, you got the sand but you don't have the smarts."

Jess was stung but didn't let it show. "I'm closing down the White Elephant this morning for the constant violation of City Ordinance 328, which forbids the throwing of trash from business properties into adjoining alleys."

"Hell, everybody does that," Luke said.

"And everybody breaks the law," Jess said. "Waste in the alleys attracts rats and rats attract coyotes and all sorts of vermin, as you well know, Mr. Short. Coffee?"

* * *

It was Jess Casey's intent to ask Dr. Bell to
attend Luke, and then he would carry out his
plan to close down the White Elephant. It would
be a setback for Dunn and would stop his new
drug from reaching the street—at least for a
while.

Luke was as weak as a kitten and wasn't going
anyplace. Jess took a shotgun from the rack,
filled his pockets with shells and stepped onto the
boardwalk. The day was overcast, ashen and
dreary, and the wind from the north bore a cool
promise of the coming fall. Main Street was busy
as always with massive drays, lighter freight wagons
and a few carriages. People, busy as ants, crowded
the boardwalks and street vendors loudly hawked
their wares. Yellow dust rose from wheels and
hooves and slowly covered everything.

The shotgun under Jess's arm drew a few
glances but no questions. A stylish, bustled belle
smiled at him and commented on the weather
and Jess agreed that it was shaping up to be a
gloomy day. One of the sporting crowd, looking
pale, made his way home one careful step at a
time and smelled of stale whiskey and cheap
perfume.

It was still early morning but Hell's Half Acre
was awake and rarin' to go.

Jess noticed the small, ragged man lounging
with his back to the wall of a flower shop, his
cloth cap pulled low over his eyes, a matchstick

between his teeth. The fellow was unshaven and his thumbs were stuck into the armholes of his vest and Jess dismissed him as just another out-of-work loafer.

It was almost a fatal mistake.

As Jess got close to the man he suddenly lurched off the wall, turned swiftly and lunged with a knife. By no means in a relaxed state of mind, Jess was quick. He moved to his left and the blade, aimed for his heart, raked across his right upper ribs. Not getting the flesh-and-bone resistance he'd expected and off-balance, the would-be assassin stumbled then regained his footing. He swung around, the knife coming up fast. Too late. Jess reached across his body, grabbed the shotgun from under his left arm and smashed the muzzles into the small man's face. His aim was true. The barrels hit the bridge of his nose, smashing bone, and the man cried out and stumbled back, his hands to his face.

Jess Casey was not in a mood to be polite. He raised the shotgun and said, "Back against the wall or I'll blow your guts out."

The little man bent his head and let the blood drop freely to the boardwalk. "Don't kill me," he said.

"Who put you up to this?" Jess said.

"I'll tell you, just don't—"

Blam!

The rifle shot and the round hole in the middle of the little man's forehead occurred in the same instant. Jess swung around, spotted a drift of smoke coming from a window on the second story of a tenement opposite, and cut loose with both barrels. Glass shattered and by the time it tinkled onto the boardwalk opposite, Jess was running toward the building, feeding shells into the Greener as he went.

He felt wetness under his armpit, figured it was sweat, then saw blood all over his shirt. It was his best shirt and that hurt.

By the time he reached the second floor the killer was gone. The Acre tenements were dark warrens where a man could easily lose himself and then leave by one of the rear exits. The bird had flown and Jess was left to curse his luck.

After a horrified glance at Jess's bloodstained shirt, a scrawny, gray-faced woman, her collarbones standing out in sharp relief, identified herself as Mrs. McGinty and showed Jess an empty apartment where the rifleman may have holed up. She was right. Jess found an empty .44-40 shell casing on the rough wood floor, and also a few drops of blood. It looked like nothing serious, but he'd stung the man.

Mrs. McGinty, hands on her bony hips, demanded that Jess tell her who was going to pay for the broken window and said she had eager tenants waiting to take possession.

"Now what do I tell them?" she said.

She also took time to note that Hell's Half Acre had gone downhill in recent years, that all the decent people were leaving and what if her new tenants, respectable white folks that they were, had been breakfasting at the window, enjoying the view, when an officer of the law blasted them with a shotgun.

"I rather fancy that blown-off heads would be the result," she said.

Jess placated the woman by offering to pay for the window. "Just get it fixed and have the bill sent to me."

"Then I'll do that," Mrs. McGinty said. "I swear, it's getting to the stage where the lawmen in this town are just as bad as the outlaws. I'm afraid to sleep in bed with Mr. McGinty for fear that we'll wake up with our throats cut and just the other day Mrs. Bradshaw was telling me that . . ."

The woman was still talking as Jess left the room and returned to the boardwalk where the dead man lay, surrounded by a gawking crowd.

CHAPTER THIRTY-NINE

A belligerent gent stepped out of the crowd of onlookers and said, "Did you kill this man, Sheriff?"

"No, I didn't, but he tried to kill me," Jess Casey said. "Now all of you people stand back and give me room here." He kneeled beside the dead man. "Anybody recognize him?" he said.

"I've seen him around," a man said. "I think he did odd jobs now and again."

"Anyone else?" Jess said. His side hurt like hell. He drew a blank on the question and went through the man's pockets. He found a couple of dusty pennies and two bright, shiny double eagles . . . forty dollars, the price of a man's life in the Acre. There was nothing else.

Jess got to his feet and immediately had to grab for a wall to support himself. He'd lost blood and his head spun.

"Sheriff, you'd better sit down," the belligerent man said.

"I'll take him back to his office." Big Sal and her assistant, attracted to the sound of gunfire like buzzards to a gut wagon, elbowed their way through the crowd. Sal looked at the dead man. "He called himself Charlie. He wasn't much. You do for him, Sheriff?"

Jess shook his head and then wished he hadn't as Main Street cartwheeled around him. "No . . . someone else did."

Big Sal, wearing men's pants, bent over and picked up the knife. Her butt was an ax-handle wide. "He get you with this?" she said to Jess, holding up the blade.

"Yeah, but he mostly missed."

"Looking at your shirt he didn't mostly miss by much," the woman said. "Come on, Sheriff, Sal is taking you home." Then to her assistant, "Barnabas, take care of this. And then tell Dr. Bell to come to the sheriff's office."

"Sure will, Miss Sal," Barnabas said. A tall, lank, gray man, he looked like a cadaver himself and an individual of a nervous disposition might fear that one day Big Sal might bury him by mistake.

"I've got a saloon to shut down," Jess said. "I'll go on by myself."

"You're as weak as a day-old kittlin' and you'll do no such thing," Sal said. "You can go around shutting down saloons when Dr. Bell says you can, and not a moment before."

"I can manage, Sal," Jess said. "But thanks for your concern."

He took a step, another, and then the earth moved under his feet and he frantically reached for the wall, his breath coming in short bursts. Sal glared at Jess from her great height, her arms crossed under breasts that hung like sacks of flour and strained the cotton of her plaid shirt.

"Right, that's enough," she said. "If some ranny decides to draw down on you today, you're a dead man." Sal took the shotgun from Jess and tossed it to the belligerent man. "You, take this and follow us."

The man was indignant. "I certainly will not. I have things to do."

Sal advanced on him, her fists clenched. "Mister, am I going to have trouble with you?" she said.

The belligerent man cringed at the sight of an angry woman standing six and a half feet tall and stoked up hotter than the coals in a stage depot stove. "I'll make the time," he said.

"Wise choice," Big Sal said. She turned, effortlessly picked up Jess in her arms, and her boots pounded on the boardwalk as she headed for the sheriff's office.

Jess, imprisoned in arms with biceps as large around as nail kegs, gave up struggling and endured a gauntlet of taunts, jeers and downright impertinences.

"Hey, Sal, found yourself a man at last?"

"What's up, Sheriff, sell your hoss?"

"You gonna bend him over your knee for misbehavin'?"

"Sheriff, it's you who's supposed to carry Sal over the threshold."

"Ride her, cowboy!"

Jess, shamed beyond measure, had half a dozen faces burned into his memory for a future reckoning by the time they reached his office, where Sal laid him gently in his chair as though he were a baby.

Then a voice from the cell area. "Who's there? I'm Luke Short and I'm armed and dangerous. Damn it, state your intentions."

"It's Sal. I brung in Sheriff Casey after a feller stuck him with a blade. Is that really you, Luke? I heard you got et by coyotes or some such."

"Damn it, woman, I'm shot through and through and I need a drink," Luke yelled. "Is Casey still alive?"

"I reckon."

"Too bad," Luke said.

When Dr. Bell arrived he examined the knife cut under Jess Casey's armpit, declared it a superficial wound, cleaned it with something that stung and applied a bandage. He then changed the dressing on Luke Short's waist and gave him a salve to apply to the coyote bites.

When he snapped his bag shut, he said, "It

looks like a hospital ward in here. Sal, are you taking good care of them?"

"Yes, especially this one," the woman said. She laid a massive, hairy hand on Jess's head. "My very own baby Bunting sitting right here behind his desk like a brave little soldier."

Dr. Bell caught Jess's eye and said, "We have something to discuss, Sheriff."

Jess nodded, then said, "Miss Sal, your company is a sweet distraction, but—"

"I know. Men talk." She smiled. "Jess, remember, as soon as you're up to it I'll expect you to come over to my place and we'll rock the joint to its foundations."

Jess felt his cheeks redden and Sal said to Dr. Bell, "He's such a shy little cowboy and I just love him to pieces." In the close confines of the office, Sal looked like a she-grizzly. "Until later, little darlin'," she said.

She kissed Jess on the cheek and he felt her mustache scrape his skin.

After the woman left, Jess said, "As you can tell, I have a problem."

Dr. Bell nodded, "Yes, you surely do. And now I'm afraid that I'm bringing you another."

Jess saw the serious cast of the doctor's features and said, "Tell me, Doc."

"I was called in to treat a girl this morning, but she was already dead when I got there," the physician said. "I'm certain she died of a drug overdose."

"A whore?" Jess said.

"No, not a whore, a young lady of good family. Three years ago her father, a retired railroad director, built a large house on Summit Street and that's where the girl lived. She didn't have to work and as far as I can tell, lacked for nothing. It seems she was one of Fort Worth's most fashionable belles and in this fall she and her mother were to embark on a grand tour of Europe."

Dr. Bell reached into a drawer in Jess's desk and found nothing.

"The other one," Jess said. "Nate Levy brought me another bottle. Nice of him."

The doctor opened the other drawer and produced a bottle of Old Crow and glasses. "How is Nate doing?" he said.

"Just fine. He's spent a lot of time resting up in his hotel room but now he's looking around for another prizefighter to replace his boy Zeus." Jess smiled. "Before your time, Doc."

"You must tell me about it sometime," Dr. Bell said. He poured whiskey into three glasses. "By the way, the dead girl's parents have agreed to let me perform an autopsy. By this time tomorrow I'll know for sure if she died from an overdose of the new drug."

"How old was she?" Jess said. "Who was she?"

"She would have turned twenty-one in the fall. Her name was Lucia Monroe and now you know as much about her as I do."

Jess shook his head. "How the hell did she—"

"Buy heroin? Lucia Monroe probably never set foot in the Acre, but one of her housemaids could have bought it for her. There are plenty of servants in the house."

"She was a morphine user and then somebody introduced her to a drug she'd never used before," Jess said.

"That would be my guess." Dr. Bell handed a glass to Jess and then walked back to the cells with another for Luke Short.

Jess had time to build and light a cigarette before the doctor returned.

"Luke says the Jasper Dunn ranny who took over his saloon is the source of the drug in the Acre," Dr. Bell said.

"That isn't a stretch," Jess said. "The trouble is that Dunn isn't breaking any laws. I can shut him down temporarily for a city code violation, but that's all. Even then I'm pushing it."

"What about Dunn being the direct cause of the deaths of two people?"

Jess spoke behind a cloud of smoke. "I don't know, Doc. I have no idea how the law stands on that. And Jethro Tull, the only lawyer I could ask, is a crook."

Dr. Bell pointed to Jess's bandaged side. "Do you think that was done on Dunn's orders?"

"I'm sure of it," Jess said. "The man who stabbed me had two double eagles in his pocket."

"You're in Dunn's way, Sheriff."

Jess dropped his cigarette butt to the floor and rubbed it into shreds with his boot. "That's how it's supposed to work, isn't it?"

"Give Luke Short a gun, Sheriff Casey," Dr. Bell said. "He's a good man to have at your side."

Jess smiled. "He has no love for me, Doc."

"Maybe so, but he knows that you're the only man in town who can help him get his White Elephant back."

CHAPTER FORTY

"If I'd known the rube had missed with his knife I could've gunned the sheriff real easy," Silas Topper said. "But by the time I realized what was happening the damned Mick had cut loose with a scattergun."

"You did the right thing," Jasper Dunn said. "The rube, what was his name? Well, it doesn't matter. To save his neck he would have spilled everything he knew."

Topper held a bar towel to his bleeding cheek. "Casey scratched me." His eyes glittered. "He gets a bullet in the belly first chance I get."

"Hello. What's this?" Dunn said, staring over Topper's shoulder.

Three men walked across the saloon floor. One was Jethro Tull, a man Dunn knew, with him a tall, distinguished-looking gent he pegged as a second lawyer. Trailing behind hurried a meek-looking man who had the pale face of a clerk. Dunn dismissed him as a nonentity.

It was the tall man who spoke. "Do I have the pleasure of addressing Mr. Jasper Dunn?" he said.

Dunn rose to his feet and said, "Yes, you do."

The tall man stuck out his hand. "My name is Professor James Carnes. I was appointed by the governor to check up on the progress of the convicts recently released from Huntsville." He smiled. "I consider you a shining example of how men released from prison can reenter society and make good."

"Well, thankee and take a seat," Dunn said. He smiled like a cobra. "Despite the persecution we face, my fellow ex-cons and I are doing our very best to rejoin society."

"Excellent, Mr. Dunn," Professor Carnes said. "Is it not, Mr. Tull?"

"I have many times told Mr. Dunn that very thing," Tull said.

Carnes placed his gloved hand on Dunn's arm. "Just one small thing, Mr. Dunn. I wish, and the governor agrees with me, to change the term *ex-con* to *returning citizen*. It's a small thing, but I believe it will save the formerly incarcerated individual from a great deal of embarrassment and discouragement as he tries to reintegrate into society."

Dunn nodded, grinning. "Sir, that's a fine plan and I'm sure my fellow returning citizens, despite the terrible persecution they face, will be most pleased."

"I was told by attorney Tull that by sheer hard

work and industry you have obtained a share of this saloon," Carnes said.

Pretending mild embarrassment, Dunn said, "A small share to be sure, but the proprietor, Mr. Luke Short, was most anxious to sign the contract."

"You are making wonderful progress, Mr. Dunn," Carnes said. "And how are our other returning citizens?"

Dunn exchanged a glance with Tull, who had a slight smile on his lips, and said, "I'm happy to say most are gainfully employed . . . but . . ." Dunn waved his hands in front of his face. "No, no, I better not say it."

"You can say anything you wish to me," Carnes said. "Mr. Dunn, you and I are perfect friends."

Turning his eyes heavenward, Dunn said, "Oh dear, I am so conflicted."

Tull said, "There is no conflict in the truth, Mr. Dunn, painful though that truth may be."

"Very well, I'll say what I know is true," Dunn said. "The lawmen in this town, City Marshal Kurt Koenig and Sheriff Jess Casey, badly want me and my fellow returning citizens to fail." Dunn buried his face in his hands, and then exclaimed, "Sweet Lord, we are being persecuted!"

"This is outrageous!" Carnes said.

Dunn, a consummate actor and con man, flung his words across the table. "Look at the face of returning citizen Topper. Show the professor what happened to you this morning."

Topper removed the towel from his cheek. It looked as though he'd been raked by claws.

"Such an atrocity cannot stand," Carnes said. "What happened to this poor man?"

"It happened this morning," Dunn said. "Sheriff Casey was attacked by a knife-wielding madman and was badly wounded. His assailant was readying himself for another stroke of his murderous blade when Mr. Topper saw him."

Dunn slowly shook his head as though the horror of what happened next was too painful for him to reveal. He tried to talk but his voice faltered and he fell silent.

Jethro Tull, quick on the uptake, glared Topper into keeping his mouth shut and continued with the story. "Mr. Topper was in a building across the street from where the attack happened."

Dunn said, "Dear Silas was trying to find a suitable home for one of our older returned citizens who is unfortunately ailing and he happened to be looking out of the open window when the assassin tried again to impale the sheriff."

Tull said, "Drawing his trusty revolver, Mr. Topper fired at the fiend and struck him down stone dead with one shot."

Dunn again took up the story. "And that was when Sheriff Casey whirled around and saw that it was Mr. Topper who stood at the window. Enraged that his life had been saved by a returning citizen, the sheriff fired his bloodthirsty shotgun at the window."

"And laid poor Mr. Topper low," Tull said. "But thank God he recovered sufficiently to flee the building and escape with his own life," Tull said.

With an air of finality Jasper Dunn pointed to Topper's bloody cheek and said, "There! I say there is the result of Sheriff Casey's homicidal savagery."

"This persecution will end," Professor Carnes said. "If I have to, I'll go all the way to the president of these United States and ask for federal troops. But be assured, Mr. Dunn, one way or another, the oppression will end."

Suddenly Dunn was alarmed. The mention of federal troops was not something he'd wanted to hear. Quickly he said, "Troops will not be necessary, Professor." Then, in a moment of inspiration, "For a prisoner release program to succeed, it must be done at a local level. It's not the law—hard-bitten, violent men—but the people themselves who must welcome returning citizens in their midst. The presence of soldiers would suggest that the people need to be forced into acceptance and we all know that is not happening. We are welcomed with an open door into every home. Is that not so, Mr. Tull?"

"Indeed it is," the lawyer said. "As Mr. Dunn says, the returning citizens are met with open arms and open doors everywhere they go."

By whores maybe, Tull thought, smiling at Carnes.

"Very well, there we will leave it for the moment,"

the professor said. "Mr. Dunn, at a future date I'd like to address all the men who arrived from Huntsville. Can you arrange that?"

"Bless you, sir, of course I can. You will do us a great honor," Dunn said.

Carnes rose to his feet. "I will now go and have harsh word with Sheriff Casey. He will rue the day he viciously assaulted poor Mr. Topper."

After the professor left with his assistant and Tull, Jasper Dunn said to Topper, "This is our chance. With Carnes on our side we just can't fail. Silas, Fort Worth is as good as ours."

Luke Short, hurt and feeling like hell, was not nearly as polite as Jess Casey. He sat in the sheriff's chair, his newly acquired Colt in his gun hand and an I'm-gonna-spit-in-your-eye expression on his drawn face.

He'd been listening for fifteen minutes now to Professor James Carnes's tirade about police brutality and how he would not stand idly by and let prejudiced lawmen interfere with the excellent progress being made by Jasper Dunn and the other returned citizens.

When the professor halted to take a breath, Luke thumbed back the hammer of his Colt and said, "Mister, your chances of making it to the door alive are slim to none, but I want you to try it anyway."

"This is an outrage!" Carnes said. "The governor will hear of this."

Luke was primed to shoot and Jess quickly stepped in front of Carnes. "I'm only going to say one thing, Carnes—"

"Professor Carnes to you, Sheriff."

"And it is that Jasper Dunn took the White Elephant by force and I intend to close the place down," Jess said. "Now my talking is done because no matter what I say you won't listen."

Carnes's face purpled with anger. "Lies, a pack of lies put out by yon killer you harbor in your office. My entire reputation rests on this grand experiment and I do not intend to fail."

"Is that all?" Jess said.

"No, it's not all. I have much more to say, but I won't cast pearls before swine," Carnes said. "I do assure you, Sheriff, you won't wear that star for much longer. Now good day to you, sir."

"You should've let me plug him, Casey," Luke Short said.

Sam Waters, who was now living with a widow woman and making only rare appearances at the sheriff's office, said, "You'd get hung fer sure, Luke. Carnes is a big man, important, friend of the governor an' all, and if what he's trying in this town works, it will be used by penitentiaries all over the country. Hell, he'd be so famous he could run for president." Sam shook his head. "Gun anybody you like, Luke, but not the perfesser."

"What the hell did he call them rapists and murderers?" Luke said.

"Returned citizens," Jess said. "And you heard what he told me—he doesn't want to hear the word *ex-con* being used in the Acre or anywhere else."

Luke shook his head. "I reckon I'll take my chances and shoot him in the belly anyway."

CHAPTER FORTY-ONE

It was Destiny Durand's idea to take Joselita Juarez out of the Acre for a while and away from the confining four walls of the Silver Garter saloon.

"We're going only as far as the sweetshop on 11th Street for cake and ice cream," Destiny told Kurt Koenig. "Joselita needs an outing to be around normal people."

Koenig smiled. "The people who patronize the Silver Garter aren't normal?"

"Far from it," Destiny said.

Koenig looked up from the ledger he was studying. Almost absently he said, "I'll send Tim Tyrone with you."

"No, Kurt," Destiny said. "We don't need a Panther City Boy and his gun in a sweetshop. And it's the middle of the day."

"You sure?"

"Yes, I'm sure. We'll only be gone for an hour or two and we'll be perfectly fine."

Koenig dipped his pen into the inkwell, his eyes scanning columns of figures. "Just be careful."

"We will, and I have my derringer," Destiny said.

To say the least, Joselita was excited. "I've had cake before, but I've never tasted ice cream," she said. She lifted her skirts to avoid a patch of mud on the boardwalk. "What is it like?"

Destiny smiled. "You'll find out."

After a while Joselita said, "Destiny, why do the older ladies look away when they see you? It seems none of them want to pass the time of day."

"I suppose it's because they think I'm a kept woman," Destiny said.

"And are you?"

"No. I'm my own woman. Nobody keeps me or owns me."

"Not even Mr. Koenig?"

"Especially Mr. Koenig."

Joselita thought for a spell, then said, "I suppose I was a kept woman once."

"You were an enslaved woman," Destiny said. "There is a difference between kept and enslaved, not much of one, but a difference nonetheless." She smiled. "Enough of this talk. We're going for ice cream and you're wearing your new dress. It's a time to be happy. Who knows, maybe we'll meet Red Stark."

Joselita laughed. "In a sweetshop? I doubt it."

* * *

"That," Joselita Juarez said, "was the best thing I've ever eaten in my whole life."

"I should think so," Destiny Durand said. "Three scoops of ice cream and two pieces of cake. I was afraid you might burst."

"Or end up looking like Mayor Stout," Joselita said.

That made Destiny laugh but then two men stepped into their path and the laughter stopped.

"Howdy, pretty ladies," Loco Looper said. "You out for a stroll?"

"Let us pass," Destiny said.

"Can't do that," Jim Turner said. "Y'all got to come with us."

Around this scene the Acre's busy life went on and if people in the crowded street noticed anything at all, they saw a woman in a yellow dress and a younger one in blue talking to two rough-looking men on the boardwalk and thought nothing of it. Hell's Half Acre was full of rough-looking men and women who wore colorful dresses.

Destiny tried to reach into her purse, but Loco Looper took it away from her. He removed the derringer and passed the purse back. Then Dark Alley Jim Turner made his move.

The man moved closer to Joselita and stuck the point of a dirk into the girl's ribs. "Miss Durand, you and the Mex come with us real quiet or I'll cut her liver out."

"Kurt Koenig will kill you for this," Destiny said.

"Don't count on it," Turner said. "Now let's move along the boardwalk like we were kissin' kin. This little gal cries out, tries to run away or any other sich, I'll gut her."

"Where are you taking us?" Destiny said.

"To a nice, comfortable warehouse," Turner said.

"They hang men for rape in this town," Destiny said.

"Rape? Did you hear that, Loco? She thinks we're gonna have our way with her. Why do women always think that?"

"I don't know, Jim." Looper pushed Destiny's back and made her stumble forward. "We got bigger plans than rape for you, little lady. Come this time tomorrow, you'll be the talk of the town."

CHAPTER FORTY-TWO

"Nate, you're gonna love this guy," Dirty Dick O'Rourke said. "He can dance like a bobber on a line and he's got a twenty-pound sledgehammer for a right hand."

"So you say, Dick," Nate Levy said.

"I ain't kiddin," O'Rourke said. He was an untidy, unshaven, odorous man who chose his cigars according to their stink. "His name is Kid Nevada and if you know of a fighter out there who thinks he can beat him he better bring his lunch because it's gonna take him all day."

"I'm looking for a new boy," Nate said. "You heard what happened to Zeus."

"I surely did, Nate. And I was broken up about it. You see this eye, this one here? Well, for the first time in its life it shed a tear. That's how I felt about things after Zeus was killed."

"A good boy," Nate said.

"Pound for pound one of the best I ever seen," O'Rourke said.

A young black kid who was laying into a punching bag, showing incredible hand speed, attracted Nate's attention. He smiled. "I need somebody like him, if he was twenty years older."

O'Rourke turned and followed Nate's gaze. "Oh, him. He reckons he's about ten years old, come up from Galveston, and I let him do odd jobs around the gym in return for his grub and a place to sleep."

"He looks good," Nate said. "Punches well."

"His name's Jack Johnson and he's game, but he'll never make it as a fighter," O'Rourke said. "He ain't got the smarts. You take Kid Nevada now, he's smart as a whip and as game as they come."

"Trot him out, Dick," Nate said. "I'll take a look at him."

Dirty Dick's gym smelled of ancient sweat, vomit and liniment. A ring was set up in the middle of the floor, some changing rooms to the rear, and the place was crammed with iron weights, Indian clubs and slop buckets.

"Ned Shoemaker here is the Kid's sparring partner," O'Rourke said. "You met him before?"

"Oh sure," Nate said. He stuck out his hand. "How's it going, Ned? How's the missus and the two young 'uns?"

"Doin' just fine, Mr. Levy," Shoemaker said. He was a shy young man with the build of a heavyweight but he'd never developed the boxing ability to elevate himself from the lowest rung of professional pugilists. "I was sorry to hear about Zeus. He hit harder than any man I ever sparred with."

Nate smiled. "Funny thing, he said the very same thing about you."

Ned smiled. "He was joshing you, I think. Ah, there's the Kid. I better not keep him waiting."

Kid Nevada was a tall young man, heavy in the arms and shoulders, his blond hair cropped short. He touched gloves with Shoemaker . . . and then disaster struck.

The Kid feinted with a right hook and then telegraphed a straight left that Shoemaker easily avoided. Shoemaker countered with a left hook to the Kid's chin. It was a punch of no great power but it caught the Kid as he took a step inside. The Kid's head snapped back and he went down flat on his back onto the canvas, canaries singing in his head.

Shoemaker was horrified. His gloved fists at his side, he said, "Mr. O'Rourke, I didn't hit him that hard. Honest."

Nate Levy smiled at the stricken O'Rourke. "Seems that your boy has a glass jaw, Dick. Sit him up and put his head between his knees for a spell."

"I don't believe this," O'Rourke said. "I had the Kid pegged as a future champ."

"He's a southpaw with a glass jaw," Nate said. "That's not a good combination, Dick. Hell, you've always got Shoemaker. A journeyman fighter can keep you in steak and eggs."

O'Rourke shook his head in disbelief. "This is the worst day of my life."

"You'll have plenty more if you stay in the boxing game," Nate said.

On the way to the door he called over the little black kid. "Jack Johnson, huh?"

"Yes, suh, that's what they call me" the boy said.

"You got style, young feller," Nate said. "Keep up with the punching bag and the footwork. Study the fighter's trade and learn it well and you'll make your mark one day." Nate fished in his pocket, then gave the boy a silver dollar. "I hope I live long enough to see you fight one day."

"So do I, suh," Jack Johnson said, touching the coin to his forehead. "An' I'll make sure you get a seat at ringside."

Nate Levy stepped outside the gym and lit a cigar. His attention was drawn across the street where Destiny Durand and the girl Jess Casey had rescued walked on the boardwalk with two huge hard cases, probably Kurt Koenig's men.

When Destiny looked in his direction he lifted his hat but the woman didn't seem to notice and the young girl, much prettier than he remembered, looked straight ahead.

Nate didn't think anything of it. One wrinkled old Jew was not a man young women would remember.

"I didn't think anything of it, Jess," Nate Levy said. "I figured their minds were on other things."

"Probably out for a stroll, I guess," Jess Casey said. "Kurt Koenig always sends a couple of bruisers with Destiny."

"I don't blame him," Nate said. "She's a beautiful young woman."

"She's all of that, and Joselita Juarez is turning into quite the young lady."

"Damn it to hell," Luke Short said. He collapsed into Jess's chair. "I can't walk two steps without getting tired."

"If it's any consolation I don't feel much better," Jess said.

"How are two cripples going to get my place back?" Luke said.

Nate said, "Not easily."

Luke's eyes were unfriendly. "Nate, I didn't really want an answer to that question."

"I'll shut down the White Elephant," Jess said.

"When?" Luke said.

"We'll rest up for a couple of days and then get it done."

"I hope I can walk in a couple of days."

"You can ride my horse," Jess said.

Luke said, "And what about Jasper Dunn?"

"He'll fight," Jess said.

"Good, because I plan to gun him," Luke said.

Jess shook his head. "Professor Carnes will fight his battles."

"As I told you before, I plan to gun him as well," Luke said.

CHAPTER FORTY-THREE

"My name is Jasper Dunn and I'm so sorry we can't offer better accommodation for ladies. But hopefully your time as my guests will be of short duration."

"We're not your guests," Destiny Durand said. "Your toughs kidnapped us in the street. One of them has my derringer. And I want it back."

"In due course, dear lady," Dunn said.

His men crowded around the two women and studied them with hot eyes, especially the curvaceous and beautiful Destiny. Ford Talon held back. This was a bad situation and it could only get worse.

"Why did you bring us here?" Destiny said. "Do you know you're playing with fire?"

Dunn smiled. "Playing with fire. How very quaint." He stared at Joselita with speculating eyes and then said, "How are you feeling, young lady?"

"I'm just fine, thank you," the girl said.

"How would you like to feel better? I mean better than you've ever felt in your entire life?"

"That would not be hard to do," Joselita said.

"I can send you to the stars, little lady. I promise that you will soar so high you'll never, ever want to come back down to earth again," Dunn said. Then, over the barely suppressed laughter of his men, "Would you like that?"

"No, she would not," Destiny said. "Joselita has had a hard, terrible life. Why would you make it even worse?"

"That is none of my concern," Dunn said. "My only intent is to force your . . . ah . . . paramour to step aside and let me take over this town with the minimum of fuss and bother. Understand me?"

"Kurt Koenig will never step aside for a damned lowlife like you," Destiny said.

Dunn's backhand slap across Destiny's face was just hard enough to sting and draw a trickle of blood from the corner of the woman's mouth.

"Perhaps it would be better for you, Miss Durand, if you held your tongue," he said.

"Kurt will kill you for this," Destiny said.

"I don't think so, after he reads the letter you'll write to him."

Destiny's blue eyes glowed with hate. "I won't write a letter for you . . . you scum."

Dunn ignored that. "Mr. Topper, the case, if you please," he said.

Grinning, the rat-faced gunman handed Dunn

a small, rectangular box covered with red velvet. Dunn opened the lid and removed a syringe, the attached needle glinting.

"Ah, Miss Durand, are you familiar with the wonderful new German drug named heroin? No? Well, it's called after the word *heroic*, you see, and it's becoming very popular." He feigned concern. "Unfortunately since no one in this country knows the correct dosage, it can be quite deadly if injected to excess."

Dunn turned to Topper. "Hold the girl and bare her right forearm." Then, "Ah, that's excellent, Mr. Topper. Now, just a tiny prick in a vein and I'll open the gates of paradise for you, Miss Juarez. You may think me cruel now, but later you'll thank me for such a wonderful, shall we say magical, experience and demand it again and again."

Joselita shrank away from the needle, her face scared.

"Stop! Do it to me," Destiny said. "The girl has been through enough in her life."

"I'm afraid not, Miss Durand," Dunn said. "You're a strong woman and you could resist the drug, even when it's coursing through your rather magnificent body."

"I'll write the letter," Destiny said. "If you leave Joselita alone."

"Is that a promise?" Dunn said. "A pretty promise?"

"Yes, yes, it is, you fiend."

Dunn placed the syringe back in the case. "Miss Durand, you have no idea how fiendish I can be and I hope you never find out. Mr. Topper, show the lady to my desk and supply her with paper, pen and ink." He turned to Joselita. "And how are you, my dear? Have you quite recovered from your scare? Well, here's another one—if Miss Durand makes one slip of the pen, one sputtering inkblot, I'll stick the needle in your arm and pump you so full of the drug that you'll fly, all right. But, alas, I fear you may never come down again."

Dunn rose to his feet and followed Destiny and Topper to his desk.

Ford Talon let his hand drop from his gun. If Dunn had proceeded with his plan to inject the girl he would have killed him. There were a dozen gunmen in the basement, including the deadly Silas Topper, and Talon knew he'd have died an instant after he pulled the trigger. He didn't want to throw away his life like that to save a girl he didn't know, but the ways of the Southern officer and gentleman run deep and are never lost.

Still, Talon was much relieved that the moment had passed.

Jasper Dunn stood behind Destiny Durand, looked over her shoulder and said, "That's right . . . you're doing well . . . *Dear Kurt, Joselita*

and I have been captured and unless . . . no, make it
captured by ruthless men . . . perfect . . . *and unless
you sign over the deeds to the Silver Garter and the
Green* . . . B-u-d-d-h-a, my dear . . . *Buddha by midnight we will both be killed.*" Dunn clapped his
hands. "There, it's finished. Now sign it. What a
good girl!"

Destiny looked up at the man. "Kurt will never
sign away what he owns. He'll come looking for
you, Dunn, with a gun in his hand."

"Even knowing that I'll kill you, quite horribly
let me add, if he comes anywhere near this place."

"That won't stop him, Dunn. You're already a
dead man."

"Then let us agree to disagree," Dunn said.
He walked away from the desk and said, "Oh,
Mr. Talon, I want to speak to you." When Talon
stepped closer, Dunn said, "What made you
change your mind?"

"About what?" Talon said.

"Why, about shooting me, of course. I can read
a man, Mr. Talon, Huntsville taught me that. I
can tell by the way he stands and the expression
on his face what a man is thinking. You were
thinking about shooting me if I stuck the needle
in the girl's arm. Is that not so?"

"I didn't intend to let you carry out your
threat," Talon said.

Dunn nodded. "So you would have shot me."

"Yes. I would have shot you."

"Now, do I have you killed, or do I still need

you?" Dunn said. "I'll think about that and let you know. Many of my men have left me, the lily-livered ones, and I can't afford to lose another gun."

"It's your decision to make, Dunn," Talon said. "You'll lose more men, because I won't go down without a fight."

"I know that, Major," Dunn said. "That's why you're still breathing. But don't push me any further."

"Let the women go, Dunn. Your war is with Kurt Koenig."

"My dear sir, there's no war, just a business proposition. Koenig gives me everything he owns and I give him back his woman."

Talon smiled. "Maybe he thinks she isn't worth that much."

"Then I'll hang her and pursue a different plan," Dunn said. "Life is simple, Talon, if one makes it so."

CHAPTER FORTY-FOUR

Life was not simple for Sheriff Jess Casey. He'd just been informed that two bumbling, would-be bank robbers were holed up in a box canyon, in other words, one of the many blind alleys off Main Street in Hell's Half Acre.

The man who brought the news was a City Hall clerk, an excitable young fellow with thin, pale hair and protuberant blue eyes.

"They're both wounded, Sheriff, and a feller by the name of Professor Carnes is trying to talk them out of the alley," the clerk said. "It seems they're two of them Huntsville returned citizens. Now I got to go or I'll miss all the fun. What a lark!"

"Wait, tell me how it happened," Jess said as he buckled on his gun belt. The pain of the wound under his armpit nagged at him.

Words tumbled out of the young man's mouth at a rapid rate and Jess finally got them sorted out in his head.

It seemed that the two men had robbed the Cattleman's Bank & Trust on Belknap Street and killed a teller. Unfortunately for the cons, when they burst outside, Mayor Harry Stout was sitting in the back of a wagon with eight other city big shots, including Professor Carnes, en route to a deer hunt and an evening supper on the prairie. A clerk followed the bandits onto the boardwalks and yelled, "Bank robbers! Murder!"

Delighted, the heavily armed occupants of the wagon and the driver gleefully cut loose at the fleeing felons, laying down such a barrage of fire that a getaway horse was killed, both convicts wounded, a passerby took a bullet through the lungs and an elderly lady called Mrs. Forbes had a bunch of fake cherries blown off her hat. Harry himself claimed the horse kill and credit for winging one of the robbers.

"The outlaws headed south into the Acre on one wounded horse, Sheriff, and when it collapsed and died they ran into the alley and barricaded themselves behind wooden crates," the clerk said. "That's all I know and now I'm outta here."

After the man left, Luke Short said, "Go ahead and do your job, Sheriff. Always remember that your duty as a lawman is to make a bad situation worse."

"Luke, one day I'll have to sit down and tell you just how much I dislike you," Jess said.

Luke loved that. He hugged himself, laughed and said, "I look forward to it, Sheriff Casey.

And then when you're all done I'll plug you out of spite."

"There's no need for violence, Sheriff," James Carnes said. "I'm sure I can convince them to come out with their hands up and then apologize to the community at large for their slip back into lawlessness."

"Slip? They murdered a bank teller," Jess Casey said.

"So the story goes," Carnes said. "I think the truth will be very different."

"They robbed the bank and a man is dead," Jess said. "That's the truth and you can't change it."

Mayor Harry Stout, big-bellied and important, stood among his stalwart riflemen and said, "Sheriff, there is now a hostage involved. I'm sorry to say that Parson Horace Hayes has been taken."

"How the hell did that happen?" Jess said.

Stout said, "The reverend wished to show them the error of their ways but they grabbed him, beat him up and now hold him captive." The mayor looked around, making sure that his words would carry to the crowd. "It's a dark day in Fort Worth. Oh, that my aim had been true. Well, truer than it was."

To Jess's surprise this drew a round of applause from the considerable crowd. Harry was a popular mayor.

"Hey, you rubes out there!" The voice came from the alley. "We have demands to make or the gospel grinder gets a bullet in the belly. The whole damned town will hear him scream."

Carnes stepped forward and called out, "My name is Professor James Carnes. You both know me. I am a friend to all returned citizens. What are your demands?"

"Then listen up, Carnes," the man in the alley said. "We want two fast horses, grub, whiskey and maybe some female company. You got that?"

"Your demands will be met," Carnes said. "You have my word on that."

"The hell they will," Jess said, angry now. "As far as I'm concerned those killers can starve to death in there."

Carnes turned to Mayor Stout. "I implore you, Mayor, to meet their demands. Once they've had something to eat and a drink or two I can talk them out of there."

"They want a woman," Stout said. "I will not sanction that."

"Then look for a volunteer," Carnes said. "I'll pay her well out of my own pocket."

"That will not happen, Carnes," Jess said. "They'll come out when they're hungry."

"And what about the parson?" Carnes said.

"He'll come out, too," Jess said.

"I agree with Sheriff Casey," Stout said. Then louder for the crowd, "This great city does not negotiate with outlaws."

Again people cheered and the mayor gave a

little bow. After he straightened he said to Jess in a whisper, "Can we rush them?"

Jess nodded. "Sure, if you're willing to step over your own dead. It's a narrow alley."

"Then that is not an option," Stout said. He puffed up a little. "Well, Sheriff, it's too late for the hunt, so I must return to City Hall with my guests. I leave it to you to do your duty and bring those killers to justice."

"No!" Carnes yelled. "That will not do, Mayor. We must meet the needs of the men in the alley. I gave them my word."

But he talked to Stout's back. Harry was already patting the older ladies on the head as he passed, and kissing the younger ones.

"One of you boys there, go get a carpenter to seal off this alley," Jess said. "Tell him he may have to dodge a bullet or two."

That last drew a laugh and shouts of approval and Jess was surprised.

Professor James Carnes was a worried man. If this standoff couldn't be resolved peacefully his entire social experiment—and his standing with the governor—was on shaky ground. He knew he had to act and act now before the entrance to the alley was boarded up with timber.

"I will talk to them, Sheriff," he told Jess Casey. "I think those men will listen to me and come out with their hands up."

"I guess it's worth a try," Jess said. "I'll tell the carpenter not to start work until you get through talking."

"Very well," Carnes said. He raised his hands above his head and quickly stepped into the alley.

"No, not that!" Jess yelled. He'd expected Carnes to stand at the entrance and talk. "Come back, Professor Carnes!"

But he was too late. The man had already disappeared into the gloom.

A minute passed . . . then another . . . Voices were raised. Then silence.

The crowd hushed and people exchanged puzzled glances. What was happening in the there?

Then came the answer.

Two revolver shots very close together shattered the tense quiet. Jess, standing close to the entrance, was sure he heard Carnes cry out, "Nooo . . ." a moment before the shots were fired.

"All right, board it up," Jess told the carpenter.

Easier said than done.

As the carpenter and his apprentice lifted the first board into place, the convicts fired again. A bullet blasted through the pine and sprayed the carpenter's face with splinters, drawing blood. The man yelped and dropped the board as though it were suddenly red-hot and he and his young apprentice scampered out of the line of fire.

"It's not possible, Sheriff," the carpenter said, blood on his cheek. "You want the damned thing boarded up, I'll give you hammer and nails and you can do it himself."

"Damn right," the apprentice said and for talking out of turn got a cuff on the back of his head from the carpenter.

Jess's short fuse was lit and he'd had enough. It was time to end this thing. A man in the crowd had a Colt stuck into his waistband and Jess said, "Let me borrow that." The man willingly passed over the revolver, a .45, and Jess thumbed a round into the empty chamber that had been under the hammer. He drew his own Colt, loaded it the same way, and stood there with the guns hanging by his sides, a tall, lanky men who looked like General Custer and wanted to be anywhere else on earth but where he was.

"You folks move away from the alley or you're liable to get shot," he said. "Clear away there."

Traffic on Main Street had come to a standstill. Horses dozed in the shafts of driverless wagons, street vendors had temporarily shut up shop and the usual cacophony of raised voices and trundling wheels was hushed to a whisper as everyone's attention fixed on the alley.

Jess remembered Luke Short's taunt and hoped he wasn't about to make a bad situation worse and get his fool head blown off in the bargain. He stepped into the alley and then hugged a wall while his eyes got accustomed to the gloom. But he'd been seen.

"Who's there?" a man's voice called from the end of the alley. Then, "Do you see him, Clem?"

A second voice, the man called Clem, yelled, "Identify yourself and state your intentions."

Jess took a chance. "This is Sheriff Jess Casey. I'm here to tell you that your demands are being met. The woman and the grub was easy, but rounding up two fast horses will take a little longer."

"Come closer, let's take a look at you," Clem said. "And get your damned paws above your head. One fancy move from you, mister, and I'll shoot the preacher."

Jess trusted to the shadowed alley and the worn finish of his revolvers not to betray the fact that he was armed. And he almost succeeded.

A startled warning shout of "He's heeled!" and a bullet came almost at the same time. A miss! But close enough that Jess heard its hornet whine. There were three shadowy figures at the end of the alley and one of them was a preacher, but Jess had no time to make a fine distinction about who was who.

He moved steadily forward and cut loose with both guns, knowing that the one in his left hand would be much less effective. His Colts hammering, bucking in his hands, ahead of him he saw a man clutch his belly and go down. But which one? A bullet tugged at the left sleeve of Jess's shirt and a second splintered into the wall to his right. The thought flashed through his head that this was mighty poor shooting. He walked closer, firing steadily, and just one man still stood. The man's knees sagged and his back was against the tall fence that closed off the alley and access to the rear of a furniture warehouse.

Jess and the man fired at the same time. The robber missed badly, several feet wide of Jess's head, but the sheriff's bullet hit the man square in the chest. The robber dropped his gun, turned and looked as though he was trying to climb the fence to escape. Finally he fell on his back, convulsed violently and lay still.

The alley was thick with gun smoke and Jess's ears rang from the concussion of the guns in such a confined space. He found the body of Professor Carnes first. The man lay on his left side, a Colt Frontier .44-40 self-cocker in his right hand. He had no wounds in front, but when Jess examined the body he saw two bullet holes in the man's back. Carnes had been walking away from the robbers when they shot him.

Jess took the gun from the professor's hand. It was still warm. He swung out the cylinder, dropped the loads into his hand and found that two cartridges had been fired. He pieced it together. As he lay dying Carnes had gotten off two shots. But he had not fired at Jess. He'd dropped one of the bandits and the preacher, the latter no doubt by mistake.

Amid the roar and flash of his own Colts in the dark alley, Jess had not seen Carnes fire. But the professor had shot twice before he died. There was no doubt about that.

A man stepped to Jess's side and said quickly and nervously, "My name is Frank Draper, Sheriff, and I'm unarmed." He started at Carnes for a moment. "Is he dead?"

"Yeah, he is," Jess said. Then, unspeakably weary, he said, "Help me to my feet." The man did and Jess saw it was the fellow who'd given him the Colt. He passed Draper his gun and said, attempting a smile, "I fired it left-handed. I don't know if I hit anybody with it."

"Well, it sure made plenty of noise," Draper said. "I know the sound of my own gun."

Jess stepped to the rear of the alley and Draper joined him. "They're both dead," the man said. "And so is Parson Hayes, shot through and through, poor old fellow."

"Seems like," Jess said.

More people crowded into the alley, jostling one another to see what there was to see. A woman held a handkerchief to her nose and sobbed over the body of the parson.

"One of you men bring Big Sal here," Jess said. "Tell her she's got work to do."

CHAPTER FORTY-FIVE

"You don't say?" Luke Short said. "Then maybe you didn't do for any of them."

"Carnes only fired two shots," Jess said. "There were three dead men."

"Why did he fire at them . . . them . . ."

"Returned citizens."

". . . in the first place?"

Jess said, "I think he realized that when the two cons robbed the bank and killed a teller they'd ruined his plans and his reputation so he tried to kill them both. And of course they'd shot him in the back and that can irritate a man."

Luke wore a scarlet smoking jacket and a round, tasseled hat of the same color. Along with other items, Jasper Dunn had thrown out the garments, but one of Luke's more loyal employees had salvaged them. The little gambler had made Jess's chair his own and looked quite at home.

"Did you identify them two fellers?" Luke said.

"Sam Waters is over to the morgue right now."

The little man showed up a few minutes later. He was eating a fried sausage on a bread roll and grease stained his mustache and beard.

"Big Sal give me this," he said. "She said identifying dead fellers can put an appetite on a man. She's right, you know."

"Who were they, Sam?" Jess said.

"Well, I pushed and pulled them bodies this way and that, to make sure like." Fat ran down Sam's hand and he licked it way. "One of them was Clem Spinner and tother is a feller who went by the name of Spade Carver. As I recollect, both were cattle rustlers and hoss thieves. They rolled drunks on the side and murdered a few, but only one killing was ever proved."

"They needed to work on their shooting," Jess said.

"I guess that's why they're dead, Sheriff, huh?" Sam said. He shoved the last of his sandwich in his mouth, chewed for a while, then said, "Seen that Perfesser Carnes's body, Jess. He'd been shot in the back."

"I didn't do that," Jess said.

"I reckon you didn't, not when I hear you tell it. But fer a while there it worried me some."

Luke Short smiled. "Casey is too much of a gentleman to shoot a feller in the back. Ain't you, Sheriff?"

The office door opened before Jess could answer that question and Kurt Koenig stepped inside. The big man wore his usual expensive broadcloth, frilled shirt and hand-tooled boots, but somehow he seemed smaller, deflated like a faulty toy balloon. Even the ivory-handled Colt on his hip failed to make its usual powerful statement.

Koenig's angry eyes went immediately to Luke Short. "What the hell are you?"

"An invalid with a gun, Kurt," the gambler said.

"Lost your place, I hear, and then got tossed out a window and got eaten by a bear or something."

"Or something," Luke said.

"Read that," Koenig said, handing Jess a crumpled letter.

After scanning the words, Jess said, "Where are they?"

"I have no idea," Koenig said. "That's why I'm here."

Jess gave the letter to Luke, who read it and said, "So now Jasper Dunn wants the Silver Garter."

"Is that his name?" Koenig said.

"It sure is, Mr. Koenig," Sam Waters said. "He's a bad one, and if he's made a threat he'll carry it out."

"Who delivered the letter?" Jess said.

"A man came into the saloon and handed it to Mark Lewis, one of my bartenders. Lewis says he'd never seen him before."

"Well, we know where to find Dunn," Jess said. "He'll be at the White Elephant. Let's go get him."

"Not so fast, Sheriff," Koenig said. "The chances

are he won't be there and if I make any move against him he'll carry out his threat to kill Destiny and Joselita."

"He will fer sure," Sam said.

Koenig's anger flashed. "Don't agree with me anymore, old-timer, huh?"

"Sorry, Mr. Koenig, but a natural fact is a natural fact."

"Kurt, how about the Panther City Boys?" Jess said. "Can you get them to help us conduct a search?"

"Don't you think a bunch of men searching the city will be noticed?" Koenig said. "It's too dangerous. I can't take that chance."

The big man looked at the faces of the three other men in the office. Jess Casey was troubled, Luke Short puzzled and Sam Waters's face was empty, as though he'd said his piece and had nothing else to add.

Finally Koenig said, "My entire life I never cared enough about a woman to love her. Hell, I didn't give a damn for anybody, male or female. The whole world revolved around Kurt Koenig and I believed that was the way it should be, the natural order of things. Then I met Destiny and everything changed."

Sam, always one to talk when he should keep quiet, said, "Woman can do that to a man. Sometimes it's for better, sometimes it's for worse, but she'll change him just the same."

"Destiny changed me for the better and for the first time I knew what it really meant to love somebody heart and soul," Koenig said. "And then Joselita came into our lives and it was like holding a little wounded bird in our hands, willing her to live. As for me, I'd found another human being to love and it felt just fine."

Luke Short, who'd listened to Koenig with growing and obvious discomfort, clapped his hands and said, "So how do we find this Jasper Dunn feller and shoot him in the belly? He wants the deeds to your joints by midnight, Kurt. I'd say time is running out on us."

"If we don't know where Dunn is, how can we give him the deeds?" Jess said.

"The man who delivered the letter said to leave them at the White Elephant," Koenig said. He stared into Luke Short's eyes. "I'm getting out, Luke."

"That doesn't sound like the Kurt Koenig I know," Luke said. "You got to choose your ground and fight."

Koenig shook his head. "I won't risk losing Destiny and the girl, and there's nothing you can do or say will convince me otherwise."

"Then maybe I can convince you," Jess said. He glanced at the clock on the wall. "It's now five after three. Give me until eleven thirty tonight. If I don't find out where Destiny and Joselita are located by then, you can hand over the deeds to the Silver Garter and the Green Buddha to Jasper Dunn."

"I don't want to put the women in any danger, Jess," Koenig said.

"I don't, either," Jess said. "I'll be real careful."

"Tall order, Casey," Luke said.

"Risky fer them women," Sam Waters said.

"Yeah, well it's better than just sitting here doing nothing," Jess said.

"Maybe just sitting here is the way," Koenig said.

"It's not my way," Jess said.

CHAPTER FORTY-SIX

Word of Professor James Carnes's death came as bad news to Jasper Dunn. The loss of such a valuable ally had weakened him worse then the desertion of so many of his men.

The blacks and Mexicans had quit early and that had come as no surprise. Dunn had little regard for inferior races and he was glad to see them go. But he'd lost good white men to gunfire and others had lit a shuck, the close confines of the warehouse basement too much like the prison they'd just left. Counting Silas Topper, his fastest gun, Dark Alley Jim Turner and the questionably loyal Ford Talon he was down to a dozen men, and most of those were rapists and murderers, not gunhands.

Dunn had confided his fears to Topper and now waited for what the little gunman had to say. Topper, as always, did not disappoint him.

"The way I see it," he said, "Koenig either values his woman highly or he doesn't. If he does, we'll have those deeds by midnight and the town is ours."

"And if he doesn't?" Dunn said.

"We keep the women as insurance and I go after Koenig."

"Can you shade him, Silas?"

"Of course I can shade him. He'll be the one to draw first and then he'll be dead. It's as simple as that."

"And then we make the woman tell us where Koenig keeps the deeds to the Silver Garter and Green Buddha. We'll say he willingly handed them over to us and then changed his mind and tried to kill you," Dunn said.

"That about sums it up," Topper said.

"It will work. If you make it look good, of course it will work. But let's wait and see if Koenig loves his woman enough to hand over the deeds. Then we can kill him later."

"Either way, I claim his women," Topper said.

"And they'll be yours, Silas." Dunn smiled. "At a minute after midnight."

Ford Talon heard the entire conversation and considered its implications. Dunn had brought in food and Talon made a sandwich of bread and beef and ate while he figured his next move. He could not leave the basement without raising suspicion and must remain where he was.

Then it came to him.

If the deeds to Koenig's properties were not delivered at midnight Silas Topper would go after him and goad the man into drawing. While Topper was gone, Talon would make his move.

He'd kill Jasper Dunn and take his chances that the other gunmen would be too stunned to react quickly and might listen to reason when he told them the game was over.

His plan was as thin as a whisper but it was all he had.

Major Ford Talon looked across the room at the frightened young women and the sight of their drawn, beautiful faces touched him to the quick . . .

Maybe some causes were worth dying for.

CHAPTER FORTY-SEVEN

A strange little man with a stranger tale to tell stepped into the sheriff's office at four in the afternoon and gave Jess Casey a ray of hope that he had not expected.

Pleasant Woodis, dressed in his usual buckskins, the huge Holland & Holland in his right hand, stopped in the middle of the floor and eyed Luke Short with little enthusiasm.

"I heard you'd been et by a bear," he said. "And then got tossed out a window. Or was it the other way around? No matter. You look hale and hearty enough to deal from the bottom of the deck."

"You need a horse to drag that cannon around, Pleasant," Luke said. "Otherwise you'll give yourself a hernia."

"I already got one o' them," Woodis said. He looked at Jess. "I was out day afore yestiddy huntin' for winter meat and I saw a peculiar sight.

Later I said to myself, 'Pleasant, you'd best go tell that young sheriff feller what you seen.' So here I am."

"I'm kind of busy right now, Mr. Woodis," Jess said. "Maybe some other time."

"You ain't too busy to hear this," Woodis said.

"Let the man talk," Luke said. "I like a good story."

Woodis said, "It ain't a good story. But it's a mighty peculiar story. Makes a man wonder if he can believe his own eyes." The old man propped his rifle against a wall then sat on the corner of the desk and said to Jess, "You got coffee on the bile, sonny? I could sure use a cup."

After he had a cup in his hand, Woodis said, "I got to backtrack a ways to the morning of the day when I seen what I seen. My woman says, 'Mr. Woodis, don't you go out there today. Last night I seen blood on the moon and this morning afore you woke up a crow came tap-tapping on the bedroom window. The crow told me the dead are walking and to stay close to home.'"

Luke nodded. "In my younger years I spent some time up Nebraska way selling whiskey to the Indians. The Sioux believe crows carry messages from a world beyond this one."

"And maybe they do," Woodis said.

Jess glanced at the clock. He should be doing something, not listening to a wild tale about crows and Indians and the walking dead.

"Well, sir, I ignored my woman's advice and rode out anyway," Woodis said. "It was a fine morning, sunny and warm with just a breath of fall in the north wind. My hoss was glad to be outdoors so everything was fine atween him and me."

"Mr. Woodis, I—"

"Hold on, Sheriff, I'm getting to the point here," the old man said. Then to Jess, "You mind that draw fighter you shot, the one they called the Second Horseman?"

Now Jess was wary. "Hiram Hartline. Yes, I remember. What about him?"

"Like I said, my hoss had been cooped up and suddenly he started acting crazy on me, buckin' and rearin' as through he'd just caught wind of a pack of wolves. He'd done that afore and I thought nothing of it, that is until I looked ahead on the trail. You make good coffee, sonny."

"What did you see, for God's sake?" Luke said. "Apaches?"

Woodis shook his head. "Nope, something far worse."

Jess was so irritated he slapped his thigh. "Then tell us, damn it."

"All right, so be it," Woodis said. His eyes took on an odd shine. "The Horseman's grave was open and I saw four women carrying his body to a wagon, drawn by the skinniest, mangiest white horse you ever saw."

"Women? Are you sure?" Jess said.

"Sure I'm sure. They were dressed in black robes and veils and crosses on chains and I took them for nuns," Woodis said. "The wagon had four posts at the corners and there was a horse's skull on each one of them. Well, the women laid the body in the wagon, real gentle-like, and then the white hoss walked on and the women fell in beside the wagon, two on each side."

"Then what happened?" Luke said.

"Nothing much," Woodis said. "They passed me and didn't even glance in my direction. After a while they were swallowed up by distance and vanished from my sight." The old man shook his head. "Sure left a rotten smell behind though."

"What kind of smell?" Luke said.

"Gettysburg," Woodis said. "It smelled like Gettysburg after the second day of the battle."

"That's a mighty strange story, Pleasant," Luke said.

"Take it or leave it," Woodis said. "I don't care."

Jess said, "It's easy to explain. Hartline was a mighty peculiar feller so it figures he'd have strange kinfolk. They came back this way to claim his body, is all. And he'd been buried a long time, so his corpse would naturally smell bad."

"That's one way of lookin' at it," Woodis said. "How did his kin know where his body was buried? And why were they all duded up like nuns? I got no answers for that. My woman knew what was going to happen, and I got no answer for that, either."

"I recollect Bat Masterson saying that he saw a whole wagon train disappear up Kansas way," Luke said. "One minute they were there, wagons, people, animals crossing the prairie, and the next they were gone. Strange that."

Jess poured himself coffee, then said, "Now we'll agree to let the dead lie, huh? Mr. Woodis, how well do you know this town?"

"I've been in and out of Fort Worth from the beginning when the Chisholm Trail first came this way," the old man said. His eyes became shrewd. "What's troubling you, Sheriff? I know when a man's got something stickin' in his craw."

"Two young women have been kidnapped and I need to find them before midnight or they will be murdered," Jess said.

"Did Kurt Koenig have a hand in this?" Woodis said.

"No. Kurt's woman is one of them."

"You mean Destiny Durand?"

"Yes, her. And a younger girl."

"Destiny is a right pretty lady and I like her a lot," Woodis said. "What can I do fer you?"

"If you wanted to keep two women prisoner, where would you do it?" Jess said.

"Right here in the Acre, fer sure," Woodis said.

Jess said, "Yeah, but where in the Acre?"

"One way is to stash them in an apartment in one of the tenements," Luke said. "I've heard that folks go into those stinking slums and never come out again."

"But people talk," Woodis said. "You couldn't keep the presence of a high-flying lady like Destiny Durand a secret for long."

"We don't have time to search every tenement in the Acre," Jess said. "That would take us to next year and we only have until midnight." Jess glanced at the clock. "Eight hours from now."

"You could lock them up in an abandoned building," Woodis said. "Plenty of those around, tenements, shut-down stores, even storerooms and warehouses."

"How long will that take?" Luke said.

"I don't know," Jess said. "But the sooner we get started, the better."

"You can count me in, Sheriff," Woodis said.

"I'm beholden to you, Mr. Woodis," Jess said. "We'll start at 15th Street and head north to 11th. In between we'll search every abandoned building we can find. I'll take Houston Street, Mr. Woodis, you take Main. We'll meet at the Waterman Hotel. Even if you've come across a likely place, don't try to go in alone."

"And I'll take Rusk," Luke Short said.

"Hell, Luke, you're in even worse shape than me," Jess said. "You stay right here."

"The hell I will," Luke said. "I want my place back and I'm not going to sit on my ass and let other people do the job for me, especially you two rubes."

Luke, unsuccessfully stifling a groan, got to his feet. He wore a nightgown that left his ankles bare, slippers and the bright red smoking jacket. He tilted the little round cap to a jaunty angle so that the tassel fell over his left ear. Then he shoved the short-barreled Colt Jess had given him into a pocket and said, "Right, I'm ready."

"You look a sight," Jess said.

"And so do you," Luke said. "Now let's go hunt up some trouble."

CHAPTER FORTY-EIGHT

What was to be the last summer thunderstorm roaring in from the Gulf hit Fort Worth at the same time Jess Casey took to the street, adding to his misery.

There were many abandoned buildings in Hell's Half Acre, from burned-out little stores to tenements and warehouses, and checking each one was a chore, especially for a man with bad knees and wearing high-heeled boots.

The homeless denizens of such run-down premises did not appreciate a visit from the law and made their displeasure clear.

One man, bearded, dirty and belligerent, who had made his lair in the back shop of a former dry goods store, went so far as to pick up a club and tell Jess that he was going to "bash his damned brains in."

The triple click of a cocking Colt convinced him otherwise. The man cursed and dropped the club but got a swift kick in the butt from Jess just the same.

The store was the fifth desolate building Jess had checked. He'd dodged missiles thrown by illegal tenants, been spooked by enormous rats and had torn a shirtsleeve on a projecting rusty nail in a doorway. Twice the stench of filthy places forced him to quit breathing until he feared his lungs would burst.

And now when he stepped outside he was welcomed by hissing rain and growling thunder, as though even the heavens resented his presence on Houston Street.

Jess thought about Luke Short in his nightgown and smoking jacket and smiled. By this time he must be as wet as the bottom of a stock tank and mad as a bobcat in a mudhole. If he ran into any belligerent tramps with clubs, there would be dead men on the ground.

Rain drumming on his hat, Jess passed 14th Street and then searched Battles Cotton Yard. He found nothing. A search of Charlie Feather's mattress factory also drew a blank.

"You're wasting your time looking at businesses, Sheriff," Feather said. "I've got workers walking around all the time and they'd have spotted two women in distress by this time."

"Call me desperate," Jess said.

"Keep to the warehouses, that's my advice," Feather said. He was a good-looking man with fine brown eyes. "A few of the older ones have basements and if I was hiding somebody that's where they'd be."

"How many of those?" Jess said, the passage of time weighing on him.

"I don't know, Sheriff," Feather said. "I guess you just got to keep looking. Here, hold on a minute." The man took an oilskin from a row of similar coats hanging from hooks. "I keep these for men who need to go out into the yard. You can return it later."

"Thanks," Jess said. He shrugged into the oilskin. "It almost fits," he said.

"Made for a big sailorman, I guess," Feather said. "Well, Sheriff, good luck."

"Yeah, you, too."

There was a disused warehouse just north of the Germania boardinghouse on 13th Street. It was set back from the road, surrounded by waste ground, but the place had not been abandoned. All the doors were padlocked and the windows shut. Jess tried peering inside, but saw nothing but darkness, dust and the occasional rat. It looked as though nobody had entered the building in a long time.

Jess sheltered under a corrugated iron awning and built a cigarette. He now faced the possibility that the women were somewhere west of the Trinity, locked up in a remote cabin. If that was the case it would take a regiment of cavalry to find them before midnight and he didn't have one of them. He smoked as the rain ticked from the awning and the sky flashed. The day had taken on a gray gloom and Jess consulted his watch. It was almost six o'clock . . . time was speeding by.

Jess's face frowned in concentration. Well, what of it? What was the worst that could happen? Come midnight Kurt Koenig surrenders the Silver Garter and Green Buddha to Jasper Dunn. He gets his women back and lights a shuck for greener and less dangerous pastures. Dunn then floods Fort Worth with his new drug, a perfectly legal product, and grows rich and powerful off the proceeds . . . even as his vile poison addicts and kills people.

Jess tossed his cigarette butt into the teeming rain, his mind made up. He could not accept the worst. To allow what he had come to regard as his town descend into anarchy would be failing in his duty as a peace officer. No, Dunn had to be stopped and he had to be stopped tonight.

CHAPTER FORTY-NINE

Hell's Half Acre kept no secrets. Everything was out in the open. From brothels to opium dens, no shady business was conducted behind locked doors and when confronted by accusations of wickedness and depravity, the standard answer from its citizens was, "Hell, I don't give a damn."

No wonder then that the presence of Jess Casey on the street, searching abandoned buildings and even active businesses for missing women, was noted and passed along with whatever other gossip was currently making the rounds.

Inevitably, Jess's quest reached the ears of Jasper Dunn, carried by Loco Looper, who heard it in a saloon from a man who heard it from a friend who worked in Charlie Feather's factory.

"Strange that," Dunn said when he heard the news. "Has Kurt Koenig decided he doesn't want to play my game and got the sheriff involved?"

"Or Casey is doing it on his own, boss," Looper said. "He's a damned interferer."

"Mr. Talon, give me your opinion," Dunn said. "Could Casey find our cozy little basement and cause trouble?"

"I guess he could if he looks hard enough," Talon said.

Dunn rubbed his temple as though he had a sudden headache. "Do you think Koenig asked him to do this?"

"Hard to say," Talon said. "From what I've heard about Koenig he'd do it himself."

"My thought exactly," Dunn said. "That man Casey has become a growing irritant. Mr. Topper, Mr. Turner, the sheriff is on Houston Street, busily searching rat-infested hovels. Find him and kill him."

Looper grinned. "Consider it done, boss."

And Jim Turner, as mean and treacherous as a snake, said, "I'm in the mood to kill a lawman."

"Then let's go get it done," Looper said.

"Take your slickers, boys," Dunn said. "I don't want you to get wet and catch a cold."

Jess Casey passed Frank's Saloon at the corner of Houston Street and 12th, and just beyond was a crumbling tenement that looked promising. The building was not fully abandoned. About half its apartments were occupied, but it was a tumbledown, rat-ridden wreck of a place and Jess wondered if Destiny and Joselita could be in one of the vacant rooms. It seemed unlikely, but something told him that this could be a possibility. Besides, it was an excuse to get out of the rain.

He decided to start at the top and work his way down. A littered passageway led to a rickety wooden staircase that led to the upper two floors. He looked into every filthy, smelly room and wondered how human beings could once have lived in there. The Acre had no secrets, but much of its misery was hidden from view.

After thirty minutes of searching, the crown of Jess's hat gray with spiderwebs, his boots sticky with stuff from the floors, he gave up and walked down the creaking stairs again . . . into more trouble than he could handle.

Two men stood facing him, blocking the hallway. Both wore slickers that they'd swept back from their holstered guns. The taller one had crazy eyes, the other the eyes of a rattlesnake. Both were smiling but their intent was obvious. They were there to kill him.

The oilskin covered Jess's gun and he'd be painfully slow on the draw and shoot. And that would be his death. He played for time. He played for a miracle.

"Jasper Dunn sent you," he said.

"You got that right," Loco Looper said. "You've lived too long, mister."

"Mr. Dunn says it's high time he cut your suspenders, lawman," Turner said.

"Let me drop this oilskin, boys," Jess said. "Give me an even break."

"No breaks," Looper said. He drew his Colt and thumbed back the hammer. "You get it right between them bonny brown eyes."

Jess heard a crash of thunder, as loud as a cannon in the hallway.

Looper seemed to explode, as though everything that was inside his body burst through his belly and chest. So great was the devastation to Looper's lanky frame that Jess, standing five feet away, was splattered with his blood.

Beside him, though he was unhurt but his face covered in gore, Jim Turner screamed in sudden terror and swung around to face this unexpected and horrific threat, his Colt coming up fast.

Pleasant Woodis, familiar with the ways of the Holland & Holland elephant gun, had already reloaded and he let Turner have both barrels. The man was almost blown in half and was supping brimstone broth in hell before he hit the ground.

Jess watched Woodis come toward him, reloading again. The little man said something but Jess was as deaf as a post and stunned by the concussion of the big gun. Woodis took Jess by the arm and led him out onto the street and the falling rain.

The little man's mouth moved again but Jess couldn't hear him. "Huh?" he said.

Woodis made a motion with his hand, telling

him to stay right where he was at. Jess nodded
and the little man stepped back into the tenement. He was gone for a long time. When he
returned he said, "Can you hear me now?"

Jess could and nodded, though his ears still
rang.

"Both dead," Woodis said. "Big gun like this
can make a mess of a man. When Big Sal gets
here I hope she's brung a shovel."

"My gun was under the oilskin," Jess said. "I
couldn't reach it."

"You don't need to make excuses to me, boy,"
Woodis said. "I saw the fear in your eyes and knew
what was coming down. My woman makes me
wear moccasins, and that's all to the good when
you're trying to get the drop on a feller."

Woodis took the makings from Jess's trembling fingers and built the cigarette himself.
"Here, lick that," he said. After Jess licked the
paper the little man sealed the smoke shut and
stuck it in Jess's mouth. "Come back into shelter,"
he said. When he and Jess were in the hallway,
Woodis thumbed a match and lit the cigarette.

"How did you know where to find me?" Jess
said.

"I didn't, but I seen them two fellers walking on
11th Street and figured they was up to no good.
The rannies looked like they're on the prod and
I figured the chances were good they were after
you and I was right."

"They were Jasper Dunn's men," Jess said.
Then, "Mr. Woodis, when you first saw those two

did they look like they'd been walking for a spell? I mean were they real wet?"

"Well, they was wearing slickers, but come to think on it when I first saw them they looked pretty dry." Woodis thought for a few moments then said, "Yeah, I figured they didn't look like you do now. I mean like a drowned rat."

"Then when you saw them they hadn't walked far," Jess said.

Woodis frowned as he considered that, then he said, "I'm catching your drift, sonny. They must have come from somewhere on 11th Street and closer to Houston than Rusk."

"Did you see Luke Short?" Jess said.

"Neither hair nor hide. Maybe Luke decided to get in out of the rain. He was always a man who liked a saloon roof over his head."

"Mr. Woodis, show me where you first saw those men," Jess said. "I think we might be getting mighty close to Jasper Dunn."

"What about them two?" Woodis said.

"They're not going anywhere. I'll have Big Sal pick up the pieces later," Jess said.

CHAPTER FIFTY

To the delight of passersby, Luke Short, soaked to the skin and in ill humor, sheltered on the front porch of the Waterman Hotel on 11th Street and moodily watched the rain fall and the sky grow darker.

The earliest of the sporting crowd had stirred and a few of Luke's old customers passed in the street and called out sundry pleasantries.

"Hey, Luke, you been walking in your sleep?"

"The coat goes well with the nightgown, Luke."

"Where did you get the hat, Luke?"

"Hey, Luke, is it really you or a Chinaman?"

Well, that was about all Luke Short was going to take. He pulled his Colt and roared, "The next man who passes a smart remark gets a bullet in his guts! Especially you, Watson. I've got my eye on you."

One of the teasers, not trusting Luke's temper, fled west along 11th Street and almost ran into

Jess and Pleasant Woodis as they turned the corner from Houston.

"Oh thank God," Watson said. "Sheriff, Luke Short is standing outside the Waterman Hotel. He's got a gun and is threatening to shoot folks, especially me. And me who just got up from a sickbed."

"I'll go talk to him," Jess said. "He won't do you any harm."

"But he's lost his mind, Sheriff," Watson said. "He's all dressed up like a Chinaman and he's hunting trouble."

Jess patted the man on the shoulder. "Luke will be just fine. He's always been a little high-strung."

"Where the hell have you been, Casey?" Luke short yelled. "I've been stood here for an hour as wet as a rooster under a drain spout. And where did you get the damned oilskin? You didn't tell me you had an oilskin. That's because I don't count anymore, huh?"

"Luke, I think I know where Jasper Dunn is at," Jess said.

But Luke was still boiling mad and unreasonable. "Like I give a damn. I'm shot through and through and liable to get pneumonia. I'm going to be dead anyway."

Pleasant Woodis reached inside his buckskins and produced a silver liquor flask. "Here, Luke, this will help heal what ails you."

Luke chose to be suspicious. "What the hell is it?"

"Bonded bourbon, my boy. It will do you a world of good."

Not one to refuse a drink, Luke took a hearty swig and passed the flask to Jess. "Here, Casey, get some whiskey down you. You look like Custer when he first saw the Indians. Your eyeballs are as big as silver dollars."

The bourbon helped and Jess was grateful for it. "I think we'll find Jasper Dunn somewhere here on 11th Street," he said. "Luke, are you in or are you out?" He took off the oilskin. "Here, wear this."

Luke took the coat, held it out at arm's length and let it drop to the boardwalk. "If you're right about Dunn, Casey, we don't want anything that will slow us on the draw."

"Then you're in," Jess said.

"Yeah. That is, until I'm out," Luke said.

"I heard gunfire," Jasper Dunn said. "Looper should be back by now."

"Me, I heard a mighty big rifle," Silas Topper said. "You want me to go find Casey and end it?"

"No, Mr. Topper, I want you here. And you, Mr. Talon." Dunn looked around at his diminished force. Apart from the men he mentioned, there were only five others, none of then named guns. Dunn was not overly concerned. Outlaws were a restless breed, but once he took over Koenig's holdings and the big money started to roll in they'd come crawling back with their tails between their legs. "You other men, go find the sheriff and make sure he'd dead. If he's not, kill him and kill anyone else who might be with him."

The five exchanged glances. Finally one of them, a man with a terrible knife scar on his cheek, said, "Boss, I hear the lawman is mighty slick with the Colt. I don't want to brace him. Send Topper. He's the gun."

"'Send Topper,'" the little draw fighter said, contempt in his voice. He spat in the scarred man's direction, then, "Squires, you're a damned lily-livered coward."

Topper drew and fired.

The bullet clipped an arc from the tag of the tobacco sack in Squires's vest pocket. Hit hard, the man staggered back, a look of shocked surprise on his face. Grinning, Topper let him have another in the belly and then watched the man fall. Topper took a few smiling moments to savor the kill, then swung his fancy Colt on the other four.

"Anybody else too yellow to brace a hick sheriff?" he said.

That question was met with silence, then an older man with iron gray hair said, "We'll find him."

"You'd better," Topper said, his eyes ugly. "Now I got the taste for it, I'm in the killing vein today."

The four men trooped up the stairs and

when they were gone, Dunn said, "Was that really necessary, Mr. Topper?"

"Sure it was, boss," the little gunman said. "There's no room for cowards in this organization." Arrogance in every step, he strolled over to Destiny Durand, put his forefinger under her chin and forced her head up so she looked at him. "What do you think, little lady? Was it necessary?"

"You're the coward," Destiny said. "The man you killed wasn't even armed."

"Then he should've heeled himself, huh?" Topper grinned.

"You're a contemptible piece of low-life trash," the woman said.

"I take that from nobody, especially a whore," Topper said. He drew back his hand, but Dunn's sharp command stopped him.

"No, Mr. Topper! I don't want to return damaged goods."

The gunman let his hand drop. He said, "You'll be my woman one day soon and by God I'll teach you respect with a dog whip."

Topper walked away and Ford Talon relaxed. If Topper had slapped the woman he would have made a play. Dunn's revolver lay in front of him on his desk and the man could be sudden. Talon knew he'd have taken hits from both Dunn and Topper. The question was: Did he want to throw his life away? Or did he want to live?

Right then Talon had no answer . . . but it was something he'd need to think about very soon.

CHAPTER FIFTY-ONE

"Boys, we got company," Pleasant Woodis said, his voice sounding a warning. He, Jess and Luke Short were in the middle of the rain-lashed street and slowed by mud.

Four men had stepped out of the warehouse opposite, a medium-sized building with faded red paint on the across its front that said: J. S. PRINGLE & SONS, WAREHOUSEMEN.

The four men were armed with belt guns and they looked tough and capable enough. But to Jess's surprise the oldest of them, a gray-haired man, held up his hands and said, "You got no problem with us."

"State your intentions," Jess said. Like Luke, he held his gun by his side at arm's length.

"Our intention is to walk away from here without a shooting scrape." He jerked a thumb over his shoulder. "The women you want are in there. In the basement."

Rain falling from the brim of his hat, Jess said, "Where is Jasper Dunn?"

"With the women, him and Silas Topper and a feller called Ford Talon."

"You four are convicts?" Jess said.

"We were convicts, Sheriff," the gray-haired man said. In a defeated gesture he let his shoulders sag. "And we don't want to be convicts again."

"What do you say, Luke?" Jess said.

"I say we gun them," Luke said, his eyes fixed on the gray-haired man.

"Mr. Woodis?"

"I'm with Luke. They're Dunn's men and we can take them down right where they stand."

"Hold your fire," Jess said. "You men, unbuckle those cartridge belts and let them drop." The four complied without hesitation and Jess said, "Go to the sheriff's office and wait there until I return. I'll decide what to do with you then."

"Sheriff, we had no hand in the capture of those women," a younger man said.

"What about the murder of poor old Bruno Cavanni?" Woodis said. "You had no hand in that, either?"

"No. It was none of our doing," the younger man said.

"You're a damned liar!" Woodis said.

Jess saw it coming and couldn't stop it.

The Holland & Holland roared twice and the gray-haired man and another went down, shot all to pieces.

"No!" Jess yelled. "Damn it, no!" But he was too late.

His face like stone, Luke was firing, scoring hits. A man staggered back and *clanged!* against the corrugated iron wall of the warehouse. He fell in a heap, coughing blood. The remaining convict dived for the boardwalk, trying to reach his gun. He did grab it but when he brought his head up to fire, Luke shot him in the middle of his forehead.

The roar of gunfire ended and an unnatural quiet descended on 11th Street. The only sound was the steady patter of the rain, the only movement the ghostly drift of gun smoke.

Jess looked at the carnage that had been wrought in the space of several seconds and the taste of green bile was sour in his mouth.

Beside him Pleasant Woodis shoved a pair of shells into his rifle. "Last two, Luke," he said. "Got to make them count."

"Yeah, well, save Dunn for me," Luke said. "I've a score to settle with that low-down son of a bitch." He picked up a cartridge belt, thumbed out shells and fed them into his Colt. "I didn't see you shoot, Casey," he said.

"Those men had surrendered," Jess said. "They'd laid down their arms."

"We got the drop on them pretty good, huh, Sheriff?" Woodis said, smiling. "They never knew what hit them. Damned bunch of murderers."

"You get lucky and get the drop on a man you take it," Luke said, hanging a cartridge belt on his shoulder. "Live longer that way. As soon as you'd taken one step through the door of your office them boys would've done for you with your own scattergun."

"They wanted out," Jess said. "You heard them say that, Luke."

"Sure they wanted out . . . when they saw three armed fellers facing them, one with an elephant gun," Luke said. "I'd want out myself if I'd seen that there cannon in ol' Pleasant's hands."

"Sheriff, you told them to shuck their artillery and got us the drop," Woodis said. "Damn it all, boy, you done good. Now let's go finish it."

Jess Casey had thought his time in Hell's Half Acre had taught him the ways of the gun and of the hard, unforgiving men who lived by its tenets.

Now he realized he'd been wrong.

He hadn't learned a damn thing.

CHAPTER FIFTY-TWO

The warehouse door was still slightly ajar and Jess Casey pushed it soundlessly open. Gun drawn, he stepped inside—and was confronted by a huge empty, echoing space.

Luke Short silently jabbed a forefinger in the direction of a stairwell at the right side of the room and Jess nodded. His spurs chiming with every step, he crossed the floor and the others followed. He turned to Luke and whispered, "I'll go first. Keep close."

Luke nodded and Pleasant Woodis said, "Right behind you, sonny."

But then the door at the bottom of the stairwell was flung open and a man's voice said, "Come in, Sheriff Casey, and welcome. I've been expecting you."

"Is that you, Dunn?" Jess said.

"As ever was, Sheriff. What can I do for you?"

"Release the two women and then we can talk," Jess said.

"How many with you?" Dunn said.

Jess didn't hesitate. "Twenty Texas Rangers, all well-armed and determined men."

He heard the smile in Dunn's voice when he said, "Then come down by yourself and we'll negotiate."

"It's a trap," Luke said. "Don't listen to him."

"There's no negotiation involved, Dunn," Jess said. "Send up the two women and I guarantee you a fair trial for murder and kidnapping. I can't be any more on the square than that."

"Well, if you won't come down, Sheriff, then here's my offer," Dunn said. "Are you listening?"

"I'm listening," Jess said. "State your piece."

"Then here are my conditions. First, withdraw your men. Second, provide five horses and leave them saddled outside. If by midnight I have not received the deeds to Kurt Koenig's properties, you will guarantee me safe conduct out of Fort Worth."

"Dunn, forget the deeds. You're not going anywhere," Jess said. "I intend to put you on trial for the murder of Bruno Cavanni and others and I aim to see you hang."

"I'm sorry to hear that, Sheriff," Dunn said. "And now you have forced me to change my plans. At one minute past midnight I will cut the throat of Joselita Juarez. The girl's death will conclude our first round of negotiations. We will then bargain for the life of Miss Destiny Durand. Let's not, at this early stage, think about the outcome if our second round of talks fails."

Luke Short, angry beyond measure, yelled, "Dunn, you low-down son of a bitch, I intend to shoot you dead on sight."

"Is that also your answer, Sheriff Casey?" Dunn said. "For the girl's sake I hope not."

"What you ask with the horses an' all will take time, Dunn," Jess said. "I'll need a few hours."

"You have until one minute past midnight to make up your mind," Dunn said. "I await your decision."

"Let's rush the door," Luke Short said. "Barge right in there with guns blazing."

"Luke, you're in no condition to rush anywhere," Jess said. "And when I come to study on it, neither am I."

"Then what do you suggest we do, Casey?" Luke said. "Stand here and twiddle our thumbs until midnight?"

"I say rush the door," Woodis said. "I can touch off this here rifle pretty damned quick."

"Yeah, and the howitzer shells it shoots are liable to go right through Dunn and hit the women," Jess said.

Woodis scratched his hairy chin. "Hell, I never thought about that. They could, you know."

"Well?" Luke said, raising an eyebrow at Jess.

"I'm thinking, Luke."

"Then think fast, cowboy," Luke said. "Time is a-wasting."

CHAPTER FIFTY-THREE

"Boss, come midnight, let me do the cuttin'," Silas Topper said. He stared at Joselita Juarez. "You won't feel a thing, little gal."

Jasper Dunn said, "Of course, Mr. Topper, I'll leave the throat cutting to you. But let's hope it doesn't come to that."

"You're trapped like a treed possum, Dunn," Ford Talon said. "That cowpoke sheriff isn't going to let you leave here alive."

Dunn waved a hand in the direction of the two women. "I have bargaining chips. They're my ticket out of here."

"Killing the girl will cut them down to one," Talon said. "Maybe not such a good idea."

"It will show the sheriff and his cronies that I'm serious," Dunn said. He rubbed a nervous hand across his mouth. "Mr. Topper, the syringe, please."

All at once the little gunman was wary. "Boss, do

you think this is a good time to be taking that stuff?" he said.

"It will relax me, Mr. Topper, and help me face the trials to come. Now, if you please, the syringe. I'll come to my desk. Mr. Talon, keep an eye on the stairs. If anyone makes to come down, kill him."

"You can't trust him, boss," Topper said. "I've got the stairs covered."

Talon said nothing, then watched as Topper opened a desk drawer and removed the syringe from the box. "I melted the rock myself, boss," he said. "This will keep you happy for a spell."

Dunn bared his forearm and Topper plunged the needle into a vein and emptied the syringe. Dunn took a shuddering breath, then smiled and said, "I will be just fine now. As they say, it is already making me feel like a hero."

"Just you sit there and relax," Topper said. "It's a long time until midnight."

"This is wonderful stuff, Mr. Topper," Dunn said, his voice drowsy. "We'll flood Fort Worth with it, and beyond, and become very rich men. I might even travel to Europe and become a fine gentleman in Paris or Rome."

It had been long in coming, but now Ford Talon decided the time was right to make himself heard. He stepped to Dunn's desk, where the man's watch lay beside his Colt. Talon picked up the watch and said, "Dunn, can you hear what this says?"

"Yes, I can," Dunn said, smiling. "Why, it says tick-tick-tick."

Talon nodded. "That's right, Dunn, tick-tick-tick. It's ticking away what's left of your life. You'll never be a fine gentleman, you'll be a corpse in a pine box in the Fort Worth graveyard."

The drug would not permit Dunn to be angry. But his voice was vicious as he said, "No, you impertinent pup, you'll be the one rotting in the graveyard. Mr. Topper!"

Destiny Durand, long familiar with the new breed of Texas draw fighters, called out, "No! Let him be, Topper."

But the little gunman wasn't listening. He was eager for another kill. He said, "Talon, I've wanted to shut your big yap for a long—"

Ford Talon drew and fired. His target was Jasper Dunn.

Surprised and then appalled, Dunn took the hit in the center of his chest. He knew he was a dead man, and in the depths of despair he cried out, a long, anguished scream that echoed around the basement like the smashing of brittle glass.

Silas Topper was slowed by a full second, but when he drew his speed was blinding. He pumped two bullets into Talon and then a third as the man collapsed to the floor.

Jess Casey was midway down the stairs when he fired through a gap in the wrought-iron banister. Silas Topper never saw it coming. Hit, then hit again, he staggered on his feet, looking around for the shooter. Then he caught sight of Jess.

"You!" he screamed, his gun coming up.

Jess fired again and again and again until his Colt clicked on an empty chamber. Three shots. Three hits. Topper dropped to his knees, staring at Jess, who walked toward him, ejecting spent shells from the cylinder of his Colt.

Topper's ashen face took on a look of astonishment. "How . . . how?"

Jess smiled. "It was easy. I got the drop."

"I'll be damned," Topper said. Then he fell on his face, a dead man.

Joselita Juarez and Destiny Durand, who vowed that she'd take a hundred different kinds of female revenge on Kurt Koenig for taking no part in her rescue, left the basement to Jess Casey and Luke Short. Pleasant Woodis had gone to fetch Big Sal, a woman he said he secretly admired.

Luke opened the lid of what looked like a small brandy barrel and looked at the brownish black granules inside. "So that's it, huh?" he said to Jess.

"That would be my guess," Jess said.

"So Dunn figured he could make a fortune selling this stuff?"

"He did. He would have had repeat customers for life."

"What are you going to do with it, Casey?" Luke said.

"Destroy it and then have the Rangers track it back to its source."

"Maybe we shouldn't be too hasty here," Luke said. "I mean there's nothing illegal about selling it."

"No. But there's plenty that's immoral about selling it," Jess said. He smiled. "You've got the White Elephant back, Luke. Go home."

Luke sneezed. "I think I caught a damned cold."

"Seems like," Jess said.

"Let me have only this barrel," Luke said. "I want to see if there's a market for the stuff, so you can tell the Rangers."

"Go home, Luke," Jess said. "Take care of that cold."

"You're not going to change your mind?"

"No."

Luke walked to the stairs and stopped. "You did good against Topper, Casey. You're not too bright, but you're learning."

"Thank you, Luke," Jess said.

"But I still don't like you," Luke said.

Jess Casey looked around the blood-splashed basement.

Jasper Dunn sat upright on his chair, his dead face frozen in a look of horrified surprise. Silas

Topper lay on his face on the floor, as still as only the dead can be.

Ford Talon lay on his back, staring at the ceiling.

Jess kneeled, closed the man's eyes and said, "Sleep well, Major."

Then he left the basement and walked into the street, where he turned his face to the sky and let the falling rain wash him clean.

THE GREATEST WESTERN WRITERS OF THE 21ST CENTURY

*Standing for family, honor, and a way of life,
the MacCallisters have carved out a hard-won corner
of the Wyoming frontier. In the thrilling new novel
from the bestselling Western writers, Duff MacCallister
faces his most treacherous and deadly fight yet.*

KINGDOM COME

Like a murderous plague, a band of cutthroats and
criminals, led by prison escapees from New Mexico,
rages through West Texas. They're slaughtering
everyone in their path: men, women, and children.
They struck at Saragosa. Now they've taken over the
town of Boracho. The Dallas newspapers call them
the Kingdom Come Gang. In Chugwater, Wyoming,
Duff McCallister calls them his enemy.
Because one of their victims was family.

Now it's personal

Riding to Texas, Duff gathers every man he can to
make an assault on Boracho, even using a hard case
recruited from behind bars. Facing a brutal,
merciless enemy, with innocent hostages caught in
between, Duff is soon in a full-blast war, with guns,
knives, and dynamite exploding on dirt streets
soaked in blood. And it won't be over until
a hero makes a final stand.

MacCALLISTER, THE EAGLES LEGACY
Kingdom Come

by William W. Johnstone
with J. A. Johnstone

On sale now, wherever Pinnacle Books are sold.

CHAPTER ONE

Carbon County, Wyoming

Riding along, minding his own business, Duff MacCallister crested the hill and was stopped by a man holding a pistol in one hand, the reins of his horse in the other.

"That's far enough, friend," growled the man.

"*Och*, it's friend that you call me, but you've a pistol in your hand. That would *nae* be the way to be greeting a friend now, would it?"

"It's only for a couple minutes, till we get our business done. We don't want anyone comin' along to interfere with what needs to be done."

It wasn't until then that Duff noticed four more men down at the bottom of the hill, some one hundred yards distant. One of them had his hands behind his back. One was holding a rope.

"And what business would that be, if you don't mind the tellin'?"

The man nodded toward the base of the hill. "As you can see, we're about to hang someone."

"I take it he's *nae* been sentenced by a court, for I know of no court that would hang someone from a tree out in the middle of nowhere."

"Ha! You got that right. The only court this sumbitch has been to, is us."

"Who is *us*?"

"Us? That's me 'n my three friends. That's who *us* is."

"And would ye be for tellin' me what the lad's crime might be?"

"What's his crime? I'll tell you what his crime is. He's a Chinaman."

Duff frowned. "Is he now? Sure, and I wasn't aware it was against the law to be a Chinaman."

"It ain't only that. He's a Chinaman that don't know his place. He come into town drivin' a surrey 'n sittin' right there on the seat beside him was a white woman holdin' a baby."

Duff tipped his head to one side. "And was it his baby?"

"The baby didn't look Chinese, but that don't make no never mind. He had no business being with 'em."

"What did the white woman have to say about the situation?"

"We didn't give her no choice to say nothin' about it. It's more 'n likely that all she woulda done is just lie about it. Anyhow, she's done got hers." The man chuckled. "We laid the whip on her good. Now the Chinaman is about to get his."

Duff reached down to wrap his hand around his rifle. "I don't think so."

"What do you mean you don—"

That was as far as he got before Duff swung the rifle around, smashing it against the side of the man's head and sweeping him out of his saddle. He lay unconscious on the road as Duff slapped his legs against the sides of his horse, urging Sky into a gallop. As he approached the others, they looked around toward him. Not one of the men was holding a gun in his hand. Duff was holding a pistol, having slipped the rifle back into its sheath.

"Here, what is this?" one of the men asked.

"I'll be thanking you to let the gentleman go," Duff said, his Scottish brogue thick.

"Gentleman? What gentleman?"

"The gentleman whose hands you are about to untie."

"Mister, maybe you don't know, but this here Chinaman was with a white woman. We can't just let him—"

Obscenities filled the air, coming from the man Duff had encountered moments earlier. Holding a rifle to his shoulder, he fired it, the bullet frying the air so close to Duff's head that he could hear it pop as it passed by.

Duff returned fire with his pistol, dropping his assailant with one shot. He turned back to the others. "Would you be so kind as to cut him loose now?" he asked in a calm voice.

"Mister, you've got no business interfering in this."

"Do you speak English?" Duff asked the Chinese

man, who, through it all, had been sitting quietly in the saddle, awaiting his fate.

"I speak English."

"What is your name?"

"I am Wang Chow."

"Wang, it seems like every Chinaman I've ever known is a good cook. Are you a good cook, Wang?"

"Here! What the hell is all this?" cried the man holding the rope. "We're about to hang this devil, and you want to know if he is a good cook?"

"Please, don't interrupt my interview with this man."

"Huh? Your interview?"

Duff cocked the pistol and pointed it straight at the man's head. "I asked you nicely not to interrupt my interview."

The man put both hands up, palms facing out, fingers spread wide. "All right, all right, I ain't a-stoppin' you."

"Mr. Wang, I am thinking about hiring a cook. Are you a good cook"

"I am very sorry, but I am not a good cook," Wang admitted.

"I admire your courage and your honesty. All you would have had to say is that you *are* a good cook, and that would save you from being hung. So, let me ask you this. If I hired you as my cook, would you be willing to learn?"

Wang, finally realizing what was going on,

smiled broadly. "I will learn to be a very good cook."

"Mr. Wang, my name is MacCallister. Duff MacCallister. You're hired." He turned to the man who had been the spokesman for the group. "As you can see, sir, I do have a vested interest in the fate of this gentleman, as he is now one of my employees. I would be very disturbed if someone tried do something such as . . . well, let's just say, hang one of my employees. Now untie his hands."

"The hell we will!" shouted the third man. Jerking his gun from his holster, he snapped a shot toward Duff and missed.

Duff returned fire, and didn't miss. "So far this little encounter has cost you half your number," he said to the remaining two gunmen. "You can either untie Mr. Wang, *now*, or I will kill both of you and untie him myself."

"Untie him, Floyd, untie him!"

"That will not be necessary," Wang said, bringing both hands around front to show that they weren't tied.

"What the hell? How did you do that? It's impossible for you to get your hands free. I tied them myself," said the man with Floyd.

"Mr. Wang, if you would, sir, please collect their guns, including the guns from the man who is on the ground."

Wang dismounted.

"Wait a minute. I ain't about to give my guns to no Chinaman!" Floyd said.

"Oh, I think you will. You will either give them to him willingly, or I will arrange for him to take them from you just like he will be collecting them from your dead friend."

"Do it, Floyd, do it!" insisted his partner, his voice still animated by fear.

"This ain't right!" Floyd objected. "There ain't nothin' right about this!"

"Their rifles as well, Wang."

Grumbling, the men gave up their rifles.

"That horse you were sitting on. Is it yours?" Duff asked Wang.

"Hell no, that ain't his horse. It's mine," Floyd said. "We just brung it here for the hangin'."

"Can you read and write, Floyd?" Duff asked.

"Can I read and write? Hell yes, I can read 'n write."

"How much did you pay for that horse?"

"Mister, what the hell difference does it make to you how much I paid for that horse?"

"I plan to buy this horse from you, Floyd. I can't have Mr. Wang walking now, can I?"

"Buy it? You mean, with cash money?"

"Yes, of course I mean with cash money. It just so happens that I am returning from a trip where I sold some stock." Reaching into his saddlebag, Duff pulled out a piece of paper. "And by a fortuitous set of events, I also have a printed bill of sale here that is blank, left over from my business transactions. I'm going to give you one hundred dollars for the horse, and the saddle. And you are going to sign this bill of sale over to me."

"What the hell? The saddle alone is worth a hunnert dollars," Floyd complained.

"You really aren't in a position to bargain right now," Duff pointed out as he began to fill in the blanks of the bill of sale. He turned to Floyd's partner. "You. What's your name?"

"What do you need my name for?"

"You're going to sign as a witness."

"It's Durant. John Durant."

"And his name? Beside Floyd, I mean."

"It's Russell. Floyd Russell," Durant said.

At the same time Durant said *Russell*, Russell said, *"Smith."* Realizing that Durant had spoken, he added, "Damn you, Durant, what for did you give him my real name?"

Duff secured the signatures of both men, then, putting the bill of sale in his pocket, he gave Russell five twenty-dollar bills. After that, he made the men dismount.

"What the hell? You only paid for one horse. You plannin' on takin' all of them?" Russell asked.

"Just to keep you two men alive," Duff said.

"How is leavin' us stranded goin' to keep us alive?" Durant asked.

"Because if I left the horses with you, no doubt, you would try to come after us. And if you did that, I would have to kill you."

"You're a funny man, mister. You buy one horse, 'n you steal three," Russell said.

"I'm *nae* stealing the horses. About ten miles ahead, you'll come to the town of Le Bonte. I'll be leavin' the horses with the local constabulary, in your name. All you have to do is call for them and pay their keep."

"Le Bonte? That's where we come from. You show up in Le Bonte with that Chinaman on a stole horse, what do you think is goin' to happen to you?"

"*Och*, but the horse isn't stolen now, is it? Sure 'n I have a bill of sale confirming that I bought the horse from you."

Russell frowned. "You don't expect us to walk ten miles, do you?"

"Aye, you'll have to now, won't you? For 'tis a sure and certain thing that Le Bonte won't be coming to you."

"What about our guns?" Durant asked.

"They'll be with your horses. Mr. Wang, since you're having to keep up with the guns, I'll take charge of the three horses. Shall we go?"

"We go," Wang said.

Suddenly and unexpectedly, but in a coordinated move that the two men must have planned, Durant and Russell lunged toward Wang Chow in an attempt to recover their guns.

Wang dropped the guns and pivoted on his left foot while driving his right foot into first Russell's, then Durant's face. Both men went down.

"Well now, that is a neat trick," Duff said. "It makes me wonder how they were able to capture you in the first place."

"They pointed guns at the woman," Wang said as he retrieved the weapons.

"They threatened to shoot a woman? What an unpleasant lot I stumbled into today."

"As you are now my employer, I ask your permission to check upon the woman."

"Of course we will. Is she your woman?"

"No," Wang said without further explanation.

"You've got too many guns to keep up with very easily. I'll take half of them. And, seeing as you aren't armed, perhaps you should strap on one of the holsters."

Wang shook his head. "I have no need for guns."

Duff chuckled. "After seeing you in action back there, I can almost believe you."

CHAPTER TWO

La Bonte, Wyoming

As Duff and Wang rode into town leading riderless horses, people on the street and board sidewalks stopped to stare.

"Ain't that the Chinaman Russell 'n the others had with them this mornin'?" a man asked his neighbor.

"Hey, mister. Who are you?" someone else shouted at Duff. "What are you doin' with that Chinaman? Where at is Russell, McGill, Alberson, and Durant?"

Neither MacCallister nor Wang answered the shouted question. They rode directly to the town marshal's office, tied off the horses, and went inside. Two badge-wearing men were drinking coffee and engaged in an animated conversation. They looked up, the expression on their faces showing their surprise at seeing the Chinaman.

"Which of you is the marshal?" Duff asked.

"We ain't neither one the marshal," said one. "We're deputies. The marshal has gone to Cheyenne to report on a lynchin'. Only this here Chinaman is the one we thought was lynched."

"You made no effort to stop it?"

"Hell, mister, half the town was in on it. They was only three of us. What was we s'posed to do?"

"Where are the woman and baby?" Wang asked.

"If I was you, Chinaman, I'd stay away from that woman, seein' as that's what got you into trouble in the first place," the short deputy said.

"Where are the woman and the child?" Duff asked.

"Well sir, after she got whupped, she got took down to Doctor Dunaway's office. More 'n likely that's where you'll find her now."

"Thank you. Oh, you will find four horses tied up out front. Eventually two men will call for them."

"Two men? What about the other two?"

"They are dead."

Duff and Wang found the woman in the doctor's office.

Her eyes opened wide and the expression on her face was one of relief and joy when she saw Wang. "Oh! You are alive! Thank God, you are alive!"

Dr. Dunaway was just as surprised to see Wang. "What happened? I was told that the men who took you planned to hang you."

Wang nodded. "That was their plan, but this man stopped them."

"Oh, bless you," the woman said. "I have been feeling so bad about all this, knowing that it was my fault. How innocent we were. No one would listen, and this man's good deed was nearly repaid by him being murdered. Oh, Mister—" She stopped. "I never even learned your name."

"I am Wang Chow."

"Mr. Wang, you were nearly killed for your good deed. I can't thank you enough for what you did for my baby and me."

"How is the baby?" Wang asked the doctor.

"The baby will be just fine, thanks to you. He was very dehydrated when he got here, but I've been giving him water a little at a time. He's a strong little boy. It's Mrs. Harrison I've been worried about. I can't believe anyone could be so evil as to take a bullwhip to a defenseless woman."

"Has Mr. Wang told you what happened? I mean, how it was that we wound up together?" Mrs. Harrison asked Duff.

"I have not pried."

"He saved my life, that's what happened. He saved my life and the life of my baby. My husband, Lieutenant Harrison, was killed two weeks ago in a tragic accident at Fort Fetterman. I was on the way with my baby to Cheyenne to catch the train to go back home to Ohio. On the way here, the horse pulling the surrey stepped into a prairie dog hole and broke his leg. He suffered for a long time. I had not brought a gun with me so I had no way of putting the poor creature out of his misery.

"I kept hoping someone would come along who could help. I didn't think I could walk all the way to the next town, carrying a baby. By the end of the second day water and food were gone, and I knew we were going to have to try. By then, mercifully, the horse had died.

"On the morning of the third day, just as we were about to leave, this gentleman came along." She pointed to Wang. "He had water and food, which he shared, and he disconnected the surrey from poor Harry, connected his own horse to it, and drove us into town."

Dr. Dunaway took up the story. "Some of our seamier citizens took over then. They became incensed at seeing a white woman with a Chinaman. They pulled her down from the surrey and threatened to kill her if Mr. Wang didn't go with them. When Mrs. Harrison tried to protest, they took a bullwhip to her."

"Why didn't someone in the town try to intercede?" Duff questioned.

"Most were too frightened to do anything and some, I am sorry to say, agreed with what was happening."

"How long before Mrs. Harrison and the child will be able to travel?"

"Oh, they can travel now," Dr. Dunaway said. "I have put a lotion and bandages on her back to keep down the infection. And, as I said, the baby is strong as a horse."

Duff smiled at Mrs. Harrison. "Then I suggest we go down to the stagecoach depot and put you on the next coach to Cheyenne."

"Oh, I can't take the coach. If I do, I won't have enough money to buy the train ticket."

"Where is your surrey?"

"I don't know." Mrs. Harrison shrugged. "I don't know what happened to it or to my luggage. My baby and I have no clothes except for what I'm wearing."

Duff offered a suggestion. "You no longer have need of your surrey. Suppose I give you three hundred dollars for it? That will give you enough money for a coach ticket and for new clothes."

"Three hundred dollars? Why, even if I could find it, I don't know if it is worth that much."

"Don't worry about it. I'll find it."

Tears formed Mrs. Harrison's eyes. She reached out to take first Duff's hand, then Wang's hand. "I thank you both, so much. I can't help but feel that Michael is in heaven, looking down on us, and that, somehow, he sent the two of you to me. God bless both of you."

Sky Meadow Ranch, Wyoming

Duff and Wang Chow reached the ranch and dismounted.

Elmer Gleason, Duff's foreman and friend,

came out to greet them. "What's this Chinaman doin' here?"

"He has come to work for us."

"Really? Just what kind of work do you have in mind for 'im?"

"He's going to cook." Duff handed his reins to a cowboy and nodded to Wang to do the same.

"Well, Chinamen have been known to make pretty good cooks." Elmer glared at the young Chinese man.

Wang returned Elmer's gaze with an expression of trepidation.

Then Elmer smiled and stuck his hand out. *"Wei biao shi win hou. Huanying."*

Wang Chow's smile was broad as Elmer's, and he took the foreman's hand and shook it enthusiastically. *"Wei biao shi win hou."*

"Elmer, would you be for telling me what you and the young Celestial lad just said?"

"I just said hello, and I welcomed him. He said hello back to me."

"I had no idea you could speak Chinese."

"I made enough ports of call in China when I was a sailor to pick up some of the lingo." To Wang he said, *"Wo cunzai* Elmer." He pointed to himself.

"Elmer," Wang repeated, pointing to Elmer. He pointed to himself. *"Wo cunazi* Wang Chow."

Duff chuckled. "I see there's no need to introduce you, you've already done that." He motioned for them to walk toward the house.

"So he's going to be a cook, huh? That's a good idea of your'n, gettin' a cook instead of passin' it off among all the cowboys. Some of 'em is so bad it's a wonder we ain't none of us been pizened afore now."

"Wang can't cook."

"What? Whoever heard of a Chinaman who can't cook? Is he tellin' the truth, Wang? You can't cook?"

"He tells the truth. I cannot cook."

"Then why in the Sam Hill did you hire him as a cook, if he can't cook?"

"It's a long story," Duff said. "I'm going to count on you to teach him."

Elmer smiled. "All right, I'll do it. As long as I don't have to teach him none o' that nasty stuff like neeps 'n haggis."

"Elmer, how is it that a man of your experience and world travel has never been able to cultivate an appreciation of such a delicacy?"

"'Cause it ain't a delicacy is why. Neeps 'n haggis ain't worth feedin' to the hogs. Oh, by the way, Miss Megan said to tell you that her sister 'n brother-in-law is comin' to Chugwater soon. And they're bringin' her nephew with 'em."

"That's good to know," Duff said. "It will be nice meeting some of Megan's family."

Elmer chuckled. "It ain't just a meetin', you know."

"What do you mean?"

"It's more 'n likely she's brought 'em up here

to check you out, to see iffen maybe you're a fit person for her to marry."

"There you go again, Elmer, tryin' to be a matchmaker. When the time comes, I'll make my own match, thank you."

Elmer laughed again. "If you say so. Come, Wang, let me introduce you to some of these critters you'll be cookin' for, oncet I learn you to cook."

Elmer led Wang into the barn where three cowboys were standing on a board stretched between two barrels. "Boys, I want you to meet our new cook. This here is Wang Chow." Elmer pointed to the cowboys one at a time as he introduced them to Wang.

"This here feller with his nose mashed up against his face 'cause he got into a fight with someone he ought not to have, is Tom Woodward, only don't never call him nothin' but Woodward."

"It warn't no fight. I got kicked in the face by a mule. You know that, Elmer."

Elmer ignored him. "And the feller that ain't hardly got no teeth to speak of is Martin. I don't know as I've even heard his first name spoke. And this long, tall, drink of water is Adam Dewey. He's the youngest, but he ain't the dumbest."

"And just what qualifies you to pick the dumbest?" Dewey asked.

"That's easy, 'cause there ain't nearly no one dumber 'n me," Elmer said good-naturedly, and the others laughed. "You fellers want to tell me why in Sam Hill you got a board lyin' twixt these two barrels?" He pointed at the board in question.

"We're plannin' on usin' it as a wedge under the corner of the waterin' trough," Woodward said. "But it's too long, 'n none of us wants to walk all the way back to the machine 'n toolshed just to get a saw. We was plannin' on breakin' it with a shovel, but so far there ain't none of us been able to do it."

"I've only had one or two tries," Dewey said. "Here, let me try again." He swung the shovel hard at the board, but it just bounced back up. After four or five tries he handed it to Martin, who tried, unsuccessfully, to break it.

"Let's see what our new cook can do," Martin said, handing the shovel to Wang. "Here, see if you can break this board."

Wang took the shovel from Martin, held it for just a moment, then handed it to Elmer.

"No, don't give it to me. I know damn well I can't break the board."

"You want the board broken here?" Wang pointed to the shovel marks on the board.

"Yes." Elmer tried to hand the shovel back to Wang, but he waved it off.

"I do not need shovel."

Wang put the knife edge of his hand on the board and held it there for a moment.

"Ha! What are you going to do? Break the board with your bare hand?" Dewey asked.

"Haiiiiiiiiiiiiiuh!" Wang shouted, quickly lifting

his hand, bringing it down sharply against the board, and breaking it in two.

"I'll be damned!" Woodward said. "I ain't never seen nothin' like that."

"I have," Elmer said quietly. "Wang, you know *wu shu?*"

"*Shi dey wo wancheng?*"

"What the hell did he just say?" Woodward asked.

"I asked if he knew *wu shu*, and he said yes, he did."

"What the hell is *wu shu?*"

"Let's put it this way. I would advise none of you to ever get into a fight with Mr. Wang."

"Why would I want to fight a little feller like that in the first place?" Dewey asked.

Elmer laughed. "Yeah, why would you?"

"I ain't never seen nothin' like that," Woodward said again, the expression on his face reflecting his awe.

CHAPTER THREE

Chugwater, Wyoming

A banner was stretched across Clay Avenue.

CHUGWATER RIFLE MARKSMANSHIP CONTEST

The shooting had started at nine o'clock that morning, with thirty-five shooters. There were only five left, all five shooting Creedmoor rifles. For the last four rounds of shooting, all five had hit their target at dead center. The target was now three hundred yards away.

"What are we going to do now, Mr. Guthrie?" one of the townspeople asked.

Normally, Bob Guthrie was the owner and proprietor of a building supply company, but today, he was the judge of the shooting contest. "We can move the target back another hundred yards."

"Or you could just go ahead and move it on

down to Cheyenne," one of the townspeople suggested, to the laughter of many.

"We may as well. We've got the target three hundred yards away now. Another hundred yards would be almost a quarter of a mile," Fred Matthews said.

"Yes, well, pretty soon it's not goin' to make that much difference anyway, 'cause the truth is, we're runnin' out of targets," Guthrie said.

One of the shooters was Duff MacCallister, and another was Duff's good friend, Biff Johnson, who owned the Fiddlers' Green Saloon. He had given the saloon that name because he was an old cavalryman who had ridden with Custer on his last fight. Cavalry legend held that anyone who had ever heard the bugle call "Boots and Saddles" would, when they died, go to a cool, shady place by a stream of sweet water called Fiddlers' Green. There, they would meet all the other cavalrymen who had gone before them, and they would greet those who come after them as they await the final judgment. Biff had managed to avoid Custer's fate because he was part of Reno's battalion.

The other three shooters still in the contest were not from Chugwater. Jason Bowles was married to Megan Parker's sister, Melissa. Megan owned a dress shop in Chugwater, and Megan and Duff were—as the women of the town explained to anyone who might ask about their relationship—courting. Jason, Melissa, and their nine-year-old son, Timmy, lived in Eagle Pass, a small town in West Texas. Jason was the sheriff of Maverick County, and they had come to Chugwater to visit Megan.

The two remaining shooters, Louis Wilson and Roy Carter, had come to town specifically to participate in the shooting match. They were drawn there because of the award money. Seven hundred and fifty dollars were being offered for first place. Second place was worth five hundred dollars, and two hundred and fifty dollars was the prize for third place. That was a significant amount of money, and it made entering the contest worthwhile.

"You fellas ready to give up?" Carter asked. "If they move that wagon any farther back, I doubt any of you will even be able to see it, let alone hit the target."

The paper targets had been printed by the newspaper just for the occasion, and they were attached to a wooden frame that had been placed into the bed of a wagon.

"Ha! I seem to remember you sayin' somethin' like that up in Soda Creek," Wilson said. "But I beat you up there, an' I'll damn sure beat you here."

"We'll see about that," Carter replied. Their bantering was good natured because the two had competed against each other many times before. They could be considered professional shooters, so many contests did they enter. As a result of their frequent head-to-head competition, they had become good friends.

"Mr. Guthrie," Duff said. "Would you be open to a suggestion as to how to solve this dilemma that has been created in the shooting match as it is currently constituted?"

"I would be open to anything that would put an end to a match that seems like it might be goin' on until this time next week."

"I would say move the wagon back another two hundred yards. Place it five hundred yards from here, and let us continue."

Gasps of surprise and disbelief came from those who had spent most of the day watching the contest, drawn by a demonstration of shooting such as had rarely been seen before.

"Nobody can put a bullet into a bull's-eye no bigger than a silver dollar at five hundred yards," Carter said. "This is ridiculous. This is a waste of time. We will all miss, then we'll just have to reset the wagon in order to start over again. I say just move it another fifty yards and be done with it."

"I won't miss at five hundred yards," Duff said.

"What? Of course you will," Wilson said.

"I'm telling you, nobody can hit the bull's-eye from that far out," Carter said. "What do you other fellas say?"

"I don't know," Biff said. "I've seen Duff shoot before. If anyone can do it, he can."

"Impossible."

"I have a suggestion," Duff offered. "If I don't hit the bull's-eye, no matter what the rest of you do, I'll drop out of the contest. Then you can pull the wagon back to whatever distance you want and resume shooting."

"You mean even if all of the rest of us also miss, you'd still be willin' to pull out?" Wilson asked.

"Yes."

Wilson grinned. "What do you say, Carter? If he misses, he's out?"

"Yeah, if he wants to do it that way, I don't see no problem with it."

Duff wasn't finished. "However, if I hit the bull, dead center, I'll be declared the winner."

"Dead center? You mean, not touchin' the line anywhere?" Wilson clarified.

"Yes."

"Mister, you're on," Wilson said. Carter quickly concurred.

"Biff, Jason, what do you think?" Duff asked.

"Then the rest of us will be shootin' for second and third prize?" Biff asked.

"Yes."

"I don't have a problem with that, do you, Jason?" Biff asked.

"No problem," Jason said.

It wasn't until all four of the other shooters had agreed to Duff's proposal that four men went out, then half pulled and half pushed the wagon all the way down to the far end of Clay Avenue. From where the shooters stood, the entire target could barely be seen, let alone the bull's-eye. It looked like a tiny white patch.

Wilson turned to Duff. "You do understand, don't you, mister, that we're goin' to be holdin' you to your brag. Hittin' that little old piece of paper don't count for nothin'. You got to hit the bull's-eye dead center. How are you goin' to do that?"

Biff concurred. "Duff, I got to ask the same question. You can barely even see the bull's-eye from here. How are you going to hit it?"

"Mathematical calculation," Duff replied.

Biff frowned. "I know that in the artillery, the gun crews use geometry to find their targets, but I've never heard of anyone firing a rifle that way."

"It's simple," Duff said. "I know the size of the target paper because I'm the one that arranged to have 'em printed. The size of the target is twelve inches wide by fifteen inches tall. So, I just estimate my target point as seven and one half inches up from the bottom of the paper and six inches in from the left-hand side. If the target isn't a misprint, that is where the bull's-eye will be. All I have to do then is squeeze the trigger."

Everyone grew quiet expecting Duff to pause for a long time to control his breathing and lay in his sight picture. To the surprise of everyone who was holding their collective breath, Duff brought the rifle up to his shoulder smoothly, then pulled the trigger almost as if in the same fluid motion.

Some of the women let out a little startled reaction to the loud pop. It wasn't that the shot was unexpected; people had been shooting all day. What was unexpected was the fact they he had fired so quickly at his target.

Carter laughed out loud. "Ha! You missed. Are

you going to just stay here and watch the rest of us shoot, or have you had enough for now?"

"I didn't miss," Duff said.

"How do you know? You can't even see the bull's-eye from here."

"Then how do you know I missed?"

"Because there can't nobody hit a target that small, from this far away."

"Duff can, and he did." Guthrie was staring through a pair of binoculars.

"Well? How far off the bull's-eye was he?" Carter asked.

"He wasn't off at all," Guthrie said in a matter-of-fact voice. "On the contrary, he put the bullet dead center."

"Mr. MacCallister," someone called. "Swede, Clovis, and Loomis is takin' off on your China-man. You'd better come get 'im, or they're goin' to beat him up bad.

"Where is he?"

"He's down in front of the grocery store."

"Oh, Duff, don't let them hurt Mr. Wang," Megan said. "He is so much smaller than they are."

Duff, Jason, Megan, and Elmer hurried down to the grocery store. Holding a bag filled with groceries, Wang stood in the road in front of the store, surrounded by three large men.

"I'm goin' to tell you one more time—put them groceries down and walk away. If you don't, we're goin' to beat the hell out of you 'n take 'em ourselves."

"Mr. Bloomington, what seems to be the trouble here?" Duff asked.

"Your Chinaman bought the last package of brown sugar I had in the store a moment before Swede came in, looking for the same thing. When the Chinaman wouldn't give the sugar up, Swede and the two who came in with him got mad."

"Wang, do we really need the brown sugar?" Duff asked.

"Yes," Wang said.

"Well, there you go, Swede. My cook says that he needs it."

"You takin' a hand in this fight, MacCallister?"

"Me? No. Wang says he needs the brown sugar, and you want it as well. My suggestion to you is, if you want it badly enough, go ahead and take it from him. That is, if you think you can."

"Look here, MacCallister. Are you sayin' you ain't goin' to take a hand in this?"

"That's what I'm saying."

"Duff!" Megan gasped. "What do you mean? How could you?"

"Watch," Duff said calmly.

"You hear that, Chinaman? MacCallister has done give us permission to take it from you."

"That's not quite what I said, Swede. I'm sure you heard me add, 'if you can.'"

"Oh, yeah, I heard you say that," Swede said,

an evil smile spreading across his face as he raised his fists. "And we can. We damn sure can."

"Go ahead, Wang," Duff said.

Wang nodded and set the bag of groceries down, then he assumed a fighting position with his right arm bent at the elbow, his hand in front of his face, and his left arm stretched out before him. His hands were open and the fingers extended and joined.

"Ha! Look at him, Swede!" Clovis said. "I think he's going to slap us."

"I almost feel guilty about fightin' someone that fights like a woman," Loomis said.

"No need to feel guilty," Duff said. "Go ahead, teach this Chinaman a lesson."

"Duff, I can't believe what I'm hearing," Megan said with a gasp.

"Don't worry none, Miss Megan," Elmer said. "I've seen how these Chinamen fight before. It's different from anything anyone around here has ever seen, but Wang will be all right." To Wang he said, *"Yījue cíxiong, Wang, pengyou."*

"What did you say to him?" Megan asked.

"I told him to fight well."

Swede was the first to commit himself, using his size and strength in a bull-like charge.

Wang bent his knees, lowering himself so the roundhouse swing went over his head. He shot out his right arm and drove the point of his fingers deep into Swede's solar plexus. Swede, with a sudden expulsion of air, bent over trying to breathe, out of the fight.

Wang's right foot smashed into Clovis's face, taking him down, while he stopped Loomis with a knife-edged blow of his hand to the Adam's apple. All three of his attackers were immobilized in less than five seconds.

As everyone looked on in shock, Wang picked up the grocery bag. "I understand that you are having guests, Mr. MacCallister."

"I am."

"I will make something special for dinner."

"That's why you needed the brown sugar?"

"It is."

"I appreciate that."

Wang walked over to the buckboard, put his purchases in the back, then drove off.

"Did you see what that one little Chinaman did to them three big men? I ain't never seen nothin' like that in my livelong life," someone said.

"You knew he could fight like that?" Megan asked.

"I knew."

"And you knew as well," she said to Elmer.

"Yes, ma'am. I've seen the Chinese priests fight like that before."

"Priests. Good heavens, are you saying he is a priest?" Megan gasped.

"Yes, ma'am, but not like any priest you've ever heard of."

J. A. Johnstone on William W. Johnstone
"Print the Legend"

William W. Johnstone was born in southern Missouri, the youngest of four children. He was raised with strong moral and family values by his minister father, and tutored by his school-teacher mother. Despite this, he quit school at age fifteen.

"I have the highest respect for education," he says, "but such is the folly of youth, and wanting to see the world beyond the four walls and the blackboard."

True to this vow, Bill attempted to enlist in the French Foreign Legion ("I saw Gary Cooper in *Beau Geste* when I was a kid and I thought the French Foreign Legion would be fun") but was rejected, thankfully, for being underage. Instead, he joined a traveling carnival and did all kinds of odd jobs. It was listening to the veteran carny folk, some of whom had been on the circuit since the late 1800s, telling amazing tales about their experiences, that planted the storytelling seed in Bill's imagination.

"They were mostly honest people, despite the

bad reputation traveling carny shows had back then," Bill remembers. "Of course, there were exceptions. There was one guy named Picky, who got that name because he was a master pickpocket. He could steal a man's socks right off his feet without him knowing. Believe me, Picky got us chased out of more than a few towns."

After a few months of this grueling existence, Bill returned home and finished high school. Next came stints as a deputy sheriff in the Tallulah, Louisiana, Sheriff's Department, followed by a hitch in the U.S. Army. Then he began a career in radio broadcasting at KTLD in Tallulah, which would last sixteen years. It was there that he fine-tuned his storytelling skills. He turned to writing in 1970, but it wouldn't be until 1979 that his first novel, *The Devil's Kiss,* was published. Thus began the full-time writing career of William W. Johnstone. He wrote horror (*The Uninvited*), thrillers (*The Last of the Dog Team*), even a romance novel or two. Then, in February 1983, *Out of the Ashes* was published. Searching for his missing family in a postapocalyptic America, rebel mercenary and patriot Ben Raines is united with the civilians of the Resistance forces and moves to the forefront of a revolution for the nation's future.

Out of the Ashes was a smash. The series would continue for the next twenty years, winning Bill three generations of fans all over the world. The series was often imitated but never duplicated. "We all tried to copy the Ashes series," said one publishing executive, "but Bill's uncanny ability, both then and now, to predict in which direction the political winds were blowing brought a certain immediacy to the table no one else could capture." The Ashes series would end its run with more than thirty-four books and twenty million copies in print, making it one of the most successful men's action series in American book publishing. (The Ashes series also, Bill notes with a touch of pride, got him on the FBI's Watch List for its less than flattering portrayal of spineless politicians and the growing power of big government over our lives, among other things. In that respect, I often find myself saying, "Bill was years ahead of his time.")

Always steps ahead of the political curve, Bill's recent thrillers, written with myself, include *Vengeance Is Mine, Invasion USA, Border War, Jackknife, Remember the Alamo, Home Invasion, Phoenix Rising, The Blood of Patriots, The Bleeding Edge,* and the upcoming *Suicide Mission.*

It is with the western, though, that Bill found his greatest success. His westerns propelled him onto both the *USA Today* and the *New York Times* bestseller lists.

Bill's western series include *Matt Jensen, the Last Mountain Man, Preacher, the First Mountain Man, The Family Jensen, Luke Jensen, Bounty Hunter, Eagles, MacCallister* (an Eagles spin-off), *Sidewinders, The Brothers O'Brien, Sixkiller, Blood Bond, The Last Gunfighter,* and the new series *Flintlock* and *The Trail West.* May 2013 saw the hardcover western *Butch Cassidy: The Lost Years.*

"The Western," Bill says, "is one of the few true art forms that is one hundred percent American. I liken the Western as America's version of England's Arthurian legends, like the Knights of the Round Table, or Robin Hood and his Merry Men. Starting with the 1902 publication of *The Virginian* by Owen Wister, and followed by the greats like Zane Grey, Max Brand, Ernest Haycox, and of course Louis L'Amour, the Western has helped to shape the cultural landscape of America.

"I'm no goggle-eyed college academic, so when my fans ask me why the Western is as popular now as it was a century ago, I don't offer a 200-page thesis. Instead, I can only offer this: The Western is honest. In this great country, which is suffering under the yoke of political correctness, the Western harks back to an era when justice was sure and swift. Steal a man's horse, rustle his cattle, rob a bank, a stagecoach, or a train, you were hunted down and fitted with a hangman's noose. One size fit all.

"Sure, we westerners are prone to a little embellishment and exaggeration and, I admit it, occasionally play a little fast and loose with the facts. But we do so for a very good reason—to enhance the enjoyment of readers.

"It was Owen Wister, in *The Virginian*, who first coined the phrase *'When you call me that, smile.'* Legend has it that Wister actually heard those words spoken by a deputy sheriff in Medicine Bow, Wyoming, when another poker player called him a son of a bitch.

"Did it really happen, or is it one of those myths that have passed down from one generation to the next? I honestly don't know. But there's a line in one of my favorite Westerns of all time, *The Man Who Shot Liberty Valance,* where the newspaper editor tells the young reporter, 'When the truth becomes legend, print the legend.'

"These are the words I live by."